CLAN

Giovanni

JUSTIN ACHILLI

author	justin achilli
cover artist	john van fleet
series editors	john h. steele and stewart wieck
copyeditor	anna branscome
graphic designer	aaron voss
cover designer	aaron voss
art director	richard thomas

More information and previews available at
white-wolf.com/clannovels

Copyright © 2000 by White Wolf, Inc.
All rights reserved.

No part of this book may be reproduced or transmitted in any form or by any means, electronic or mechanical — including photocopy, recording, Internet posting, electronic bulletin board — or any other information storage and retrieval system, except for the purpose of reviews, without permission from the publisher.
White Wolf is committed to reducing waste in publishing. For this reason, we do not permit our covers to be "stripped" for returns, but instead require that the whole book be returned, allowing us to resell it.

All persons, places, and organizations in this book — except those clearly in the public domain — are fictitious, and any resemblance that may seem to exist to actual persons, places, or organizations living, dead, or defunct is purely coincidental. The mention of or reference to any companies or products in these pages is not a challenge to the trademarks or copyrights concerned.

White Wolf Publishing
735 Park North Boulevard, Suite 128
Clarkston, GA 30021
www.white-wolf.com

First Edition: April 2000

10 9 8 7 6 5 4 3 2 1

Printed in Canada.

Tears, idle tears...
Tears from the depths of some divine despair
Rise in the heart, and gather to the eyes...
[T]hinking of the days that are no more

—Lord Tennyson, "The Princess: A Medley"

For someone, presumably.

Giovanni

part one:
vegas
9

part two:
dig your own hole
107

part three:
the middle of nowhere
185

part one:
vegas

Sunday, 20 June 1999, 1:50 AM
Faust Nightclub
Manhattan, New York

"What's cover?" Julie had one hand deep in the pocket of his Oleg Cassini slacks.

"For you?" Tony the doorman shot back with a look of disinterest. "Twenty bucks."

Julie looked down at the line of people there before him. He pushed his sunglasses up the bridge of his nose and hid behind the collar of his overcoat. It was a wet night, a bit chilly. Julie's breath puffed around him in ephemeral wisps of steam.

"I sure hate waiting in line," said Julie deliberately.

"Funny. These guys love it." Tony jerked his thumb at the queue.

Sarcastic bastard, but he's probably heard it all before.

"I'm sorry. What was the cover? Fifty dollars?" Julie peeled a bill off the roll of money without removing his hand from his pocket. It wouldn't do to have the rubes noticing him too much.

"That's right," Tony said, taking notice now that it wasn't idle banter. "Coat check's right inside." Tony took the fifty and opened the door, releasing a thunderous welt of 150-beats-per-minute deep house music.

A girl in line started complaining, but Julie was inside before he could hear what she said. Patting the bump that was the wallet with the fake ID, Julie passed his overcoat to the check girl. She smiled, handed him a ticket—number 231—and winked. Julie blew her a kiss and lurched toward the bar.

"*Absolut screwdriver*," Julie shouted at the bartender, hoping to be heard over the din.

The A-list was out in full force tonight: club kids, speedheads, spectacular drag queens and other beautiful people stalked the dance floor and displayed themselves at the booths that dotted the club's mezzanine.

Bingo. Julie's eyes met his mark.

"*I said seven bucks, sunglasses.*" Julie threw a ten on the bar, took his drink and moved toward the back of the bustling room.

Frankie Gee sat at a table to the rear of the dance floor. Julie would have to move past him to get to the bathroom. He looked up at the DJ booth, where a pair of androgynes in shiny shirts flitted back and forth, clasping headphones to their ears and twisting the knobs on their mixing boards. The air was heavy here, fresh cigarette smoke, the reek of alcohol and the omnipresent bass of the sound system making oxygen a valuable commodity.

Drink in hand, Julie shoved his way toward the end of the row of booths and into the restroom. Under the first stall he could see a pair of feminine legs on their knees facing a decidedly male pair of shoes. The second stall remained unoccupied. A pair of young club crawlers in baggy pants stood before the urinal trough.

"Help you sir?" asked the attendant, a Mexican or Puerto Rican who was a hundred years old if a day.

"I think I left my hat here last night."

"Ah, yes sir. I get it."

The attendant opened the cupboard beneath the sink and produced a New York Yankees baseball cap, which contained a brown paper package tied shut with twine. Julie tipped the man a twenty. The attendant looked up at him with a smile and a knowing—if misunderstood—thumb of the nose. Julie's sunglasses hid the disgust in his eyes.

He stepped back into the open stall, ignoring the slurping and throaty moans next door. Dropping the cap to the floor, Julie ripped open the package, dropping the shredded brown paper into the toilet. He took the pistol and shoved it into his pants at the small of his back, patting it to make sure it didn't bulge too much from under his suit jacket. To keep the attendant in the dark, he took a few loud, staccato sniffs. *Let him think I'm a coke fiend—whatever.*

Julie steeped out from the stall; the boys at the urinal had left already. The attendant smiled at him and gave him a towel after he washed his hands. Julie made to leave, but the attendant remarked, "Bad karma!"

"What?"

"Bad karma! Leave a tip."

"Fuck you. I just tipped you." Julie couldn't believe this guy.

"That was before. Tip for towel. No tip; bad, bad luck."

"Here's a tip: Shut the fuck up." Julie barged back out to the club proper.

The smoke got in his eyes, bothering him.

Frankie Gee still sat at his booth, which was up against a mirrored wall. Two guys from his crew sat with him, and each man had an overly made-up skank at his side. There were twenty, maybe thirty drink glasses at the table—mixed drinks, shots, martini glasses. Quite a party. The whole group laughed. The men made exaggerated gestures with their hands. The women blinked frequently.

Julie moved to flank the table, so he could approach it unnoticed with any luck. He jostled people out of the way, moving through the bodies on the floor like Moses through the sea.

A foot in front of the table, Julie stopped. The goons looked at him, as did the women, all with expressions of interrupted laughter. Frankie Gee looked into his drink, a full glass of—vodka?—with a twisted lemon peel in it.

"We know you, sporty?" grated one of the goons.

"You know my boss."

The girls scattered. The blonde one climbed over the back of the booth to get away. This wasn't going to be a fistfight, they knew; this shit was about to get serious.

"Who's your boss? He's got real balls hiring a guy wearing shoes like those," shot back the other thug.

"Big Paul."

"Fuck you, punk. You're no Gambino. Big Paul's been dead for ten years."

"Call me a loyalist."

"I'm about to call you an ambulance, fucko," said the first tough. He went to his coat pocket, but Julie was quicker. Grabbing his own gun, Julie put three bullets into him before the man's hand made it out. Four more shots into the other one, one of which took off about a quarter of his head. Ten shots left. Julie heard the screaming; out of the corner of his eye he saw people rushing past him, desperate to make it out before they got shot, too.

Frankie Gee just sat there. "You cocksucker. You just killed two perfectly good men."

"They didn't do *you* much good, Frankie."

"I guess you're right. Fuck 'em."

Ten shots, all in Frankie's chest. The man flipped over the back of the booth as Julie's barrage walked him up and over the leather seat. Blood and gore spattered the mirror beside the booth.

Julie walked around the side of the booth to inspect his handiwork, the work of God's calling.

Something was wrong. Frankie Gee lay in a heap, twisted over himself, looking up at Julie with a smile on his face. He gathered himself up from his awkward position, got to his feet and looked down at his chest. Ten holes, unmistakable, clear as day.

"You fuck. You kill my guys and ruin my shirt? Nice grouping, though." Frankie put his finger into one of the holes.

"What the fuck?" Julie stammered, pointing his useless pistol at Frankie. This didn't happen. People don't get up with a quarter pound of lead in them. He was in over his head: Julie felt a dull, knotty horror in his belly. He was going to die. Bad karma.

"How witty," Frankie said, looking Julie in the eyes. "I gotta say, though, I didn't expect much else from a third-rate buttonman like you. Joe was right about those shoes. You're the second one this week. What the fuck is it with you wackos? You been crawling outta the fucking woodwork lately...."

What was this guy? His gorgeous suit, desecrated with his own blood; his showpiece girls and armed companions; a hundred-thousand-dollar Mercedes in the valet lot. He was everything Julie had expected, except tougher, more powerful. More *evil*, Julie realized. The devil picks his servants wisely. Frankie's got something...*unholy*.

Summoning that unholy power, Frankie smashed Julie in the mouth with a fist that felt like it had a five-liter V12 behind it. Julie flew—literally—ten feet and crashed into a freestanding table, crumpling among capsized chairs. He looked up, blood marring his sight and giving him the feeling that his ears were seeping off his head. Frankie Gee loomed above him, bending down to grab his collar and lifting him from the floor.

"Pete! Come here!" Frankie shouted.

"Yeah, Frankie, what's up?" Julie wondered why this guy wasn't shaken, like the rest of the crowd that had panicked and fled.

"Tell Tony he's fired."

Pete ran off. Julie's vision faded completely; the last thing he saw was a lusty look in Frankie Gee's eyes as the man moved his face toward Julie's throat.

Julie felt an intense pain—as if his soul had caught fire. Every nerve that could still feel blazed with the torture, and Julie knew his blood was running out of him in rivers of red—was Frankie *drinking his blood?* It didn't matter anymore. Julie was done. The devil had won this round.

Sunday, 20 June 1999, 5:00 AM
A private car
Manhattan, New York

Nickolai smiled. Sometimes, the simplest ruses were the best.

"Hello."

Click.

And so it went, several times over. Nickolai knew he was driving Benito Giovanni mad with the incessant and untraceable, if perhaps a bit rudimentary, prank.

Finally, Benito grew exasperated. The fourth—or was it the sixth?—time Nickolai called, the Giovanni answered the phone in a very businesslike manner.

"Why now?"

Oh, masterfully done, Benito, Nickolai thought to himself. *Put me on the defensive this time. Still, you haven't yet played to my satisfaction. Through another flaming hoop, you dog!*

"I've been waiting. Why now?"

Nickolai laughed. "How could you know it was me?" Had he truly known? Or had Nickolai simply taken pity on the poor necromancer, given what he was about to ask the Giovanni to do? "If only you'd seen through things so well a couple of years ago, Benito." *If only I didn't have to do what I'm about to*, Nickolai smiled wickedly to himself, trying hard to erase the tone of malicious glee that edged his voice. *Oh, the hell with it. I'm going to enjoy this.*

"You used subtlety then," Benito replied, almost too quickly. "Now without shame you reveal your bullying nature."

A puzzled look came over Nickolai's face. Subtlety? Such was the Kindred's stock in trade! Subtlety played as much a role now as ever. Didn't this bullheaded fool realize that Nickolai had cracked the Giovanni code? That he knew the isolated, secure-network PCS area prefix that the Giovanni were using for their mobile phones? *Don Giovanni, you are playing a foolish game, one that you cannot win.* Surely Benito realized that the endless nights grew long and that a fellow Kindred must take his mirth where he could find it. Eternity weighs heavily on the souls of the damned, or so some elder or another had told Nickolai during his brutal Tremere's apprenticeship. Only the worthy choose to do something with their time other than squander it, and isn't laughter the greatest medicine?

Enough.

"Miss Ash and her party—you will be unable to attend. I need you. Cancel your plans. Do what you have been told." *Terse, but effective.* Nickolai hung up the phone without waiting for Benito's reply. *And now, on to greater things. I have a plane to catch.*

Sunday, 27 June 1999, 9:57 PM
Roma Classico Import/Export
Brooklyn, New York

Frankie Gee said Las Vegas, so Vegas it was. His exact words were, "Talk to Milo and find Benito." Chas Giovanni Tello thought it would be easy.

Chas talked to Annie, the girl who handled the travel arrangements, and she took care of it.

"You're a pretty girl, Annie, but a bit wrong in the head to be hanging around hardcases like Frankie fucking Gee. A lot of you kids today, you like to mix with bad elements. You think it makes you tough. It doesn't make you tough, Annie. It just wears you out early." Chas lit a German cigarette—Shepherd's Hotel—and blew a puff of smoke over Annie's head.

"Fuck you, Chas. I can take care of myself. Your badass gangster-act doesn't fool anybody, by the way. I bet David could drop you like a bad habit, you and your suit and case." David was Annie's boyfriend. Chas, head tilted up to finish exhaling smoke, looked down at Annie through slitted eyes.

"David's a punk-ass piece of shit, Annie. He looks like a fucking broom, what with those skinny shirts and giant pants he wears. You little boys and girls—your fads don't mean shit. One night—one day, you'll finally grow up and realize that you wasted all your energy and youth on being dumbfucks. If you don't have a suit and case by the time you're thirty, you got no fucking sense." Chas tapped his temple for effect. "I was young like you once. I thought I knew everything; I had that ignorant invincibility that being young gives you. And you know what? I grew up. I'm not so much older than you, Annie," Chas said, smirking inwardly. Well, maybe he didn't *look* that much older than Annie. "This mind still remembers shit like foolish youth."

"Fucking-A, Chas, you want these tickets or not? I can't fucking call the travel agent with you here yelling at me. Now shut the fuck up, so I can get this done." Annie looked up at Chas with an expression of boredom, chewing her gum with her mouth open.

Chas wasn't interested in backtalk from this little bitch, though. "Annie, maybe you forgot. Maybe you're a little confused, here. I'm your fucking boss, as far as you're concerned. Yeah, yeah, you work for Frankie Gee, but so do I, and I pull a little more weight than whatever cunt in a tight skirt answers the ad this month. You talk to me like that again, and I'll fucking slap the smart right out of your goddamn mouth."

Annie, for all the pretty she could muster, was just another dumb kid. Chas wondered how long it would be before something accidentally happened to her—something like Frankie or himself.

"And make sure the flight lands *at least* three hours before sunrise, Annie."

Annie popped her gum, rolled her eyes and waved Chas away.

"Girlie, you don't know who you're fucking with. Gimme the goddamn phone. Gimme the phone, Annie." Chas grabbed the receiver and punched a number into the telephone.

"Jerry? Chas. I need a favor. You know Annie down here at the office? Red-haired girl?" Chas stared at Annie, who crossed her arms and curled her lip at him. "Yeah, you remember her boyfriend? Guy we sent down to Sallie's to pick up that thing? Yeah, him.

Find him. Find him; cut off both his pinkies. Send 'em to the office here, attention Annie. Put the fingers in some kinda jewelry box. Annie needs to know I'm not fucking around over here. Thanks." He dropped the phone in Annie's lap.

"Now get my tickets, Annie." He stubbed out the cigarette on her desk and flicked the butt in the trash.

Later that evening, the tickets arrived. "Who the fuck delivers tickets at night?" Chas asked no one in particular. "Ah, fuck it. Who cares?"

Frankie, Victor and Chas shared a nip of vitae and anisette while Frankie made sure they knew what they were supposed to do. Victor, a ghoul in Chas's service, was to meet the Rothstein contact in Las Vegas and apply whatever pressure was necessary to locate one Benito Giovanni, missing for five nights going on six. If Milo Rothstein proved too difficult, Chas would lean on him, too. If he still wouldn't crack, Milo would take the big nap. No guns, no onlookers, no police.

Las Vegas was a crab-ridden crotch of the undead—vampires from the Camarilla laid some kind of bullshit claim to the city; Anarch punks from California sowed their oats there; the Giovanni had as many operatives along the strip as they had in all of Boston; and the Followers of Set maintained some freakish temple beneath the sands of the valley desert.

Vegas. Bright lights, big city. A population large enough to host maybe a dozen vampires reasonably, but the very nature of the town drew thirty times that number. Benedic, prince of the city, didn't mind, so long as those transient vampires acted in accordance with the traditions. Not that he was any staunch supporter of the Camarilla, but rather, he understood the purpose behind all those old and seemingly arbitrary laws.

Las Vegas claimed perhaps a score or so "permanent" Kindred who made their havens there. The Giovanni were a constant thorn in Benedic's side, however, for a faction numbering so few. The local branch of the family, the Rothsteins, had claimed a stake in the city ever since Bugsy Siegel had gotten the idea in his head to build a gambling paradise in the middle of the desert. Now, Benedic was no slouch—he had his vast array of contacts keep him constantly apprised of Vegas's winds of change—but he couldn't seem to get ahead of the Giovanni. To his credit, he kept the "race" fairly even. Indeed, many of the Las Vegas Kindred suspected that, if Benedic didn't have to worry about the minor, pressing details of princedom, he would have edged the Rothsteins out years ago.

It was only this sketchy knowledge that Chas Tello took with him to Las Vegas during his trip to "find Milo and Benito." Frankie Gee had requested that Chas do everything by the book—present himself to the prince upon arrival, state plainly what he planned on doing there, do it, and fly back home. "With any luck," Frankie Gee maintained, "those Rothstein fucks will never know you're there, except Milo. Unless you have to talk to them, don't. Let Victor do all the work. This isn't any of their business."

"Gotcha, Frankie. And if things get ugly?" Chas asked.

"Don't let them get ugly. Get the fuck out of the way. Don't let them roll over you, but don't take anybody out of the picture unless it needs to happen. Milo, I don't give a damn about—if Milo gets hurt, nobody's going to be upset. But don't go there thinking you're going to deal with Milo. You're just the insurance."

"You're the boss, Frankie."

Chas knew that Frankie had people above even him. He wasn't quite sure how the hierarchy worked out—apparently the "family affair" the Giovanni had going on went outside the old limits of organized crime. More than once, Chas felt like a very small fish in a very big pond. After all, if vampires—which was tough enough to wrap his mind around, even if he was one—older than Frankie pulled *his* strings, how far back did the ranks go? He'd spoken before with Giovanni who weren't part of the American *cosa nostra*, but he didn't know who they worked for or what they did.

Chas's cousin Robert had told him that once you got past the Mafia part of the family, the rules became very different. In fact, most of the family—which wasn't Mob-connected—looked down upon the "goombas" who were happy to "waste" their unlives playing gangster. Those old ranks of the family had their own interests and hobbies, for which the Mob branch seemed only to generate income. It worked like the old system always had, with the Giovanni bigshots taking their *pizzu* from the guys who ran the rackets themselves in exchange for protection. But Robert had told Chas that the whole thing was more like an investment company, and that "this thing of ours" was only one entry in some old guinea's ledger somewhere. Neither Chas nor Robert even knew how the Giovanni had become involved with the Mafia, given that the family had its ancestral estate up north in Venice while the wiseguys were still centralized in Sicily.

But such problems weren't part of Chas's list of current situations to solve. Do the Benito thing and keep the money rolling in. Easy as pie.

Delta Flight 2065 to Atlanta became Flight 893 to Las Vegas, which arrived a few ticks before midnight. Chas and Victor traveled lightly, intending to stay only two nights, three at the most. Milo Rothstein expected them on the evening of Tuesday, the 29th.

They killed time with plane talk. Hunched over, Chas whispered to the ghoul.

"Frankie Gee makes me fucking cringe, Victor. Me—and I've done it all. You see, the thing about Frankie is that he doesn't just do shit, he makes everything he does an exclamation point. You fuck over Frankie, and he doesn't just hurt you, he hurts you *bad* in front of your family or your boys.

"This one time, back when I was just a ghoul sucking blood off the Giovanni family tit, Frankie had me bring in this kid who borrowed money and skipped a few points on the vig when he made his last payment. Just a fucking kid, this guy was, and something like six hundred dollars shy. Fuck it— chump change, right?

"Not to Frankie Gee. He sits the kid down and I duct tape the dumb son of a bitch to the chair. Frankie starts talking, and the kid goes ghost white if you know what I'm saying here. Ghost fucking white. I figure he's seen too many gangster movies, and he thinks Frankie's gonna go *Pulp Fiction* on him. Me, I'm thinking Frankie's gonna slap him around, take whatever money the kid has in his wallet, maybe break a thumb or two and turn the kid loose. It's kinda funny to me, Victor. I'm laughing at how scared this kid is because I know the shit going on in his mind is way the fuck worse than anything Frankie's gonna do. It works well like that, from where I stand. You scare the fuck out of the guy who stiffed you and you let him go—he thinks he's just had the luckiest break in the world and he never fucks with you again.

"Frankie, I guess, doesn't see things the same way.

" 'Whattaya think I'm gonna do to you, boy?' Frankie says to this kid. 'You think I'm gonna break your knees? I'm gonna shoot you in the face?' Frankie's all smiling, and I'm laughing a little louder, because he's really sweating this kid. 'You owe me six Bens and you try to skip out on it? That's not so responsible of you.' The whole place has this weird gasoline smell about it.

" 'Hold his fucking eyes open, Chas,' he tells me and I do. I have to reach around his head and kind of pinch them open. I guess he knows the shit's about to get rough and he's trying like all hell to close them. No good, because I work my finger there beneath his eyelid and pull back, like what's that movie where they make that criminal kid watch those Nazi movies?

"Anyway, I got his eyes pulled open, right? And we're in this warehouse. Frankie has this van pull in; somebody in the back opens the door and pushes out this girl. She's in pretty good shape—they haven't beat her or anything, but she's tied up in phone cord or that string you pull your blinds up with, you know? Frankie picks her up and holds her in front of the kid. It's his girlfriend or his sister—I don't know. Frankie Gee takes out this survival knife or Bowie knife or whatever and starts waving it around, like he's about to really put the hurt on the girl.

"Now, see, here's where it gets really fucked up. Me, I would have stopped by now. The kid's already shitting bricks just to have been caught up in the whole thing. Then we catch him and tie him up—he's ready to pay whatever he's got and sell his ass into slavery for the rest. *Then* his girl shows up—maximum density, you know? His mind's going a million miles an hour wondering how—not if, but how—Frankie's going to kill him and the girl. I would have collected right there and let the kid think a miracle saved his life. But Frankie was pissed at being screwed over. He wanted to get this kid but good. Make a statement, you know?"

Chas paused.

"Victor, Frankie knife-fucked that girl. Stabbed her thirteen times in the pussy. The first time, her eyes bugged almost right out of her fucking head. But that didn't do it—he got her a dozen more times.

"The kid's totally out of his mind when this commences to go down. He's jerking in his chair and crying and his cheeks are all poking out from beneath the duct tape. He tips himself over—I couldn't even watch the shit and I had to let go. I only knew about the thirteen times because I fucking *heard* that knife make that sick stabbing sound.

"Then, as soon as he's done stabbing, Frankie's through with the whole situation. He cuts the kid loose using the same knife, and me and him get in the van and the mook at the wheel drives us away. Didn't even mess with the kid—he put the whole weight of the situation right between that girl's legs.

"I'm not trying to fuck you up, Victor. I'm just wanting to let you know how this works. What you're getting into. I don't mean to get all weepy or sentimental or any of that bullshit, but I'm telling you the God's honest truth when I say that a part of you dies when you get involved in this.

"Fuck, just yesterday, I had Annie's boyfriend's fingers cut off because she talked back to me. How fucked up is that? Now, I wish I wouldn't have done it, Victor. I can feel something inside that *likes* that sort of fucked-up shit, like I'm making it happy when I do it.

"I know you're not one of us yet, Victor, but that may come up after we come back from Vegas. You need to think long and hard about this shit. The world doesn't need any more of this, but Frankie might try to put it on your shoulders. Just remember that you won't be able to stay who you are. You'll be something else altogether, and the only hope you'll have is to hang on to the memory of what you were before. And that's a hard fucking thing to do.

"I know, I know. I'm talking in circles here. I'm being—what is it?—*cryptic*. But we got secrets we have to keep. Just remember that you don't want to know those secrets, no matter how good a deal it sounds like. I promise you."

Victor swallowed, not wanting to speak. Chas waved down a flight attendant and ordered a whiskey and water for him.

Tuesday, 22 June 1999, 11:43 PM
The Mausoleum loggia
Venice, Italy

Isabel peered down the vertiginous airwell, from which no cooling gust or stale exhalation issued. This house, the loggia, the ancestral home of vampires of Clan Giovanni, had stood for a literal millennium. Over the intervening centuries the house had grown—burrowed, rather, twisting in upon itself and crawling beneath its old basements and sub-basements in a gruesome parody of the Giovanni family's own genealogical tree. By the time Isabel stood at the top of the stair that descended into the bowels of the house, the family had added no fewer than thirty floors, and indeed, far more of the manse rested below ground than above.

The excavations had been made to accommodate not only the swelling ranks of active clan members (from a mere handful at their inception during the—Renaissance?), but also the corpses, ashes and other legacies of Giovanni both dead and undead who deserved no harbor other than a memorial enshrinement. Failed Giovanni Kindred and fallen scions of the clan alike occupied their final resting place beneath the Mausoleum, which had a complex code of categorization understandable only by the keepers of the crypt. The ashes of Catherine Giovanni, who had masterminded the family's immensely profitable role during the Babylonian Captivity and the following schism of Roman popes and Avignonese popes of the fourteenth century, occupied an urn in an alcove next to the preserved tongue and genitals of Marco Gracchus Giovanni, who had deserted his critical alliance with the Desert Fox and fled the sands of northern Africa. Only the keepers understood the placement of the remains, but almost all Giovanni understood the circumstances of their fallen forebears. Ancestor worship (and, as often, revilement) played a very important role in the nightly affairs of the clan's members. Even ghouls and mortals of the Giovanni, who might very well be ignorant as to the blood-sucking nature of the family's darkest secret, knew at least some small degree of the Giovanni's history. From their humble beginnings as harbingers of Western Europe's emerging post-medieval middle class through the affluence brought about by Crusade war profiteering, from their tenuous relations with the Roman and Spanish Inquisitions to the glory of the Age of Exploration, the Giovanni family claimed a broad and grandiose history, of which little was wasted on its young.

That very history concerned Isabel Giovanni on this very night. Since their rise to prominence, the Giovanni had been haunted, oftentimes literally, by the ghosts of its past. For with the Giovanni's prominence had come depravity, the most obvious symptom of which was their study of the Black Art, *nigromancy*. As the story went, as the Giovanni amassed more and more wealth, their tastes became more and more jaded. On the road to their debauchery, the Giovanni took pleasure in acts scorned by society at large. Giovanni annals were rife with litanies of sodomites, pederasts, incest enthusiasts, coprophiles, corpse-fuckers, snuffers, slave masters, kidnappers, and practitioners of veritably every other deviance on the list. These practices had carried on into the modern nights, so great was the Giovanni wealth and so ingrained was their ennui that could be challenged only by flouting grave social mores. Isabel herself had, in life, borne her brother's child, pleasured her father and her aunts and uncles, smoked Oriental opium with the gigolos of Milan before fucking them to exhaustion, and severed the tendons of those among Garibaldi's Red Shirts who earned her displeasure. And the family annals didn't record every deed perpetrated in the name of Giovanni debasement or ambition—Isabel's daughter's death was not truly the result of chronic colic, and anyone inspecting that tiniest of white coffins would find only the bones of a sheep. But even these aberrant tastes could quell the insatiable lust of the Giovanni for so long before *nigromancy* took a firm root. As the family tree grew ever more upon itself, so too did the family's mastery of Dead Magic grow. What had started with the summoning of simple shades had become a cottage industry and then blossomed into a full-fledged aptitude.

Clan Giovanni had no qualms with this. Its rude Epicurean tastes accommodated such things as the handling of entrails and intercourse with corpses. Indeed, *nigromancy* even had a purpose beyond simple indulgence—by provoking the ghosts of the dead, the Giovanni could master them. Their invisible tormentors-turned-servants proved the ultimate boon in their transactions. Whether gleaning secrets from supposedly secure back offices or plaguing their contacts with nightmares and more physical haunts, the dead spirits offered a myriad of possibilities to the

Giovanni that those with whom they did business (or conducted other affairs) could not harvest. When one trafficked with Giovanni, like as not, one also trafficked with a host of his unseen allies.

But those unseen allies had become capricious of late, which upset the prominent members of the clan. And rightly so! Their previously reliable and ubiquitous aces-in-the-hole had suddenly become peevish or, more frequently, simply gone missing. It was as if a convocation of ghosts had been convened…elsewhere. While once the Giovanni could have easily called upon a host of wraithly spirits, their powers had suffered some sort of unexplained limitation that now allowed them to call upon only one at a time, if that. Thanatologists among the clan speculated that an enormous upheaval was taking place in the Underworld, the chthonic spirit-world of the dead. Others postulated that in the frenzied final nights, as the Gehenna foretold by other, older families of Kindred approached, the Giovanni ancestors had turned against them. Still others surmised, somewhat fancifully, that magic was changing or eroding completely, and that the old ways had simply become too dated or ineffectual in the modern world: In a faithless age, mysticism lost its potency.

Whatever the case, Isabel Giovanni numbered herself among the Kindred concerned with the sudden impotence of necromantic power. In less than a month, she was supposed to serve as liaison between the Boston branch of the Giovanni empire and a few important representatives of the Camarilla, a vampiric organization from which the Giovanni cordially abstained. It simply wouldn't do to go without her resources. And so, in search of answers to this particular mystery, Isabel had come to the one place where she knew she could count on the dead magic working. Ever since the mausoleum had been built—ever since its first crypt had been scraped from the silty rock of the ground beneath sodden Venice—the spirits of the family had watched over the family, and later, the clan. And so it was that Isabel Giovanni descended a score or more flights of stairs, to prostrate herself before the bones of her grandmother Giulia. Giulia had never been Kindred herself, which was why her bones still existed, but she had been "sensitive" to the spirit world.

On her knees, dressed in a light wool robe and bent before the alcove in which Giulia Giovanni Abruzzina's remains rested, Isabel whispered her grandmother's name.

And again.

And once again.

Had the damnable, secret affairs of the wraiths not taken precedence, Giulia would have come. As it was, however, something more pressing must surely be occupying her. Isabel needed her insight, though, and she had no choice.

When the spirits failed to heed a necromancer's call, the only alternative was to force them to manifest. The surest way to do so was to anger the ghost, who could later be placated and dealt with constructively. Isabel had some reservations, but as always in the mind of the Giovanni, the end justified the means.

Isabel gathered Giulia's bones from the niche and made a pile of them on the floor. Torches in the sepulchre flickered, leaving momentary trails of black smoke. Atop the pile, Isabel placed the lower mandible of the skull. Walking thrice counterclockwise around the pile, she made the sign of the cross with her left hand and whispered Giulia's name three times again.

Still nothing.

Growing frustrated, Isabel knocked over the pile of bones, gathered them once again and placed them in an incorrect alcove. Turning her back on the niche, she opened the folds of her robe to expose herself, adding, hopefully, an appropriately lewd touch that would attract the wraith's attention with its vulgarity.

It worked.

A cold breeze wafted strongly into the room, extinguishing a torch and coalescing the smoke into a long, thin face with drooping eyes. "Slatternly child!" the face's mouth cried, with a voice that sounded as if it came from the bottom of a chasm. "I have ignored your call with reason! How dare you assume that your selfish wants take precedence over my cold purpose?"

"I am sorry, Grandmother, but your wisdom is incomparable." Isabel knew that flattery never hurt when dealing with the impatient souls of the departed. Only by inflated estimations of their worth could ghosts be calmed, as many still had profound attachment to the physical world in some form or another. Still, one could never be too careful around the Restless Dead—they had no qualms about giving one's secrets to another in exchange for their favor.

"What is it, then? Speak your mind!" Clearly, something was pressing on the other side of the veil between the worlds of the living and the dead.

"It is this urgency, Grandmother, that concerns me. What is it that transpires in your Underworld?"

"Ah, so those who walk the lands of the living have noticed...." Giulia began, but trailed off apprehensively.

"Yes, Grandmother, we have." Isabel left the comment to hang in the air, hopefully prodding the wraith to further insight. But none seemed forthcoming. "Does something beneath the shroud of death compel you?" she ventured again.

"Powerful forces shake the realm of death," Giulia whispered, her manner becoming furtive. "I cannot say any more, because the truth evades me. But I can say this: Our armies move each night. The tides of blackness whirl and eddy in a manner I have never seen before. Lightning strikes and thunderheads make too much noise. Great change is on its way."

"Grandmother, help me. You're not making any sense," Isabel pleaded.

At once, Giulia became angry again, losing the fearful cast her smoky features had taken. "I have spoken what I can, my ill-mannered descendant. Cover yourself! The dead have no duty to tell you of our private affairs. I will warn you though, contemptible whore, that an old evil has found a new body. Even if the war beneath the living doesn't plague you with its aftermath, those who wait beyond the grave will. Augustus has damned his brood in more ways than one: Your unwholesome traffic with those of us whose life has left is but the first of your blights. The knife of treachery is hot, especially to cold, undead hearts...."

"Crone, you're speaking in riddles!" Isabel decided to shift her tactics. Giulia was either under the influence of the darker half of her consciousness, or she was deliberately trying to occlude the issue. Isabel knew that the ties that bound wraiths to the living world, the objects that fettered them and prevented them from going on to their true rest after death, held great import. Giulia's bones were all that remained of her grandmother, and the only tie she knew that bound her to the living world. The Giovanni blood that sat lifeless in her veins held a great potential for depravity, and Isabel hoped that her own capacity for violating taboo exceeded that of her grandmother's ghost. "You leave me no choice."

Isabel pulled the bones rudely from the niche in the wall; they clattered like the keys of a macabre xylophone. She shed her robe and opened one of the veins in her arm, spraying cold, dead blood over the bones and her nakedness.

"Prurient slut!" shrieked the spirit, at which Isabel grimaced lewdly. Slowly, lasciviously, she dropped to her knees, sprawling on all fours over the scattered pile as a mortal woman would a lover.

"Just speak frankly with me, Grandmother, and I'll stop." Isabel ran her fingers over individual bones, mocking the caress with which the living fondled each other during acts of passion. Each gesture was an impurity, hands stroking the phallic skeletal remains, blood soiling them. With every lustful pass over her lifeless body, Isabel enraged her long-dead grandmother by defiling the ivory pieces of her legacy. She licked them, tasting her own vitae; she prodded herself with them, passing them over the gash in her arm, her breasts, her barren and hairless sex. She favored some in her blasphemous acts and cast others aside, spurned and impotent tools that gave her no pleasure. But beneath such hellish, wanton acts, Isabel's mind remained her own. Even the most carnal of acts could not satisfy her Kindred's lust for blood. Mortal sex—no matter how insidiously parodied—provided her no orgasmic joy. These vulgarities served only to demonstrate superiority over the wraith. For every memory of the debased mortal ecstasy this would have caused her were she alive, Giulia's ghost felt a spasmodic shudder, as the remnants of her earthly body served merely as a vehicle for the concupiscence of another. The ghost's remaining vengeful resolve withered as her grandchild, the fruit of her once-living mortal loins, pressed the pelvic bone to her own pubis, mimicking the advances of a lover atop his naked paramour.

"Enough, wanton! I'll tell you what you want to know. End this display."

Isabel braced herself for the pang of guilt she knew should come after such a horrendous act. To caper so whorishly with the corpse of the woman who helped bring you into the world! To make such rude and carnal gestures with *the pieces of corpses*! Unthinkable!

And yet, the rush never came. She had ensured the wraith's compliance—seized what she wanted—and felt no remorse. In nights past, she would have brooded seemingly without end, but not this time. The time she had simply—taken. And that was it.

"The spirits of the dead wage war, Granddaughter," Giulia spoke while Isabel pulled herself into a standing position and covered herself with the robe. "The struggle between factions is not a monopoly the Kindred hold. A storm brews in the dead realms that threatens not only to overwhelm this world, but to poison the one in which you exist as well. Several of your kind have taken up residence here—constructed a stone city they sacrilegiously name after one of the cities of God's first. They are unwelcome in this world, as much as I would be in yours. The time has come, it would seem, when the lords of this dead kingdom would have them removed, driven from the Underworld. But those lords are too shortsighted to know the effect this would have. The storm—it will come now, for tempers have flared unchecked for too long. It will claim us. And it will cross the veil. Your world will know the vengeance of that which is greater than men or any who walk among him. God will judge many before the night of His wrath is felt wholly. May He have mercy upon unworthies like yourself. And until then, we must prepare."

Tuesday, 29 June 1999, 3:14 AM
Caesar's Palace
Las Vegas, Nevada

The plane had arrived without a hitch, delivering Chas and Victor safely to McCarran International Airport, and from there to the hotel via a quick cab ride.

"I hate this city," Chas said idly, in the back of the cab.

"Why?" asked Victor.

"You'll see."

Check-in had likewise gone smoothly. Chas had decided to try his luck in the casino, maybe earning a few bucks and seeing if any disastrous turn of chance portended ill omens for him.

If the cards and dice were any indication, this trip would be a good one, Chas decided. He had won six hundred dollars at blackjack, half of which he tipped the dealer, and two hundred at craps, half of which he tipped the croupier.

"I just do it for fun," he explained, gracefully deferring their questioning gazes.

It wasn't like he really needed the money, after all. Plus, it'd be a good cover story if something big happened while they were in town and they made a few dollars on that—he could say he'd won big, and heavy tips would corroborate that.

It was still next-to-last shift at the table, and the drinks (surreptitiously switched with those of neighboring gamblers—they watched their cards and chips but never their cocktails) still flowed freely. Pretty soon, however, the Bad Time would come, after all the sport gamblers had gone to bed and the desperate gamblers crept like cockroaches into the casino. Pale, pasty-faced insurance salesmen and middle managers from Iowa, their wives dropping coins into video slot machines while they themselves tried vainly to win back next month's mortgage payment on a lucky deal or throw of the dice.

Easy pickings for the casino, and easier pickings for vampires like Chas.

Not that he had to worry about feeding. The city was full of similar desperation; it was an undercurrent that ran through the whole town, touching the oil barons and the rogue drifters alike. At one moment, any of them could be Lady Luck's favorite suitor and at the next, they could be penniless and drunk on the curb out front. The only thing that separated them as individuals was where they stood on the spectrum of destiny.

Fuck. A seven. Crapped out. Chas left a twenty for the croupier and left the table. It was getting late anyway. Where was Victor?

Chas rode the elevator back to their hotel room, running his hand through his hair and looking at himself in the mirror on the wall. He sniffed, which startled an old woman in the elevator to consciousness. She exited on the nineteenth floor.

Lady, Chas thought to himself, *You just rode an elevator with the devil and you never knew the difference. You're lucky to be alive.* He smirked, a self-deprecating little twist of the mouth yet somewhat sincere, and leaned back against the rail.

Floor twenty-six.

He slid the electronic key through the lock and heard the tumbler whir, then opened the door.

Victor shot up, naked, from the bed, his cock limp and his eyes and nose rimmed with red. Burst blood vessels. Beneath him, a girl of maybe seventeen bent on her hands and knees, rough white lines on her ass and a fine cloud of white powder that settled slowly onto her thighs and the bed. Beneath *her* lay another girl, this one on her back, flat-chested and with pupils so big Chas could see them from the doorway.

"Shit, Chas, I thought you wouldn't be back for another couple of fucking hours."

"Victor, you stupid piece of shit. What the fuck did you bring these hookers in here for?"

"Hey, mister, we're not hookers, we're *escorts*," said the one on top, standing semi-erect now, though on her knees and still straddling her partner.

"Bitch, shut the fuck up or I'll put out your fucking eyes and skullfuck you. All right, ladies, party's over. Get dressed. Come on, get dressed. Pack up. Time to go."

Chas was clapping his hands and barking at the girls, prodding them into movement. They responded sluggishly, but were obviously wound up, as the coke or crank or whatever played havoc with them and they acted impishly to see what would happen.

"I'm fucking serious here. Victor, put your fucking clothes on. Cover that thing, would you? Jesus Christ."

"What's the fucking problem, Chas? I mean come on, we're in Vegas; this shit's legal." Victor led the top girl back to the bed, bending her over, rubbing white powder from her ass into his gums with one hand and working his dick to some degree of attention with the other, readying himself to take the girl from behind. The skinny, flat-chested one—bottle blonde, for the record—giggled and leered at Chas, dry-humping her friend's leg.

"Yeah, come on, Chaaaas…" She drew out his name, making an impossible three-syllable word out of it. "You're in Vegas."

"Shut the fuck up, slut. I've been coming to Vegas since you were a twinkle in your daddy's eye." He looked her over, noticing track marks on her arms as she squirmed beneath the other whore.

"Come on, baby. You like it rough?" She smiled, crawling out from beneath the other girl and stepping toward him. Yellow teeth. Cigarettes and heroin. Bad news. *Not this one*, Chas found himself thinking.

What? You're not serious, he said silently to himself. Still, he couldn't deny the truth—must have overlooked it in his anger. He could feel the girls' blood calling to him, hear the pulse of it through their veins. He looked out the window: desert lightning behind the neon and halogen.

Chas shook himself. "You don't know how rough, girl. Now pack up and take your sister with you and get the fuck back to the street corner."

"Victor," the skinny girl crowed, "I think your friend's a fag. Is that so, big meany?" She leaned in, taking a rude handful of Chas's crotch. "Do you like boys? I'm kind of shaped like a boy…I've even got a dildo in my bag that I could use to—"

Chas batted her away, this time fighting with the urge that could only end in trouble. Victor wasn't even paying attention—couldn't be trusted to defuse the situation. He was working his hips back and forth behind the girl on the bed, who looked at Chas lasciviously, her mouth open, pupils and irises half-circles obstructed by her eyelids. Chas smelled the musky odor of sex, which mingled with the sharp tang of what he now figured was cocaine.

Enough. He felt the red rush rising.

His throat constricted; he had to force out words. "Victor, did these whores have a pimp?"

Victor was still stabbing away with his groin at the other girl's upended ass. "Fuck." He grunted. "What? Fucking what?"

"A pimp, you no-account motherfucker. Did you buy these whores from a pimp?" Pressure rising…losing sight…

"No. No. They were…." Grunting. "They were solo."

Good. No one to care about finding them in pieces.

"I told you, Mister Chaaas," the skinny one piped up, "we're *escorts*, not who—"

Chas snapped. He tore the phone off the nightstand, grabbing the receiver and base in one big hand. The cord to the wall went taut and pulled free in a shower of drywall dust. Chas brought the whole assembly down on top of the skinny girl's head. Again. Three times. By the fourth, her head had given in like a ripe melon, blood running from her shattered skull, spraying the carpets, tainting the wall, misting the other girl's swinging breasts as her lusty look immediately became one of horror.

Even Victor stopped his fervent rutting, eyes going white and mouth slack. He pulled out of the girl, a trail of lubricant following him briefly. "Fuck, Chas what are you—"

Chas whirled around, bringing the phone high as if he meant to stave in Victor's head, too. His eyes were wild, his face contorted, his mouth a snarl of vicious fangs. "Fuck off, Victor." He dropped the phone as the ghoul feebly brought up his arms to ward off an attack that never came.

In a flash, Chas had the other girl by her neck, lifting her from the floor to viciously impact her head against the ceiling. Out like a light she went.

Chas tore into her throat, just above where her neck met her clavicle. Skin parted and blood flowed from the wound, spilling down her naked body in torrents, washing away little rivers of the white powder that still dusted her hips and haunch. He drank deeply, in huge gulps that he knew would have reduced her to screaming fits were she still conscious. The taste overwhelmed him, its salty bite and rich consistency, almost like a metallic burgundy...

...And then he stopped. Too much would kill her, and she was already going to be a problem. He licked the messy wound carelessly, and it closed. Then he dropped her to the floor like a sack of garbage.

Victor cowered, naked and shaking in the corner. His face was pale and his mouth still slack in shock. But there was no anger. No regret either, really. Just undiluted disbelief.

Meanwhile, Chas toweled off the blood that stained him. Then he changed his suit and adjusted his watch, glancing briefly at its face.

"Clean this up, Victor," Chas said as evenly as possible. "Then meet me in the casino. You have forty minutes."

Tuesday, 29 June 1999, 5:22 AM
Caesar's Palace
Las Vegas, Nevada

Chas was upset in the lobby lounge. He was almost one of the cockroach people, he could tell. Freaked out in Vegas, went a little beyond the boundary, and now had to worry about how to fix it. Even though Victor got fucked into doing the dirty work, it was still his operation. One dead, maybe two— dammit! Why? He didn't even need the blood! Just a bad situation and he lost control, wasn't it? He briefly tried to console himself by entertaining the thought that they deserved to die. They probably would have mickeyed Victor and left him in a tub full of ice, duct tape on his back and a bloody hole where his kidney used to be. Or they would have stolen the luggage and money and everything else in the room, and then bought *chiva* with the profits.

But Chas knew he was grasping at straws. He knew he'd fucked up and this was just one more step on the way to hell, into the devil's carriage house. His head fell into his hands. Christ, he even *looked* like one of the cockroach people.

Through his fingers, past the bar, he saw Victor walk into the room. Down the dais, toward him Victor came, with the coke fiend's look of paranoia held in check only by the knowledge that if he flaked, things would become even more nightmarish than they already were. He looked tired, the bags under his eyes red with drugs and fatigue.

"Everything done?" Chas snarled, looking out of the corner of his eye.

"Yeah. It's done. Room's clean." Sniff. "Phone's gone, towels and sheets and all that shit's on its way to Long Beach."

"And the girls?"

"I got the one being carried out on a stretcher. Told the EMTs she's in some kind of amphetamine freak-out, which a blood test should support. Oh, and she's rambling about somebody tearing somebody up, which I think they'll dismiss as drug dementia."

"You called EMTs? How the fuck did you get away from them so quickly?"

"It's fucking Vegas. I gave them a hundred dollars apiece. They think I'm just some cokehead john who wants to get away from his scummy whore with no questions asked."

"All right. And the other girl?"

"Um… If you end up at the steak house here, I wouldn't order off the menu. At least not till tomorrow. I'll make a phone call and things should clear up by the time you get up for the evening."

Chas forced a sigh and pursed his lips. Thank fucking God *that* was over with. Now to just ride it out and talk to the Rothsteins' crew tomorrow….

"This is fucking why I hate Vegas, Victor."

Tuesday, 29 June 1999, 5:36 AM
Caesar's Palace
Las Vegas, Nevada

"Oh, fuck." Chas gurgled as a torrent of blood ran backward, *up* his throat, and spewed from his nose and mouth. "Fuck. Victor. Fuck me, Jesus Christ, Victor, I don't feel so good."

Victor knew—this wasn't how things normally happened. He didn't know *what*, though; bad blood or something. "Look out! This man is sick. Stomach ulcer. I'm his attorney and he has a heart problem!" Whatever. Just to get these people the fuck out of the way.

Chas stumbled, his legs feeling like jelly. His vision narrowed to a tunnel and everything, everyone in the tunnel seemed to be staring at him. He could feel every ridge on his fingerprint, every thread of his shirt. He could feel where the blood he had vomited was thin and where it was viscous and coagulated. Fragments of the cockroach people's speech found their way into his hearing, but he remained oblivious to the larger noise around him. "Fucked up," the voices said. "Look out—what a mess." "Did they shoot him?" "…Card-counter…" "…Too much to drink…" "…Gangsters!" "…Someone should do something…" "…That man removed…" "…Don't look, Gladys…" He felt the tacks that held the soles to his shoes, the minor gradations where the carpet had been laid over an irregularity in the floor's foundation. Another gout of blood-puke found its way up and everyone looked at him. A horrified waitress dashed out of his way and two bouncers looked at him disapprovingly as they waved him and—who the fuck was holding his arm?—out of the casino and into the lobby.

Victor. It was fucking Victor. Chas peered, his eyes narrowing to slits as he focused on Victor's face. Victor shoved Chas into an elevator—puke—and two greasy-haired roach-men in cheap slacks and sport coats dodged to get out of the car.

"Jesus, Chas, what the fuck happened to you?" Every detail of Victor's face stood out as Chas stared at it, the pores, the individual minute strands of hair that would make up his beard once it grew out more, the lines at the side of his mouth and at the corners of his eyes. The still-red rims of his nostrils.

"It's the hooker's fucking crank. Or mescaline. That whore must have been tripping. Fuck, Victor, get me to the room before I—" More vomit, spraying across Victor's shirt and the mirrored wall of the elevator car. Chas grabbed Victor by the front of the shirt—wondered if he could tell the thread count by feeling the individual fibers. "The fucking room, Victor. Shit."

"Calm down, Chas." Victor pushed him back, as much to keep him from crashing into the walls as to remain on top of the situation. "I got everything under control. Victor's in charge, you hear me? Don't fight me, because I'll have to hold you back and you'll probably fucking kill me."

They burst into the hotel room, a few indignant rays of sunlight already climbing through the crease where the drapes met. Blood-sweat drenched Chas's forehead and welled through his shirt where it wasn't already stained with blood-sick.

"Fucking hell, Victor, are we—" puke "—done?"

"One minute, Chas. One fucking minute. Almost there."

Victor kicked open the bathroom door, noting that the floor was still a bit wet from where he'd had to mop it with towels earlier. Oh, well. It would have to do. He pushed Chas into the bathroom, casting him inelegantly into the tub. As a quick afterthought, he hung the "Do Not Disturb" sign on the outside of the room's door and pulled shut the lever-lock that worked like a door chain. *Fort fucking Knox, this place is,* he grinned. The he pulled shut the bathroom door, making sure to put the bedspread in front of the crack beneath the door.

As Chas collapsed into a fitful, twitching unconsciousness, the devil ran through his mind. The devil, lord of the cockroaches.

Tuesday, 29 June 1999, 11:56 PM
Caesar's Palace, Senate Boardroom
Las Vegas, Nevada

Milo Rothstein sat at one end of the enormous stained-oak table, flanked by his *de facto* counsel. Prince Benedic's Nosferatu flunky, Montrose, sat to his left, looking like a skinned and twisted war prisoner in designer clothes. One of the lesser Rothstein Giovanni sat to his right, nervous and ill-informed. He knew that, in the event that things got out of hand, he was probably going to be thrown to the wolves. He was there only because he had learned the keen power of scrutinizing the auras of others. He had originally learned his "little trick," as Milo called it, to use as an edge while hunting the casinos and streets. It had proved to be an ersatz gift, however, as it made him a prize commodity in the petty squabbles between the family and the *other* vampires who wanted Las Vegas to be their playground only.

At the far end of the table, Victor Sforza tapped the note pad sitting before him with his pen. Chas stood behind him, playing to their ruse of mouthpiece and enforcer.

The Giovanni neonate leaned toward Milo, whispering, "The one standing up is a vampire. I'm not sure about the one sitting at the table. He's playing his cards pretty close to his chest. I'm guessing he's either Kindred or a ghoul."

Milo nodded. "To what do we owe the honor of this visit, Mr. Sforza?"

Victor rose, smoothing his tie. "Well, Mr. Rothstein, it would seem that our employer, Francis

Giovanni, has come to learn that an acquaintance of his has gone missing. Mr. Giovanni suspects that he may have taken refuge here, or that you might know where he has gone…to. Gone, I mean."

Milo smiled and looked past his steepled fingers into his lap. "And why would your employer's friend come to see me?"

"Because Mr. Giovanni knows that you have had dealings with him in the past."

"Have I?" Milo raised his eyebrows. "Such guarded speech! What exactly is my connection with Benito, anyway?"

Victor shot back before Chas could warn him with a cough. "I never said Benito. You must know what we're talking about, or the individual's name wouldn't have come to your mind, would it?" Chas tensed. The ball had always been in Milo's court, but he'd chosen to pull his initial punches, to see what his guests had to offer. Chas suspected a set-up, that bad blood between Frankie Gee and Rothstein in the past was being settled by proxy. Willing blood into his limbs, he felt the flush of undead potency course through him.

"No, Mr. Sforza, I'm afraid you don't quite see the full truth. I know precisely why you're here, and my *apparent* slip-up was intended to indicate that I know more than you believe me to. If a simple underestimation were your only error, you might have come out of this meeting ahead."

The freak, Montrose, watched Chas bristle, and made to rise. Milo outstretched a hand, as if to calm him or to keep him seated. With an almost imperceptible narrowing of the eyes, Montrose looked to

Milo. Chas caught the minute display and raced to put the pieces together in his mind: Montrose wasn't happy with Rothstein. Rothstein might know where Benito was, but had some reason to keep it quiet, which might be the reason for the tension between them. The quiet fellow who hadn't been introduced was either the linchpin or a red herring. More likely the latter given his visible discomfort. But then, that could be part of—Chas halted his thoughts, choosing not to second-guess himself. Better to let everything play out than to go off half-cocked.

Victor backed down, a good move. "I mean no disrespect, Mr. Rothstein. I came at the request of my employer, who seemed to think that this matter would be easily resolved on amicable terms. Perhaps I've misjudged you, but your manner seemed defensive. I apologize for my presumptuousness." That seemed to calm Rothstein, but Montrose remained agitated. Chas relaxed a bit, cursing himself for so quickly invoking the power of his undead vitae. He knew the rush would remain there, but he tried to shrink himself visibly. The room's recessed fluorescent lights flickered briefly beneath the yellow wash of the main lamps. Montrose raised a warped eyebrow.

Victor continued. "It is Benito we're after, but only to settle a debt with my employer. I'm afraid that if you give him reason to think you might be harboring the debt, he won't take that as an act of comradeship."

Chas winced—Frankie hadn't said anything to him about a debt. Either he was keeping Chas in the dark, or Victor was making this up on the fly. He hoped this last was the case, because if Frankie had sent him out here to play back-up man to a fucking ghoul without giving him the full picture…

"I'm sorry, Mr. Sforza, but I can't help you." Milo's statement broke Chas from his reverie. "Benito Giovanni stopped here briefly more than two weeks ago, but stayed for only one night before taking his leave."

"I see. Well, then I am sorry to have wasted your time. My employer will be disappointed, but perhaps your recent sighting of Benito will provide him with some new insight." Victor rose, made a show of scribbling something on his note pad, and turned to leave. "Thank you for your hospitality, Mr. Rothstein. My associate and I ask for one more evening to conclude our affairs and to afford us ample time to return home without fearing the rays of the sun." *Good play*, Chas thought; *let them think you're Kindred*. Victor could certainly think on his feet.

"But of course. Where are you staying?"

Chas flashed a brief look to Victor. Either Rothstein hadn't known about the problem last night or he was trying to lull them again.

"We're staying here in Caesar's Palace. In the tower—twenty-sixth floor. A grand view of the Strip," Victor remarked casually, buttoning his suit coat in preparation to leave. *Please, please, please*, Chas thought to himself, *don't take a shot at Treasure Island*. Montrose apparently made his haven there, according to information gleaned before things had acquired their current state between the Rothsteins and Frankie Gee's faction.

But he hadn't to worry. Victor kept his mouth shut.

As they left, heading toward the elevator, Chas

clapped Victor on the shoulder. "Not bad. You even had me fooled for a minute. With any luck, he's underestimated *you*. Or maybe even overestimated you, which will take the attention off…well, whoever it's supposed to be on."

"Damn, Chas, give me some credit," Victor returned. "It's possible to make a deal without cutting someone's nose off. I just hate talking to Kindred who believe what they tell other people about themselves. Half of the conversation is flattery and the other half is trying to get them to take your bait. Kindred like Milo Rothstein talk in circles; you just have to hope they get dizzy. I made that shit up about the debt—I don't know why Frankie's after Benito, but I don't want to look like some ignorant messenger boy. The better I play the game, the more opportunity I give Milo to trip up on his end."

Chas just looked ahead with a slight, bemused smile on his face. Victor was right—sometimes the Kindred fooled themselves better than anyone else with their charades.

As the elevator climbed to the twenty-sixth floor, Chas hoped Milo hadn't left the table thinking the same thing.

Wednesday, 6 October, 1999, 11:47 PM
Si Redd's Resort Hotel & Casino
Mesquite, Nevada

Dan Nussbaum bellied up to the bar. The bartender noticed that he had "that look" about him—the look that signified he was about to hear some kind of story. Maybe a divorce story, maybe some other hard-luck story. Or maybe something *really* weird, which you sometimes heard from a freak who's too strange to be seen under the bright lights of the bigger gambling towns.

Dan ordered a draft.

"Something on your mind, friend?" prodded the bartender. Best to get it over with.

"Yeah, I guess I see a lot of things. Every once in a while, though, some things stick out. I mean, I suppose I'm jaded; Pop says I am. I think he's just old, though. I've seen junkies and drag queens and kids who stole their parents' cars. Pop must have seen it all dozens of times more than I have, but it still shocks him. That's his generation, I reckon.

"The family has a gas station and convenience stop up U.S. 95, outside of the city—Vegas—up by the Air Force range. By 'family' I mean me and Pop. Ma died of cancer six years ago or so. Darlene lives in Los Angeles; she never calls or writes.

"So anyways, that's how I see the stuff I do—it just comes to me. Middle of the night, before the slots get hot, after breakfast, whenever. It comes in from all over.

"Like this one time, I'm behind the counter, looking over the baseball magazine—I've got a bookie in

Vegas—when this real strange fella comes in. It's night, but he's wearing sunglasses. He comes in the front door and his long hair flutters behind him—he even has to stoop a bit to make it under the doorway. I could smell the leather and marijuana on him like he ain't had a shower in a good day or two.

"He nods as he comes in; no sense not being friendly, I suppose. I look past him, out into the lot, smiling at him like 'welcome.' Out there, under the neon lights of the metal awning, parked amid a cloud of bugs and road dust is a Cutlass, front passenger side missing a hubcap. There's a woman in the front seat, but she's asleep or preoccupied, looking forward, or maybe sleeping.

"The guy shuffles around the store a bit and I don't pay him any mind. If he needs something he'll holler. Most people on that road just want to settle their business and get back to the highway.

"He comes up to the counter out of the snack-food aisle and puts his items in front of me: a box of black garbage bags, a roll of duct tape and a pack of Twinkies.

"'Eight sixty-three,' I says. 'You a hitman?' I kidded him.

"He digs a couple of bills out of his greasy pocket and drops them on the countertop.

"'Vampires. Keep the change. You got a john?' is what he says in response.

"'Yes, sir, right around the corner.' I hand him the '64 Impala steering wheel with a key dangling from it.

"He leaves, opens his trunk, throws in his stuff—hard—and yells something. The girl doesn't move, so I guess he wasn't talking to her. He slams the trunk shut, but it bounces open, and he slams it down again. Must've been something in the way. Like a vampire." Dan Nussbaum laughed into his beer.

"The fella lumbers around the side of the building and returns two minutes later. He comes inside, puts the steering wheel on the counter and leaves.

"I blink, and he's gone, nothing but taillights and dust clouds. But that's none of my affair."

The bartender washed a few mugs, unfazed. All the good stories had at least a dead ex-girlfriend. But maybe that's what was in the trunk....

Wednesday, 30 June 1999, 12:52 AM
Caesar's Palace, Room 2604
Las Vegas, Nevada

Chas and Victor returned to their room to find the message light blinking on the telephone. No doubt it was Frankie Gee with some new revelation or a request for them to stop somewhere on the way home.

Chas checked the message at the front desk: *Call Frankie back in New York, urgent.* Something about that unsettled him—nothing ever got Frankie so worked up he needed to do something immediately. He was the kind who, if he got fucked, would sit and ruminate, letting his devious mind conjure a suitable revenge while feeding itself on cold hatred. Frankie was the sort of guy who'd come back at you six weeks after you gave him the short end of the stick. He'd make a big show of it, too—something you thought was trivial or that had passed like water under the bridge had instead been smoldering in Frankie's gut, and now you were going to be paid back in spades.

So Chas called Frankie's office immediately. "Hey, Frankie. This is Chas. What's the problem?" He idly wondered why Annie didn't answer the phone.

"This thing's bigger than I thought, Chas. Apparently, Benito owes people more important than me. I just got word from some of the old-town guineas on high that we better be extra fucking careful with this shit."

"What do you mean? What, he's in the hole across the board?"

"No, nothing like that. I'm small potatoes with some of these old motherfuckers, you know what I mean? I didn't tell them I had you out there, but if Benito's anywhere near Las Vegas, these guys are going to send a crew out your way."

"Well, what do you want me to do? Rothstein's talking like he doesn't know shit but there's someone else in the picture, I'm pretty sure. He had one of his little men there to shake us up, but he also had a freak job in there. Real piece of work, this Nosferatu. Does the name Montrose mean anything to you?" Chas scratched a hotel pen across the note pad on the nightstand. No ink.

"No, nothing to me, but it might to the goombas. Keep your eyes and ears open for someone named Isabel. She's some bigshot with the old family out of Venice."

"Isabel Giovanni?"

"As far as I can tell. She'll be there, like I said, if Las Vegas is worth anything at all."

"Rothstein says Benito came and went. He was here, but then he disappeared. Nobody knows where he is."

"Well these old motherfuckers are all up in arms about it. Wherever he is, they need to just leave him there."

"You don't want us to stay any longer, do you?" Chas remembered the previous night, Victor's escapade and his own encounter with Las Vegas unique brand of lacquered, mediocre vice.

"Well, now that you ask, I do. You stay there a couple more nights, see if any of the old crew make it out there."

"Fuck, Frankie, that's not going to get me in trouble with them, is it? I mean—"

"Hey, you do what I tell you to do, you hear me? Don't you fucking cry to me like a girl because I tell you to stay a few more nights. What the fuck is your problem, Chas? You going soft?"

The question sent Chas's mind racing. *La cosa nostra*, particularly the Giovanni brand, wasn't something people retired from. When you were done, you were either a pile of ash in jail, a pile of ash on the street, or a pile of ash in the oven of your own fucking haven. If Frankie though he was going soft, the old man might have him taken out of the picture before he had a chance to fuck anything up. He shifted the focus from himself.

"No, Frankie, I'm not saying that. I'm saying that if these other guys are making it their case, they might not want us around. Family or no, their dirty laundry is still their dirty laundry, and I don't want to put my nose in it if it's going to fuck up their operation or ours."

"Well, it's good you're thinking, Chas, but you let me take care of that end of things. You and Victor stay out there, and keep your eyes open. I got a suspicion that this is bigger than they're wanting it to seem. They've already made it big by stepping in, going over my head; but it's like you say, it's their problem. If they can't handle their problem, well, maybe I can find someone who can and they'll end up owing me, *capice*?"

"Yeah, I got it."

"One more thing, Chas," Frankie added, trying to seem off-the-cuff.

"What's that?"

"You watch out."

It was like the kiss of death. One simple statement, delivered with such finality and such strained irreverence. Chas knew, like as not, he wouldn't be coming home from this. Easy as pie had suddenly turned into something altogether different.

Wednesday, 30 June 1999, 1:12 AM
Caesar's Palace, Room 2604
Las Vegas, Nevada

Fifteen minutes later, the phone rang.

Victor had wandered down to the casino, wanting to avoid going stir crazy, and taken out a twelve-thousand-dollar marker on the room, which made Chas a bit suspicious. After his conversation with Frankie he wasn't very interested in trusting his own family, let alone a cokehead ghoul who was probably fucking cocktail waitresses at the blackjack table right this very moment.

Second ring.

Chas got up quickly and went to the window, looking down from the guest tower to the parking lot. No sirens, no Crown Vics or government Chevys, no ambulances, and only one white limousine, which he was sure he'd seen earlier. No telltale shadows just under the doorjamb. Just some Bruce Willis movie on TV, in which everything was blowing up or getting punched.

Third ring.

Chas sniffed at the air. A faint whiff of—almonds?—but nothing otherwise. Not that he could be poisoned, at least not by conventional means. He had gone through these paranoid drills a million times before, finally convincing himself, perhaps fatalistically, that if someone really wanted him dead—finally dead—he'd be dead, and there was nothing he could do about it. Whether they were subtle enough to use one of the Kindred contract killers, traditional enough to riddle him with bullets in the street, or brazen enough to set his hotel room on fire, they'd get him. No, the true secret to immortality, or even long mortal life, was to evade attention. Prince Benedic of Las Vegas did it—he kept a quiet, tasteful estate outside the city limit. Frankie Gee did it, hiding behind ranks of *capos* and *caporegimes*, looking every bit the part of a low-class thug and not one bit like a hundred-and-twenty-year-old don who had sailed into Ellis Island half a century ago. Sometimes the invisible people got hurt, but nobody ever set out to do it. Just keep quiet and let someone else take the bullet.

Fourth ring.

Enough with the paranoid bullshit, Chas reasoned, and picked up the phone.

"This is Chas."

"Good evening, Chas. This is your Aunt Isabel. Do you have time to come down for a quick cup of coffee with your favorite aunt?"

Once again, Chas's mind shifted into high gear. She relied on him to know her by name, which means she probably figured Frankie (or someone else) had tipped him off that something was going down. She'd asked him to meet her, however, and in a public place, which was either to cover herself because she'd dealt with Frankie's boys before, or to reassure *him*. He flattered himself and decided upon the former, even though he knew otherwise. She didn't ask about Victor, though, so he'd keep that part quiet and see what played out.

"Sure. I'll be right down."

"Marvelous. I'll be waiting."

She sounded sweet, Aunt Isabel did. So sweet,

Chas decided to play it safe. He checked the clip and chamber of his big automatic—hopefully it would at least buy him some time if conversation became too tense—and left the room, closing the door deliberately behind him.

Yeah, the room had smelled like almonds.

Wednesday, 30 June 1999, 1:19 AM
Caesar's Palace, Nero's Restaurant
Las Vegas, Nevada

Isabel had been waiting for only a few minutes when Chas arrived. He looked pleasant enough, in that sort of big-boned, rough-hewn American way. He wore a simple, clean-lined black suit, but no tie, and his collar was open. How mortal! And didn't these coarse gangster-types ever get over their black suits? *When someone sees a man in a black suit*, thought Isabel, *they know he's either with the government or quite against it.*

No matter, Isabel figured. Las Vegas was lousy with high-rollers and their would-be emulators, and nothing about Chas aroused immediate suspicion. In the end he was just a resource, and once she was done she would probably never see him again.

Wednesday, 30 June 1999, 1:19 AM
Caesar's Palace, Nero's Restaurant
Las Vegas, Nevada

Chas figured he'd play the part of the flustered underling for pathos. He had left his shirt open and his hair somewhat tousled. After taking the elevator downstairs, he thought he'd make a quick pass throught the casino before joining Isabel in the steak house. Better see what Victor was up to with twelve large riding on the boss's name.

But Victor was nowhere in sight. *Worry about that later*, Chas told himself.

And so, somewhat preoccupied, he wandered into Nero's, telling the host he'd come to meet his aunt, who was to be waiting for him.

"Aunt?" the host had asked.

"By marriage," Chas replied. What the fuck did that mean?

He soon found out. Isabel looked far too young to be his aunt in any conventional sense, in her late twenties or perhaps early thirties. She looked very continental, with faintly olive skin (*so that's what undead Europeans look like*), brown hair almost black, and lithesome arms crossed before her. She hadn't noticed him yet, and her head was turned in repose, giving him a plain view of her classical beauty made all the more interesting by minor curiosities of feature that only generations of quiet inbreeding could bestow. *Slightly weak chin*, he observed, *and dangerously high cheekbones*. He also noticed the youthful curve of her small breasts and the arch of her shoulders, from which a silk dress hung in a manner best described as salaciously. A green bottle of Pellegrino sat in front of her, on the table, open but unsampled.

Shit, thought, Chas, almost aloud. *I want my aunt.*

He sat down, her head turning at his arrival, and she favored him with a slight smile.

"Don't gentlemen ask before they take a lady's company?"

"Erm…" Chas relied wittily. "They told me that you were waiting." *Oaf.*

"Well it is a pleasure to meet so handsome a cousin. Or nephew. Or whatever you might be. I can't keep the relationships straight, myself," she said through a laugh.

Chas noticed her scent.

"House of Givenchy," she spoke.

"I'm sorry?"

"Givenchy. My perfume."

"I'm familiar with Givenchy, but I didn't know—"

"Your nose moved. I saw it. I notice the little things."

"You must think I'm a clown. I'm not usually so taken aback, but tonight's been full of revelations."

"I'm sure it has." *Good*, thought Isabel, *Get right down to business. A wise choice, and one that allow you an early lead. My move.* "And what revelations were those?"

"Well, I got a call from my boss who said you might be on your way out here, and that I should be aware that hospitality might be in order." Chas smiled. "It would seem that we're both looking for a mutual acquaintance."

"So your boss knows you're out here?"

"I'm sorry?" Chas repeated. *Damn, she's ahead of me by too many steps. What's she talking about?*

"I wasn't told that your branch of the family had anyone here."

"Well, then, why did you know you could find me?"

"Because, Chas, our family is full of liars. Omission is no less a lie than any other alteration of the truth."

"I suppose you can look at it that way. But Frankie's got me mobile looking for Benito. I figured this was a good place to start. Vegas pretty much springs to mind when you think of the Ma—my family's business, and Benito didn't strike me as the super-creative, I'll-break-the-mold type. At least from what I'd been told."

"I see. Mmm. Yes, well, 'acquaintance' is a bit of a strong way of describing him. Benito is a commodity to those above him. He and his type are common enough among our ranks."

Chas found himself put off by this. He didn't know what to make of Isabel's statement. Apparently, she occupied some other position in the family than Benito did, but she was simultaneously more and less than he? Her words indicated that she was not "above him," but that he was somehow less valuable than she.

"I'm afraid you've lost me, my dear aunt." Chas hoped she took that in the spirit with which it was intended. "Could you maybe give me a bit more to go on? I can't help you unless I know what I'm supposed to be doing."

"Oh, that's quite the contrary, Charles." *My full name*, Chas reasoned, *turnabout is fair play*. "If you simply do what you're told, you're far more efficient and valuable. The world has two types of people: those who lead and those who should follow. It's all right— there's no shame in being one of the followers. It's simply the role to which you're best suited. I myself am a follower, having long since lost my special gift of insight. It's part of the family curse, if you know what I mean."

Chas did, indeed. She was talking about the Embrace. While becoming a vampire offered many gifts, it more than made up for them in drawbacks. For someone like Chas, many of them didn't matter: He didn't care if he never saw the sun again. Of late, he'd even become somewhat enamored of the idea of the Giovanni Kiss—Kindred of his clan caused great pain when they fed from vessels, as opposed to other Kindred, whose bite caused ecstasy once the vessel yielded to it. In the end, however, no matter how any individual looked at it, the Embrace was damnation, plain and simple. Even if the Kindred was able to take some small solace in the potency of his undead, immortal form, that was nothing more than God's ironic and spiteful sense of humor. As the legends told it, the Curse of Caine was levied upon the first vampire, slayer of his brother Abel, during the days of Adam, Eve and a garden full of snakes. As far as Chas was concerned, that meant only one thing—the God of the Old Testament created vampires, back when He was one angry, badass motherfucker. The Old Testament was full of demonstrations of God's wrath. He was always smiting or cursing some group of people for the licentiousness or greed of some other group of people. It was only after the advent of the New Testament that God calmed down a little. You wouldn't find any great Biblical curses like vampires or rains of blood or turning people into pillars of salt in the modern nights, no sir. And that's probably why the world was going to hell in a handbasket. God didn't care anymore. Go ahead and fuck it up all you want, He seemed to have said. I have given you creation and you want to use it to destroy yourselves. Well, have a good time, Chas imagined Him saying before He turned his back and went away to work on something worthwhile.

Chas shook his head. Where had all *that* come from?

He looked across the table to see Isabel smiling at him.

"Did you do that?" he asked.

"Do what?" came her coy response.

"That thing that just happened. Did you fill my head will all those weird thoughts? I mean, I've never considered myself a religious man, but I just had a very…um…righteous stream of consciousness pour through my mind. Of course, now that I think about it, they were pretty much in the same vein as most of my thoughts, but why would I all of a sudden start thinking about God?"

"Chas, you heathen, I have no idea. Maybe it would do you some good to think about God once in a while. I know it's helped me."

"That's bullshit, Isabel. I mean, I guess I still believe in God—kinda stupid to believe in Kindred without Him—but it's not a big part of my…um…life."

"No one said it had to be, Chas. But do you honestly believe that the maverick act you and your part of the family put on is the be-all and end-all of life and unlife?" Isabel looked around, making sure to lower her voice so that if anyone was listening they wouldn't hear her say such curious things. Unlife, indeed. "Do you think a curse so great as the one that our family has taken upon its shoulders exists so that you can play *The Godfather* and shoot other vampires in the face for eternity? Are you so vain? Or so simple?"

"Hey, calm down, Isabel. Jesus Christ, this shit's getting strange. I came down here to talk to you about the Benito thing and the next thing I know I've got fucking Genesis 3:16 running though my head. It *was* you, wasn't it?"

Isabel made a grand show of sighing. "My boy, if I wanted to agitate you, I'd do it in some way that helped me. Sending you into a fervent rapture of self-indulgence doesn't really work for me, you know? If you simply *must* know, I can tell you what happened to you, but it's probably not going to make you very happy."

Chas stared expectantly.

"Ghosts."

"Ghosts," repeated Chas sardonically.

"That's right. Ghosts."

"Flip answer, Isabel. Very funny. Ghosts. Now, if you'll excuse me," Chas stood halfway before meeting Isabel's gaze. He stopped. "You're fucking serious."

"Watch your mouth, and yes, I'm serious."

At that moment, the table's waiter stopped by. "Have you decided what you would like for dinner? Or perhaps a cocktail to begin? Another Pellegrino?" Chas looked as if he was about to drive the waiter away, but Isabel put her hand on his. No sense in upsetting the staff and having them know you're up to something.

"I'm, sorry. We've just been catching up. It's been a long time since we've seen each other. I think we'll need another few minutes to decide on dinner. In the meantime, I'll have a negroni."

Chas looked over at Isabel almost accusingly, as if thinking *this is what happens when you meet at a restaurant*. Then he looked to the waiter and quickly asked for a bourbon and water. The waiter smiled and nodded, taking his leave to fetch their drinks.

Isabel looked impishly at Chas. "What are you having for dinner?" she teased.

"I would never eat here," Chas replied, calming a bit. "I've heard terrible things about their meat locker."

"Well, then we should probably leave pretty quickly after our drinks get here. I don't know that they'll want us taking up their tables if we're not planning to eat."

"Yeah, because they're slammed at one thirty in the morning." Chas made a sweeping gesture with his arm, emphasizing the largely empty room.

"You're wasting time," Isabel remarked, "and we should wrap up this conversation and get you on your way. You still have a lot to do tonight."

Eyeing her inquisitively, Chas wondered what Isabel was talking about.

"But first," she continued, "ghosts. I know I don't need to preface this with too much, but if you're prepared to believe in vampires, you should be prepared to believe in ghosts."

Chas smiled dryly, crookedly, as if the whole thing was a very clever trick.

"I'm serious. I'm sure you're the first to admit that there are things you just don't know about the Giovanni. You like it that way—I can see it in you. As long as nothing bothers you individually, you're more than content to let Clan Giovanni do whatever it wants. That's how most Giovanni like it, Chas, and it's why you're still among the Kindred rather than a heap of ashes at the foot of some elder's chair. You do your part and you don't ask questions. But the truth of the matter is going to be unpleasant, even for a rough character like yourself."

Chas's smile had slowly vanished from his face. Over the course of her few words, he had begun to watch her as a deer eyes a wolf, not as an enemy, but as a creature that knows it exists only at the whim of another. The wolf doesn't kill deer for sport, but out of necessity. The deer had only to fear the hungry wolf. But was Isabel hungry in whatever context or metaphorical sense the word implied?

"That's okay. I'm a big boy. I can take it."

"Yes, that's true. But as far as those ghosts go, Chas, that's something to which the Giovanni have inextricably tied themselves...*our*selves. You know very well that death goes hand-in-hand with much of our business and personal affairs. Well, I'm telling you that for many, death is not the end. The spirits—souls—of the dead continue to serve us even after they have left the physical world. It's one of the family's secrets from centuries ago. The Renaissance and even before. We make the dead do our bidding.

"But something's happened recently. Something that's made our power over the restless dead...I don't know what it is, actually. Our mastery of the spirits hasn't begun to wane, but there seem to be fewer spirits around, and even these aren't in the places we've come to associate with them.

"Without boring you with all the petty details, I think that's what just happened to you—a ghost was having his way with you, Chas. They can see into our world and they know things about us, which is why they're so valuable to us. But that's a double-bladed sword. They know, for instance, that you're a Giovanni, and they hate you for it. It's not necessarily anything you've said or done, though it might be the ghost of one of your victims or vessels. They resent the fact that you're Giovanni because the Giovanni can use the restless souls whenever they choose."

Chas looked positively incredulous. "You're telling me that ghosts are prejudiced against me. That's what you're telling me. That not only can the Giovanni family perform voodoo, but that the little demons don't like us for it and so they sometimes pick on us."

"Well, Chas, that's a bit of an irreverent way of saying it, but I suppose that's correct in its own fashion. I understand that it's a bit much to take at face value, but you'd do well to take it quite seriously. The dead do, after all."

Chas leaned back in his chair, his palms on the edge of the table and fingers atop it, as if he was about to push himself back in disgust. Their drinks arrived and Isabel begged another few minutes of the waiter, who was all too happy to return to the kitchen and resume gossiping with the other staff about the weird couple at table seventeen.

"What's a negroni, anyway?" Chas asked, thankful for the change in subject from the decidedly bizarre direction the conversation had just taken. He had to admit it made a twisted sort of sense—if the Kindred still walked the earth, well, why the fuck couldn't ghosts? The very thought brought to mind some of the tales told by other Kindred he'd met in passing. Stories about the *things* with which the undead shared the night, whether knowingly or otherwise; other monsters and things even less definable. Chas felt a sharpening of his mind, and sudden epiphany that other forces were at work in the world. And, accompanied by a single, cold drop of bloodsweat between his shoulder blades, he realized that he feared them. He didn't know them, didn't know what any other creature of the night—even one as vital to him as Frankie Gee—really had going on in their mind. Mortals were easy. They didn't even suspect that the monsters from their collective unconscious walked among them. But to be one of those monsters—and to know that others…

Chas didn't want to think about it anymore. Best to get back to the issue at hand and deal with the things he *could* affect. Let the world keep spinning. "What is it? Is that cranberry juice? You didn't have them fix you up a little blood cocktail back there, did you?" Even before he finished, Chas realized that she might well have. It might be another example of the far-reaching influence the supernal beings of the world possessed. He realized that maybe he didn't want to know, after all.

"It's just gin, vermouth and Campari."

Somehow, Chas found the mundanity of it calming. He shook his head.

"This place is bugging me," Chas complained. "Can we get out of here?"

"Of course."

"Good. Let's go to the casino. Nobody's going to lean on us to order dinner there, and if we don't gamble, they won't hassle us to take their free drinks, either."

Chas left a pair of twenties on the table as they walked out.

Wednesday, 30 June 1999, 2:12 AM
Caesar's Palace Casino
Las Vegas, Nevada

"Let's not beat around the bush here, Isabel. I need to get moving on this Benito thing," Chas said quietly. Even amid the racket and ping of the slot machines—the ones they hadn't replaced with that video-game shit—one had to be careful how loudly one spoke. Vegas casinos were wired to the last inch with video cameras, and some had microphones to boot.

"Have you met a Kindred named Montrose?" Isabel asked, looking at Chas directly. She still didn't know him well enough to trust him, and she kept her sharp senses on the lookout for any "tells" he might drop that would tip her off that he was hiding something. Damn this family.

"That twisted fuck? What's it got to do with him? I thought he was Rothstein's bully-boy." Chas touched his nose briefly, as if to ward away an itch.

A tell.

"What made you think that?"

"He was all muscle and ready to dust knuckles once Victor started playing haughty. He didn't look too smart, either, like he wanted any excuse to come over and toss some Giovanni salad."

"Well, that's...colorful. Could you do me a favor? Could you take it easy on the street idioms? I don't mind the cursing, to be honest, but English isn't my first language and I'd rather not spend time deciphering from English to English. And 'tossing salad' as slang means something entirely different in other situations, which I'm sure you don't mean, but which conjures amusing images nonetheless," Isabel responded, looking around the room over Chas's shoulder.

"You're talking about that prison fag shit. Yeah, I've heard all that before. Now if you want to make an accusation—"

"Oh, calm down. Let's get back to Montrose. He's got more at stake in Benito's disappearance than Rothstein does. Rothstein's a front Montrose is using. Of course, Rothstein thinks that he's using you as a favor to Montrose. Yes, I know, it's convoluted. Bear with me. Milo Rothstein represents a significant amount of Giovanni influence in Las Vegas, which he thinks will protect him. It won't: Milo's made too many enemies by skimming off the top of what's already being skimmed off the top. It's actually costing the Giovanni to keep him here, but Las Vegas is still profitable, given the amount of money other Giovanni interests in town generate. You know, other Rothsteins. Their family's just as complicated as ours, only a bit smaller.

"Anyway, Rothstein knows that Montrose is in on Benito's kidnapping, so he thinks he's putting the Nosferatu in debt by leading you on. The bottom line is that Milo probably doesn't know the first thing about Benito, but he's not going to tell Montrose that or Montrose will know that Milo's fooling him and deserves nothing in return.

"The problem is that Montrose already knows Milo's a patsy, and is, in turn, keeping *that* a secret from Milo. Montrose is playing you through Milo and Milo through you."

Chas, squinting one eye a bit, cut in. "That

doesn't make any sense."

"No, it doesn't. Which is why he's doing it. To keep you pointed at each other, when he's the real problem to both of you."

"How's he a problem to Milo?"

"Think it through, Chas. Milo has other Giovanni coming into his town to investigate the Benito affair. You're not the only one. The Scots have someone here, too. Since Milo's skimming too much, having any outside Giovanni here puts him in the position of having that maybe found out."

"But how do you know that?"

"Well, Jesus, Chas, you think I'm not as clever as Montrose, at least? I play this game, too. You'd better learn if you have any intentions of staying involved very long."

Chas raised his eyebrows.

"Okay, but one more thing."

"Yes, my darling nephew?" Isabel made a crooked smile with one half of her mouth.

"How do you know it's Montrose who's behind the whole thing? Or at least behind the part he's, um, behind…of. You know what I mean."

"Because he's sloppy. The night Benito was kidnapped, security at his building reported a delivery attempt by Trans-State Expediters, and that the delivery vehicle returned after about five minutes but didn't attempt to drop off its shipment. Trans-State Expediters is a subsidiary of The Architects' Group, which is a venture-capital consortium here in Las Vegas. Sitting on its board is one Theodore Benedict, an alias maintained by Las Vegas's Kindred prince, Benedic."

"So? Is Montrose also the prince? No, wait, it's another alias."

"No," Isabel smiled smugly, "Benedic doesn't have anything to do with it. Benito crossed Montrose a few years back on an art deal or something that went sour. I think Benito had offered Montrose an investment opportunity on a cache of hidden originals that his ghouls had found in Nice, France. Apparently, someone had hidden them to keep them from falling into the state's hands during the French Revolution. There's a Millet among them, I think, and maybe a David. It doesn't matter. Benito edged Montrose out of the deal before it became final, so Montrose has a grudge. Also, Montrose had recently been found out for putting one of his spies in the prince's haven, so he's obviously got a grudge against Benedic, too, or he at least wants to even the score. In light of that, my guess is that Montrose was either setting Benedic up to catch some of the flak in the Benito affair—possibly making Giovanni matters here very touchy—or he was just setting up another layer of blinds between himself and the game's pawns."

Chas stood, staring at Isabel.

"You've got to be kidding me..." he said, trailing off at the end to indicate that surely she *was* kidding.

Isabel just rolled her eyes coyly.

Isabel said earnestly, "It's not so difficult once you put a few of the pieces in place. Then you start to see the big picture."

Chas shook his head. "Yeah, but that's some series of guesses you've turned into pieces. Even hearing all that, I don't know if you've put together a big picture, or just a stack of little pieces that's part of one even larger piece, or whether it's all just a stack of shit that doesn't mean a damn thing except that it's easy to tell a good story with a handful of speculation."

Isabel smiled. "Well, nephew," she chimed, kissing her hand and planting it on his forehead, "I suppose we'll just have to see."

With that, she waved, turned, and walked into the Las Vegas crowd, leaving Chas to wonder if this was a second kiss of death this night.

Wednesday, 30 June 1999, 2:47 AM
Caesar's Palace, Room 2604
Las Vegas, Nevada

"Frankie, how do I get a hold of Milo Rothstein?" Chas knew he had only a few minutes before the sun came up and Frankie had to hide himself from its deadly rays. Time zones were a vampire's greatest enemy when it came down to business.

"Jesus, Chas, you know what time it is here?"

"Of course I know what time it is, but it's an emergency. Remember what you told me about those Giovanni up the ladder? Well, they're out here, or Isabel is, and Milo's in the way. Our man Benito's mixed up in something that stretches pretty far and Milo's running cover for whoever's got his number."

"What the fuck are you talking about, Chas?"

"Come *on*, Frankie, I'm trying to help you out here. Isabel thinks that playing hardball with these motherfuckers will flush them out and let us know where we stand. I agree with her. I mean, fuck, it's not like we have anything to lose. Milo and his crew are already on the outs, you said, and I got lucky finding out this little bit. It's going to let me do what you told me."

Chas knew Frankie wasn't one to fall for the false jingo ruse, but it was all he had. He'd pick up the pieces later and sort this all out once they made it back to New York. Right now his concern was keeping a step ahead of the game, because he knew Milo wasn't about to let Frankie Gee's bloodhounds leave town with Benito's trail on their minds.

"Chas, this is fucked up. I'm going to give you the number and I'm going to pray you know what you're doing. You do know what you're doing, right? This shit just can't wait until tomorrow night?"

"No, Frankie. We still got three, four hours before dawn here, and I don't want to give those fucking Rothsteins the benefit of first move. Even if nothing happened tonight, their people are all over this town, you know? They'll have a good sixteen hours on us before we can even step up to bat. Vincent's good in the clutch, but we don't know this town and nobody's in our pocket."

"Why don't you guys back off the situation then and let it cool down?"

Chas stopped for a moment. Frankie wasn't one to change gears if a golden opportunity presented itself. What was this hesitancy all about?

Frankie didn't have any love for the Rothsteins— it was old-world greaseball shit between the Giovanni Italians and the Rothstein Jews. Even though the Rothsteins were part of the Giovanni *clan*, they weren't family. What was good for the pocketbook wasn't necessarily good for the table conversation, as Frankie used to say. The Giovanni turned good money from the Rothstein connection, just like they turned good money from the Mafia guys, just like they presumably turned good money from their other interests. It all came down to that.

So what was Frankie's beef? He'd already said that Chas might need to take Milo out of the picture— what was the cause for reversal? The whole situation had changed in so few hours. What was supposed to be a quick and forgettable bit of pressure had turned into a crisis in just a few hours, with those few hours marking a total reversal on Frankie's position.

"Come on, Frankie, you're leaving me out like half a fag over here. You told me that Milo can go if he needs to and he does. What's the problem?" Chas knew he was overstepping his bounds a bit, but he relied on Frankie's lack of time and hopefully confusion over the situation to give him something to go on.

Chas heard a few clicks from the other end of the phone and then a quick inhalation.

"All right, Chas, listen and listen good." Frankie's voice had become husky, like he was leaning over and whispering and tucking the phone in toward his body so someone else wouldn't be able to hear. "I can only tell you this once. You talk to Milo and you make it perfectly clear to him that if he doesn't give you the straight dope on Benito's situation, you're going to do him. If he doesn't tell you where Benito is, you do just that—you put a big, long hurt on him; tell him it's for me—then you make sure he don't see no more moonrises, *capice*? And then, even if he tells you where Benito fucking Giovanni is, you kill him anyway. Here's his number." And Frankie whispered the ten digits (or actually seven, as the area code was a unique secret—**#—held by Giovanni Kindred, who needed secure lines).

Blinking twice, Chas hung up with no parting good-bye. He had written down the number, though only half was visible. Cheap fucking hotel pens. But he had indented the paper enough to have everything that mattered. He tore off that sheet, ran the sink, and threw the rest of the tablet in the water. Nobody else needed that number. Or they wouldn't after tonight.

Frankie Gee had never told Chas to kill anyone before. It had always been a matter of opportunity or survival. If someone got in the way and Chas couldn't work around them, *then* maybe they got hit hard enough to never get up again. But this time was different. This time it was a mandate. Frankie had killers. Chas was more of a menacing mouthpiece. But Chas was the only one there, and Frankie wasn't about to have Victor do the deed. Victor wasn't even full family—some Giovanni somewhere had married his sister twelve, thirteen years ago. No, Frankie trusted Chas to do this all by himself. What was going on back at Frankie's that made everything so delicate?

Fuck it. Answer that later. Right now, Milo awaits.

"Let's go," Chas called to Victor, who had watched the whole thing but obligingly tuned out what he wasn't supposed to hear. Good boy. "Grab the bag."

Victor's eyes widened. The bag meant trouble. "What's up, boss man?"

"We're going down to the lobby to make a phone call and to wait on our fella Milo Rothstein. Then we're going to go somewhere good and discuss the matter like gentlemen." Chas cocked an eyebrow.

The pair took the elevator to the lobby. A bank of telephones stood just outside the public restrooms. Chas took the one farthest from the facilities, turned away from the doorway and dialed the number Frankie had given him.

"Milo."

"Yeah, Mr. Rothstein, this is Earl. I'm Mr. Sforza's

attendant, from the conference room earlier?"

"Yes, Earl. I'm curious how you came across this number."

"Well, Mr. Rothstein, it's Mr. Sforza. He's got some kind of problem with, um, the home office and he said it would be best to call you and arrange for some other accommodations."

"He did? That's very strange. It would seem that our Mr. Sforza has had a change of heart."

"That's not for me to say, sir." *Come on, shitbag. Drop the niceties and send a fucking limo.*

"Well, I'd like to hear what has Mr. Sforza so worked up at…three in the morning. I'll send a car that will be there shortly. Have your things and be waiting in the lobby. You said Caesar's Palace, correct?"

Shithead. How stupid do you think I am? "I didn't, sir. Mr. Sforza said that in your meeting this evening."

"Ah, yes. In any event, wait in the lobby. My man will be there soon."

"Thank you, sir. We'll be waiting."

Monday, 21 June 1999, 9:17 PM
Boston Financial Corporation
Boston, Massachusetts

A white panel van rolled up to the loading dock of the office building that housed the main offices of the Boston Financial Corporation, Ltd. The night manager of the security team came out to wave the driver away and inform him that it had to make deliveries in the morning. As the security officer left the building, however, a black-wrapped form stole inside quietly, catching the door with long, slim fingers and sliding almost like a liquid across the concrete piling that made up the dock's ingress.

The van's driver nodded, waved goodnight, and drove away.

And around the block, returning not quite two minutes afterward. Upon his return, he pulled the van up to the dock, parked it, and proceeded to jack a pallet out of the back.

The pallet contained six long, rectangular cases bound together by plastic shrinkwrap. The driver returned the jack to the van and drove away again, this time for good.

The quiet intruder crept through the dock's shadows, clinging as closely as possible to the walls. It made a wide circuit of the dock area, remaining out of sight and finally ducking around a corner, where it silently exited the building from a bay of normal-sized service doors. Taking care to tape the retainer lock down before letting the door close, it jogged spring-legged to the pallet of rectangular cases, where it proceeded to peel away the shrinkwrap with a long knife. It then opened three of the cases, from which swiftly emerged three similarly dressed shapes. Like bats or tattered cloaks they looked, a group of ragged, quiet skeletons, all tall and thin. Without so much as the grate of concrete across metal, they opened the taped door and swept inside, like trash blown in the wind.

Once inside, the shapes made a beeline for the service stairwell. Up and up they climbed, by turns bounding like rats and scuttling like insects. The wan fluorescent light glowed horrifically on their skin, some pallid, some greenish, some mottled and tight. They had decided to take the staircase because of its lack of evening traffic. Also, the stairwell had no security cameras—although they could easily have hidden from the living eyes of the building's night staff, the coarse machines would have caught their every movements—a pack of tatter-wrapped skeletons clambering unquestioned through the halls of the building. No, such sloppiness would have brought down the wrath of other Kindred, should this ruse ever come to light. The Masquerade, held so dear by the undead who wished to remain unnoticed among the mortals around them, was far more important than the abduction of Benito Giovanni. In the end, even Benito was a mere pawn of the game, while the Masquerade was a rule observed by all sensible Cainites. Especially the horrid and twisted members of Clan Nosferatu, who looked so much like the monsters that other Kindred pretended they weren't.

Their nails and talons clicked and scraped as they sped inexorably up the stairs, sounding like nothing so much as the chittering chelicerae of hungry insects. A flapping, stinking, hideous form they were, rolling amorphously up the stairs in a scrabble of bent limbs and rail-thin appendages.

Four floors below the one occupied by their victim's office, the skeletal crew poured out from the stairwell into an empty office that was the receiving room of a civil engineer's consulting firm by day. Clearing the desk of papers and detritus, the Nosferatu clambered and clicked onto the top, where they pulled open a ceiling grate that concealed a ventilation shaft. Up the thin pipe they wriggled, using their shoulders and splayed feet to brace themselves against the sides of the tube. No normal man could have fit into the shaft, let alone undulated his body to negotiate his way upward. With the flick of a bare, prehensile foot, the last monster pulled shut the grate, leaving no evidence of their passing except for a wafting scent of rot in the office below.

Up for four floors they writhed, spilling out at their destination like a noxious puddle of body parts and wattled skin. Cloaking themselves with a suggested mental invisibility, they walked unchallenged past the desk of their victim's assistant. They pulled the door behind her open ever so slightly, allowing them a quick entry into the office beyond, while they went unnoticed by Benito Giovanni within, as he cursed at his telephones and flailed about in frustration.

And then, when the moment to strike had arrived, they revealed themselves to their prey. Benito Giovanni and a powerful but seemingly spiteful spirit made a brief but deadly resistance to the kidnapping operation. Benito managed to sound the building's alarm, but the Nosferatu remained undetected, even under the direct and intense scrutiny of the well-armed security team that responded. No matter. The objective was achieved, even if it did cost them two of their number.

Wednesday, 30 June 1999, 3:50 AM
Stardust Hotel, Room 2901
Las Vegas, Nevada

A white stretch Lincoln Continental picked up Chas and Victor from the lobby of Caesar's Palace. Neither thought that Milo would be so foolish as to have them brought to his haven, and Chas wasn't sure a car would be readily accessible at their rendezvous, so he had told Victor to bring the bag.

The bag meant that Chas intended to exact vengeance, and it was full of all manner of unpleasant implements. Duct tape, phone wire and silk cord all served the same purpose: to tie down whoever needed to be restrained. A supply of cutting instruments from the crude to the exquisite could be used to get anyone to talk about anything, as could the claw hammer, the blackjack and the "plumber's snake," which left one hellacious welt anywhere it struck naked flesh. The bag normally would have contained a lighter, but Chas figured that the hotels would have plenty of matchbooks on hand. None of it was very necessary in the end, anyway, after the binding material. Any time Chas needed to make anyone talk, tying them up and menacing them with the contents of the bag usually served the purpose. It wasn't like Chas was a master torturer, anyway. He usually let brute force and raw pain do the work. No, he was certainly no artist, but he got the job done when it needed to be. The whole ugly toolkit had been wrapped in stolen hotel towels, so the bag looked like an overnight duffel full of clothes, instead of a satchel of implements used for hurting people.

Exactly what Chas's vengeance was *for*, he hadn't figured out yet. Benito Giovanni fit somewhere into the picture, but as to his role, neither Chas nor Victor was sure. Both of their minds scrambled to make sense of the few pieces of the puzzle they had been given, but nothing clicked. Chas kept his mouth shut, making sure to continue the charade he and Victor had put on earlier, just in case the driver was privy to the situation. He pretended to be Victor's valet and bodyguard, letting the smaller man appear as the one in charge.

Both Giovanni were surprised to be let off at the front of the Stardust Hotel and Casino. They'd figured that Rothstein surely had a hidey-hole somewhere outside of town and that he'd keep them there as a form of insurance to himself. The fact that he had delivered them to such a public place reassured them, however.

"Room 2901," the driver told them as he let them out. Chas quickly checked the license plate as the Continental drove away. Legitimate tag (at least to the naked eye), no rental stickers. That boded well, too.

They took the elevator to the twenty-ninth floor. As they exited, Chas made a quick reconnaissance of the floor. No uninvited guests lurked in the vending vestibules—just a humming Coke machine. The stairwell was empty, at least on this floor, the one above and the one below.

Chas knocked at door 2901.

Milo answered the door, which Chas pushed open and motioned for Victor to step inside. Rothstein looked up at Chas. "A bit presumptuous, perhaps?" but he shrugged it off. The room was not altogether unlike the one they kept at Caesar's. The forgettable Rothstein from the meeting was also in the room, relaxing somewhat in an overstuffed chair, but the twisted Nosferatu Montrose was nowhere to be seen. On the television, the same Bruce Willis movie Chas had seen earlier played. He was going to make idle conversation about it to set the room at ease, but then he remembered that he was "backup," at least at present.

"I trust this room will do for you?" asked Milo. That must have meant that Rothstein planned to let Victor stay here, probably as a favor, as he thought Victor had turned against Frankie Gee. That is, with any luck, he thought Victor had switched sides. It was impossible to tell among the Kindred exactly who knew how much, even when they told you.

"It's fine, thank you," replied Victor. He put the bag down by the side of the bed and sat down.

"Oh, don't do that. These bedspreads are filthy," Milo said, pulling the spread from the bed and shoving it in the closet. "They never wash the things, and I'm sure you know what sorts of filth and excess go on in these suites." He smiled. Did he know? Fuck it.

"Well, if it's anything like what happens in every other hotel room everywhere in the world, I'm sure you're right," said Victor. Good. Keep up the chatter. *We're all friends here, you lying fucks*, thought Chas. *Wait a moment. Lying about what? Calm down, cowboy. No need to go off half-cocked again.*

"Very true. I'm afraid I have to ask, though. To what to we owe this sudden shift in allegiance? Your

justin Achilli 91

man," Milo motioned to Chas (or Earl, as he hopefully knew him), "said that you had an unpleasant telephone conversation?"

"More or less," Victor shrugged. The nameless Rothstein turned off the TV and rose from the chair. "I'm sorry, I missed your name at our last meeting."

"Benjamin. Or Ben, rather. Ben Rothstein."

"Pleasure to meet you, Ben, but I have to say I wish it were under other circumstances." Victor looked to Milo. "My plans seem to have fallen apart, but I hope I can repay your last-minute and largely undeserved hospitality. If you'll pardon my gross tongue, I thought I was all but fucked about an hour ago."

Milo laughed. Ben took the cue once it was obviously okay to do so and gave a nervous smile of his own. How this dumb little freak ever got Embraced into the clan—if he was a vampire at all—was beyond Chas.

"Well, it's never too late to play the game, I always say," Milo mused.

I'll bet you do, Chas thought.

"But to get back to the matter at hand, I'm still curious why. I don't need the full story—you can tell me the rest of the details tomorrow night. Well, I suppose it's actually tonight, but you know what I'm saying." Milo paced absently at the foot of the bed.

"Long story short, Frankie wanted me to lean on you guys hard about this Benito character. I said that you obviously hadn't seen him after a few weeks ago, and that you were already one up on us and why we were here. Any hardball on our part was just going to piss you guys off—again, I'm sorry for the coarse talk, but I'm a little tired—and we're basically in your back yard. I know the Rothsteins and Frankie have some bad blood in the background, but that's not because of me, and it's not my job to fix it. I think you guys should just kiss and make up, but whatever this is came before me, and I know how this business makes people carry grudges. But Frankie, he's insistent, and I told him outright that I'm not willing to be the guy who starts a war. Benito's going to turn up sooner or later, and even if he doesn't, *someone's* going to see him and that's not worth opening old wounds for, you know? So then Frankie gets all bent out of shape and I figured it would just be good to keep my options open. It's not like I'm walking out on Frankie—you know that it doesn't work like that in our line of business—but I'm not going to burn any bridges if I don't need to, right?"

"Very sound reasoning, Mr. Sforza. And I admire your loyalty. It seems that such things become rarer and rarer in these modern nights."

Chas smiled inwardly. A good enough story, assuming Milo wasn't one of the paranoid-just-below-the-surface types. If he was, he was a fucking Oscar-quality actor, because he didn't have any of the tells, any of the pantomimes that subtly betrayed a lie as it was told or motioned. Victor could be good when he wasn't blown and fucking hookers.

"I trust you'll give us a call when you wake, Mr. Sforza? It's getting late and we'll leave this evening without asking any more of your time. Benjamin, would you go ahead and bring the car around?"

Bang. Just like that. Milo Rothstein's vanity

signed his death warrant. He was so intent on looking like a bigshot in front of his rival's men he didn't bother to keep Ben in the room to keep the score even.

Ben left to have the valet fetch the car. Chas took off his jacket as the door shut behind the exiting Rothstein, noting the mechanical buzz of the electric lock doing its work. He hung his jacket and unbuttoned his cuffs, beginning to roll them upward. Milo noted him with the faintest hint of apprehension.

That's right, fucko. Time to die.

"I'll take my leave, Mr. Sforza. Feel free to enjoy the casino for the rest of the evening—I've arranged a small marker to make your stay more convenient and comfort—"

"Wrong, cocksucker," Chas sneered. "You're going to fucking answer a few questions before you go home." Victor moved like an old pro. He had the bag open and the phone cord out before Milo turned to look back at him. Chas favored the phone cord, he had told Victor on the flight. It's tough as all hell to break, and even if someone did manage to burst the strong plastic sheath, it was full of copper wire that cut flesh to ribbons if you tried to force your way through it. The only way to avoid shredding yourself with it was to hope that it burst when and if you managed to break the plastic skin, too.

Chas took a swing that clipped Milo on the chin, knocking his mouth open and sending him tripping backward. Victor took advantage, looping the wire over Milo's head and around his arms, pinning them to his sides. This he pulled tight, then looped it twice again around Milo's body. Victor knew he had to be careful—the Rothsteins were Giovanni after all, and Giovanni Kindred were able to call on inhuman strength. Not that he'd ever seen it before, but if Milo was a hidden powerhouse, he might be able to snap the cord and break Victor's neck before Chas could subdue him.

But that wasn't the case. Victor completed five more loops by the time Chas had dragged the chair from the desk over to where Milo was still standing, bound as he was.

"Victor, tie him up. Milo, you talk to me and give it to me straight so I don't have to break anything I don't need to." He admired his handiwork. The punch—augmented by Chas's own appreciable Giovanni strength—had broken Milo's jaw and a jagged piece of bone jutted through the skin of his chin. Before his eyes, however, the bone submerged beneath the skin and the gaping laceration closed as Milo defiantly healed himself.

"You might want to save that precious vitae, kike. If you keep acting like that you're going to need it."

"If I do say so myself, *Earl*, this is a completely obnoxious way to behave in someone else's domain." Milo suddenly didn't seem the type to give up so easily. Think and keep talking was Chas's best course of action. If he let Milo fluster him, that would make the whole exercise a waste of time.

"Okay, Milo. Here's the rules. Rule one: Unless I ask something of you, you shut the fuck up. You break rule one, you get one of these." Once again, Chas hammered Milo with his fist. This time, he caught Milo to the side of his left eye, breaking the bone and blowing his pupil. Milo chose not to heal it immediately and winced, his eyes looking wild as the one pupil first shrank and then rapidly grew many times the size of the other.

"Rule number two: When I'm talking, no interrupting. You break rule number two, you get one of these." Chas delivered a matching blow to the other side of Milo's head. This time, however, he didn't crack the skull, but Milo's other eye reacted in the same manner.

"Rule three is I'm the fucking boss. And you don't fuck with the fucking boss, understood? Break rule three, and you get one of these." Once more Chas bludgeoned the bound Milo with his fist, this time straight in the face, breaking Rothstein's nose and showering an explosion of blood down the front of his shirt and jacket.

"That's the rules. You got it?" Milo didn't move.

"That counts as yes. Good. I like that." Chas bent down to lick some of the blood from the front of Milo's ruined face. Kindred vitae—much stronger than the thinner blood of mortals. But Chas reined himself in. He needed to hear what Milo had to say, and if he lost control now, he'd fuck up the whole plan.

Somewhere in the back of Chas's mind it occurred to him that he said that to himself a lot lately. He had to talk to the devil to keep it in check, just like he had to keep Milo quiet until it was necessary for him to speak. Or so he figured.

"So, down to brass tacks. Where's Benito?"

"I don't know," Milo sneered, eyes moving groggily over Chas's form.

"Wrong answer." Chas slapped him this time,

shaking loose a trickle of blood-spit and spraying blood from Milo's running nose across the room. "Take two. Where the fuck is Benito?"

"I told you, I don't know." Milo looked blearily up at Chas. He almost looked like he was challenging Chas, or perhaps enticing him to ask something more. But Chas wasn't interested in playing to the crowd. This was his own private hellshow. He was in charge; he called the shots.

"Not what I wanted to hear, Milo." Another slap dislodged a coagulating gobbet from under Milo's nose, which landed on the carpet like a slug dissolving in salt.

"It occurs to me, Earl, that if you want a specific answer, you should ask the question that leads to it. One does not find the Seven Cities of Gold by asking directions to Detroit." Detroit? What the fuck did Detroit have to do with anything? Probably nothing. Still, it reinforced the point that Milo wasn't going to give anything up without making Chas work for it. In his bound state, this was all the Kindred had left.

Chas looked at his watch. Eight minutes had passed. He figured he had twenty before Ben got curious and mustered the courage to call the room. "You're right, Milo. But talking out of turn means breaking rule number one. Time to pay the piper." Once more, Chas rained a blow down upon Milo's head, this time impacting the top of his skull. Nothing gave, though; Chas still needed to hear what Milo had to say so he didn't hit him too hard.

"Jesus fucking Christ, you simpleton! Isn't it obvious I don't know? Why don't you ask Montrose?"

"Don't take the name of the Lord in vain," Chas smiled maliciously, running his left palm over the knuckles of his right hand. "It's a sin, I think. In fact, I'm sure it's a sin when a Jew does it. And I already know about Montrose, but we don't know how to talk to him. We had your phone number. Lucky you. Oh, and stop breaking rule number one and I'll stop hitting you." Another massive blow to the face crushed the left side of Milo's head like a jack-o-lantern. His eye sagged out, his skull bulged alarmingly in a shape that foretold massive trauma, and a well of black head-blood rushed out of his face where Chas's knuckles had lacerated his skin through sheer force. As much as was possible, Milo bit his lip to remain silent.

"Say! That's good! You're learning. Okay. We'll take a different tack now. You've already given us Montrose, but we knew that, so we need something else. Where's Montrose?"

"Fuck you."

Wham.

"Who's Montrose working for?"

"Fuck you."

Wham.

"How do you make a Manhattan?"

"Three parts bourbon, one part sweet vermouth, maraschino cherry."

Not bad, but too much vermouth. *Wham*.

"You don't understand, Milo. I'm not going to stop until you're dead or I've got something I can take home, you see? Who the fuck are *you* working for? What's the secret that's so fucking sacred that you're going to let me beat you inch by inch by fucking inch until I've killed you with my bare hands? What's the fucking story, morning fucking glory?" Chas leaned over to grin in Milo's face, pressing his forehead to the bound Kindred's. "What's the answer to the sixty-four-thousand-dollar question?"

"You really want to know?"

"No, shithead, I'm just fucking around over here."

"No, I mean you *really* have to want to know."

"What the fuck, Milo, I just told you I'm willing to punch you until you die, didn't I? You know how serious a motherfucker has to be to punch someone to death? You know how tired I'm going to be tomorrow night when I get up if I have to punch you for three fucking hours? I'm fucking serious as cancer over here."

"Okay, come here, then."

"What?"

"You heard me. Come here. Lean close so I can whisper it to you."

"You're out of your fucking gourd if you think I'm going to lean down there and let you bite my fucking ear off."

"I'm not going to bite your ear. Then you'd beat the shit out of me even after you killed me." *You're right*, Chas thought privately. "Bend down here so I can tell you."

"Milo, I swear to God, if you fucking bite me…"

"I'm not going to bite you. No, closer."

Chas put his ear up to Milo's mouth, almost hoping that the fool would dare to nip him so he could pummel the Rothstein into sticky paste. This close, Milo wasn't a Kindred anymore but a reeking, sumptuous, humid cloud of pulpy blood. *Tell me quick, motherfucker, before I bite you.*

"The secret is…"

"Yeah, spit it out."

"The secret is…go fuck yourself."

Motherfucker! Milo had him—took him for a ride. "All right, shitbag, you just cashed your fucking check. Goddammit! Fuck! Victor, you keep an eye on this son of a bitch!" As if he was going to get up and go somewhere. "Keep him right fucking where he is." Chas stormed about the room, pacing angrily and shaking his head violently with every turn for a few seconds. He turned on the TV. Same Bruce Willis movie, still going strong. Gunshots and exploding helicopters or something. The cockroach people love that shit. He turned up the volume so that it was maybe twice as loud as a conversation would have been. After that, Chas stalked into the bathroom and purposefully washed his hands and forehead, looked down the front of him to make sure he didn't have blood fountained all over his shirt.

"You fucking wait here, Milo," and Chas stormed out the door.

Milo looked at Victor. Victor looked at Milo and shrugged, as if he hadn't a care in the world. They heard a heavy, staccato scraping sound. And then another. Then a quick *bang*. And then the sound of something immense being dragged over carpeted floor.

"Mr. Sforza, what is your companion do—"

Chas kicked open the door, a sheen of blood-sweat across his forehead, something large blocking the light from the hallway from entering the room. "Yeah, that's right, Milo Tough-Guy. You're so fucking…so fucking tough, I'm going to show you what this is all about. Now you're in the big leagues."

As Chas ranted, he pushed the Coca-Cola vending machine into the room from the hall. It didn't quite fit, catching on the hollow metal doorjamb—so Chas pushed until the jamb pulled away from the sheetrock, sprinkling him and the machine with a veil of white dust.

Victor sniffed.

"You can't be serious," Milo stammered, his ruined eyes wide and his mouth agape.

"You fucking bet I can, cocksucker. I'm the most serious motherfucker you know right now." The doorjamb twisted away and Chas managed to force the big machine entirely into the room. He kept pushing, stopping only briefly to shove the bed to one side with his thigh before continuing to shoulder the machine over toward the window.

"Earl, this is patently absurd."

"Goddammit, would you shut the fuck up? I'm trying to work here. The sooner I can get this where it—needs—to—be—There!—the sooner we can wrap this up. Victor, get the tape."

Victor rummaged through the bag while Chas singlehandedly lifted Milo and the chair and slung them unceremoniously in front of the machine's dimmed façade.

Finding a virgin roll of duct tape—still in the plastic wrapping—Victor tossed it to Chas. "Is this a good idea, Chas?"

"Shut up, Victor. I'm Earl. I know what I'm doing. Earl's your own little angel of death, Milo."

Milo had nothing to say about the situation, instead goggling around in incredulity. Seven big loops of tape later, Milo found himself attached to the machine, inseparably, it seemed.

"Okay. Milo. One last time. Montrose. Benito. Gone. Make it make sense to me, eh? For fuck's sake, at least give me Montrose's phone number."

"Look, Earl, I've already told you—"

"All right. You're done. Victor, set this prick on fire."

Victor fumbled through his own pockets and turned up a silver lighter. He went to the wet bar as Chas ran quickly from the room to grab a fire extinguisher from the wall. As he pulled off the plastic sheath, a mild *beep beep beep* went off and a tiny red light blinked.

In the room, Victor had sprinkled Milo liberally with high-proof rum.

"You're going to set me on fire and put me out?" asked Milo, not knowing what to believe or even what to guess.

"No, you fucking stiff!" Chas yelled at him and hurled the fire extinguisher through the wide glass window. Glass showered downward, accompanied by the extinguisher, which surely made a clash and tinkle as it hit the ground twenty-nine floors below. "You're going out the fucking window."

Victor struck the lighter and Chas heaved upward from the base of the vending machine. Milo's eyes bugged amazingly as the duct tape held him to the machine, and his clothes and blood-damped hair went up in a fiery rush.

With an assertive, final *heave*, Chas pushed the machine up and out the window, sending Milo Rothstein tumbling toward the ground in a flaming, spiraling death-dive.

Chas and Victor bolted from the room, the latter grabbing the bag and hurling his flaming lighter to the floor to burn away the blood-evidence, and sprinted down the hallway toward the stairs. They took three flights in as many bounds, and Victor kept going, intending to call an elevator a few floors below. Chas yanked the fire alarm on floor twenty-six and then dashed down the stairs to join Victor at the elevator. Chas counted himself lucky that he didn't have to breathe or he'd be panting hugely—and suspiciously.

And then nonchalantly, amid the confusion and the fire department trucks and the ambulances and screaming vacationers, they made their way across the street to catch a cab back to their hotel. With any luck at all, Milo was old enough to be dust by now, and this would look like some rock-star publicity stunt or the work of hooligans. No one had any reason to suspect murder at all. No one except Montrose and the Las Vegas Rothsteins, of course, but that could be dealt with later.

Wednesday, 30 June 1999, 10:57 PM
Caesar's Palace, Room 2604
Las Vegas, Nevada

When Chas had risen for the night, he found Victor still in bed.

Dead.

The television was on, running through a collection of previews that would soon show and on which channels they would appear. An overturned mug of coffee sat on the nightstand. The *Las Vegas Review-Journal* and the *Wall Street Journal* lay open on the bed and stained by coffee on the floor, respectively. The smell of almonds permeated the room.

Someone had infused the coffee with cyanide.

"I told you I hate this city," Chas said to Victor's still-stiff corpse. By the time anyone found him, Victor would be turning green-red and purple as the blood pooled downward.

But that wasn't Chas's problem. He had a cargo-class flight to catch back to Boston. A quick call to Frankie Gee from the dispatch office at the airport should have whoever was in charge of such things make sure no one matching Chas's description came up in any of the police reports.

"Goodbye, cockroaches."

Poor, stupid Victor. A victim of ambition, both his own and others'.

It never even occurred to Chas to question why they'd thought to poison Victor's coffee but not to stake the Kindred sleeping in the bathroom. And even if he had thought about it, he'd just guess he had a charmed unlife.

part two:

dig your own hole

Night unknown
Mycerinus's courtyard
Memphis, Egypt

The cowled figure stepped forth from the shadows, seeming to pour out of them like wine from a pitcher. It surveyed the surroundings, sniffing a bit in the humid air.

What a curious scent, the figure thought to itself. *Like blood, only…everywhere. Pervasive. As if the air itself…*

A peal of thunder rent the night, shaking the Egyptian sands and even the pillars of the palace itself. The pharaoh no doubt slept poorly this evening, probably rousing his concubines with his nervous stirrings. For nights now, an ill spirit had fouled his temper, and no amount of pliant flesh or tender foods could calm him. Ever since the disgraced son had spoken his fateful words, the king's manner was one of discomfiture.

What was that curse again? That blood shall fall like rain? That rain shall follow blood? Something perhaps about a bloody reign? The figure trod silently across the sands from the temple to one of the lesser buildings. *In this time of miracles, almost any oath may carry literal truth. Men and gods—impossible to understand! Where one land swears by the existence of one all-powerful, its neighbors spill blood in the name of numerous divine lords. And even this simple Egypt, with its notions of the king who walks among them—how strange! That a god should stink and rut and befoul the water among his very people! Yes, how does this Egypt stretch as far as any of the nations of man? Here, far from the Father's Garden?*

Away from the palace, carved into another rock wall, a portal stood, guarded only by a small boy. The figure stood before the boy, showing him a scepter and a scarab brooch, clasping each in a thin, bony, cadaverous hand. The boy smiled blankly and ran his fingers over a bas-relief of a skull on the rocky face of the wall; the portal opened.

Dank air crept out, like the exhalation of a sick man. The figure entered, still musing to itself. *Every moment is at once an absurdity and a miracle. The spark of life that sustains the boy, that animates my flock— why does God choose to give them such a precious gift? And why does He spite me, who knows of Him and reveres Him and fears Him as he wishes? Why does He force me to walk as the dead among them, while painting them—ignorant savages!—with the colors of vibrant life? Why should He let them watch His glorious sunrise? Or sate their lusty loins beneath the flawless skies? Do You hear me, God? Are You with me in death, or have Your ears grown deaf to the voices of Your disavowed?*

If God was listening, he gave no indication. A single serpent crawled from one of the steps the figure descended, into a crack in the sandstone wall.

Oh, how very like my angry God. Always punishing the councilor for the sins of the artisan. Or perhaps, always punishing the children for the sins of their father. The figure smirked beneath its hood. *I know Your ways, God. You have turned Your back on me, yet it has allowed me to step nearer to You without your knowledge. You do not see me; You force Yourself not to hear me. And it will be Your undoing. One night, You shall feel my fangs—the very affliction with which You cursed me and my sire and my sire's sire—at Your throat. And then, great God, You will know what fear can breed in a man—even a dead one. My dead heart still beats, but it is not with mercy or love. No, my heart beats with the black blood of anger...an anger that Your wisdom has left as a scar. Better to have struck me down than to permit the kiss of—*

"Master?"

A child's voice interrupted the figure from the growing histrionics of its reverie. Taking the last step, the cowled form entered a low, arched room that stank of sweat and youth and the waste of mortal bodies. A single torch guttered against the far wall, bestowing precious little light on the squalid chamber but giving the figure far more luminescence than it needed to see. The cool stone walls bore no marks, other than a few streaks of offal and a haphazard pattern of russet hand-prints. A boy emerged from the far corner, his face obscured by unknown filth, naked as the day he was born.

"Master?" The wretch repeated his question, unaware that his master indeed stood before him. The figure shook its head. Perhaps the boy would never learn—he peered too purposefully into the darkness.

"Yes, Nusrat. It is I." The figure peeled back its hood, its head emerging, baring a rictus of teeth, like a skull plucked from a lifeless body. Which, in truth, it was....

The boy leapt into the dead man's cold arms, clambering exuberantly up them to kiss his master's face. The master turned away, sparing himself the boy's clumsy affections. He looked about, lifeless eyes leering from pitted sockets, scanning the darkness. "Nusrat, where is your sister? Elisha?" He called out, but received no response.

"She's sleeping, master. She's still sick."

"She's not sick, my dear boy." A charnel hand emerged from the robe to pat the boy's shorn head affectionately. "No, she isn't sick. She's tired. I've taken so much of her precious blood that she hasn't the power to walk." As he spoke, the dead man led his ward hand-in-hand to the corner where Elisha lay. "See? Elisha. Elisha…"

The girl sprawled in a heap on the floor, looking like nothing more than a pile of bones herself. Flies buzzed about her—*How did they find their way in?*—and crawled across her half-open eyes, in and out of her parted lips. "Elisha? Are you not well?" The dead man's skeleton-head grinned a particularly vicious smile. "Do you need your rest? She does, doesn't she, Nusrat? She needs her precious sleep." The dead man nudged Elisha's head with his foot as Nusrat stared up at him plaintively. "Oh, yes. She's very tired.

"May I ask something of you, my boy?" The dead man stroked the boy's hand, his bony fingers leaving brief, bright trails on the boy's bronzed skin. He looked down, his face a mask of deathlike serenity.

"Yes, master?"

"Take this to Djuran, at the top of the stair." He handed the boy a small scarab with a human skull in place of its head. It was a magical, alchemical elixir-tablet, fashioned from his own blood, created to augment his servants' powers and bond them to his will. "I'll have one for you when you return."

As the boy's naked feet flapped away into the darkness, the dead man turned his attention again to Elisha. "My dear, sweet girl. I am sorry to have left you so."

He lifted her—she weighed little more than a bundle of river reeds—and cradled her in the crook of his arm. Pushing the tattered shift away from her body, he bent one weakened leg away from him, exposing the flesh of her thigh and the delicate pink pucker that hid above. As a hungry man eyeing a roast and spitted calf, the dead man stared at the enfeebled girl's haunch. Carefully, delicately, he bit into the flesh of her leg and felt the musky skin give way beneath his fangs. A weak trickle of blood coursed into his mouth, at first slowly and then in greater volume. The dead man drank with a detached fervor, indulging himself in the sole passion that animated his cursed frame, lapping up the blood in rivulets. With but a few seconds' draught, the flow ceased completely, just as the boy returned from his errand above.

The robed specter dropped Elisha's body to the floor, where it came to rest with a dull thud. He rubbed one finger coarsely across his lip and motioned to Nusrat to come closer. "And now, would you please get rid of that?"

The boy answered, "Yes, master," but the dead man had already turned to go.

Before he reached the top of the stair, the dead man met the door attendant, whose eyes held a wide look of shock. "Master, you—the skies have—"

"Spit it out, boy. I don't keep idiots in my employ," the dead man snapped, nonetheless worried about the effect whatever lurked outside had had on his attendant. Djuran was not the brightest of slaves, but he was stalwart. Could it be that the pharaoh had finally tired of his cadaverous vizier's ways? Had he sent a royal guard to arrest him and press him beneath stones? Had a sergeant come to arrest him? It would likely be the gravest error of that sergeant's life....

As he ascended the stairs with the stammering Djuran behind him, the dead man saw what had the boy so agitated.

The skies were lit with brief bursts of ruddy lightning and the humid air held the tang of blood. Indeed, as the dead man looked out over the sands and walls of Egypt, they all became stained with a heavy brown-red rain.

The Lord God had caused blood to fall from the sky.

Thursday, 15 July 1999, 1:27 AM
Seasons Restaurant, Bostonian Hotel
Boston, Massachusetts

"So, you're proposing what, exactly?" Isabel looked sternly at the Kindred before her. He had been sent from Baltimore at the behest of Jan Pieterzoon to entreat Giovanni support against the Sabbat. His name was something French, or maybe Canadian, but his English certainly didn't have any accent.

"Recognition of the Giovanni claim to Boston," replied the agent. "The Camarilla will formally acknowledge the supremacy of Clan Giovanni in Boston and its immediate environs. That is, in exchange for the support of the present members of the clan against the Sabbat's efforts along the eastern seaboard. It's in your best interests, you know."

"Don't patronize us, you fucking pindick," barked Chas from across the table. This meeting had convened at the last minute, by request of Francis Milliner.

Francis was the eldest member of the Milliner family, the Boston branch of the Giovanni. Isabel believed him to be more than a bit paranoid, but she indulged him. Much had recently taken place in Boston, including the execution of one of the most dangerous loose cannons ever known to the clan. Genevra Giovanni had been a Sabbat sympathizer, having use for the Giovanni family only insofar as it served her immediate needs. Not that every Giovanni vampire—and probably every vampire, period—didn't harbor similar selfishness, but the open display had made her powerful enemies among the clan. Masterfully, the Milliners had hidden her elimination beneath a veil of organized crime violence. Isabel had to give Francis credit—he had crafted an almost century-long ruse to use as a smokescreen for whatever untoward befell him and his brood, and never thought twice about playing it out to take Genevra out of the picture. For his foresight and cleverness, the elders of the clan decided to allow him to drink the heart's blood of the rogue, bringing him closer to the power of the elders themselves. Who knows how many other contingency plans Milliner had up his sleeve?

To that end, Isabel had little interest in talking details with a second-rate yes man. Francis was the man with the plan, but she was his smokescreen, she knew. The Camarilla probably didn't even know that it was Milliners and not Giovanni who exercised the most influence in Boston. Outside a few individuals, everyone knew that the Giovanni were the preeminent power there. Of course, the Milliners *were* Giovanni, but such semantic games were the coin of the Kindred realm. Misdirection and subterfuge could take a Kindred much farther than brute force, and Isabel was walking, unliving proof of that.

"Chas, please. Settle down," Isabel remarked. He was still headstrong, ostensibly here to deal with the Benito Giovanni affair, and a liability to this discussion. Chas was a testament to the fact that sometimes nasty and brutish did the job, particularly in America. He wasn't especially strong, powerful or clever, but he had a mean streak a mile wide and had less and less reservation nightly about showing it to a rival. That had begun to shine through—his eyes had sunk in the few weeks since Isabel had met him, and his once-full lips were pulled back into a perpetual growl or sneer. His hands were always white-knuckled, as if only by the most persistent concentration could he keep the Beast in check. Isabel knew: Chas was bound to snap soon. She had planned to play her cards right, however, and unleash Chas when it was most convenient, watching him go down in a blaze of glory that would no doubt take a few others with him. The key was to do it subtly, however—again, discretion made sure one need not keep escalating her efforts—and to make sure his inevitable kamikaze took place visible only to Kindred eyes and nowhere she'd have to call upon favors to cover up among the media, police, etc. Still, he had a point. The liaison sneered at Chas, who bristled visibly.

"But don't let that mislead you—I'm sorry, what was your name again?" She put the diplomat in his place.

The guest's eyes narrowed to slits, regarding Isabel coldly. "Gauthier. Jacques Gauthier. Childe of Paul Levesque, childe of Shlomo Baruch, childe of Christianne Foy, childe of Vidal Jar—"

"Yes, yes," Isabel interrupted, "very impressive. Archbishop of Canterbury, extract of vanilla, Milk of Magnesia, and so the old joke goes. We realize that you're here to represent the Camarilla's interests and that you're supposed to butter us up and make this seem like the most fantastic deal ever to fall into our laps. But let me offer you my counterposition. Your approval means nothing to us. Your high-handed 'recognition of sovereignty' and other quasi-political jingoism won't work in this room. You're not dealing with rank neonates. Your Camarilla is not a government, nor is it a military body. It is a simple social convention, a contract supported by its members in the interests of furthering its own ends. Quite frankly, it is a civil sinecure with which bored, effete elders play games and delude themselves. Am I to believe that, if we could not reach an agreement in this room, before the next dawn Boston would face a liveried phalanx of Camarilla shock troops? It's more likely that a few rowdy insurgents of your sect would swagger among Boston's Kindred like a mob of drunken soccer hooligans for a few nights until routed by the very same Kindred whose havens they disturb.

"Your recognition means nothing. Your support means nothing. Your sect is incapable of maintaining the quiet influence it has along this entire coast of one of the most affluent nations in the world, just as it has proven powerless against the unknown Kindred of the East sweeping in from the West Coast. Oh, Jacques Gauthier, don't be so shocked—I've looked into matters. I wouldn't dream of entertaining an envoy such as yourself without knowing the full ramifications of the relations you propose. When weighed against other options, the only benefit that a loose agreement of support provides is in the hope that the Giovanni of Boston could simply turn their backs on the whole matter and allow the Sabbat and Camarilla fanatics to shred each other in the streets. How does that sound? Is that answer satisfactory?"

Jacques had risen from his seat, his mouth open wide, his head turned slightly downward and his teeth clenched. At Isabel's side, Chas twitched, undead veins bulging, like an epileptic bound to his chair in the throes of seizure.

"Do not presume that we are so powerless, Isabel Giovanni," retorted Jacques. "The Camarilla, as you say, is not a military organization, but to believe that that renders us powerless is pure folly. Neither is the

Sabbat a military power, but these are not battles fought exclusively in the trenches. For every brawling fool who sees this solely as a matter of martialry, three more Kindred behind him make their moves through quieter channels. This is a war of influence, and the resources of the Camarilla are orders of magnitude more than the resources of Clan Giovanni. We are merely interested in minimizing and localizing the influence of our enemies—and your enemies as well—the Sabbat."

"The resources of the Camarilla! Absurd. The Camarilla has no resources! The only power it wields is that which is voluntarily afforded to it by its members. Your sect is far more fractious and selfishly motivated than you would have us think. The Camarilla does nothing as an entity, and you know it."

"Nor does Clan Giovanni, by that rationale," countered Gauthier.

"True, but Clan Giovanni in this case is a community of Boston's Kindred. We will more than certainly protect our own interests, and put aside our personal grudges when opposed with a greater opposition. Whether that opposition is Sabbat or Camarilla—or both—is irrelevant. I know the man who has sent you here. I know Jan Pieterzoon. He has made quite a name for himself among the Kindred, and I suspect he may one night find himself among the—what do you call them?—archons and justiciars of the Camarilla. But he will not do it by playing the role of firebrand. Rather, he will master the game of politics, promising one thing, delivering another, and then convincing those beneath him that what they wanted in the first place was what he actually delivered. I know that Boston is only part of

Pieterzoon's larger move at this stage, but I'm not going to pretend to know what cards he still holds in his hand. Jan is a much more proficient plotter than I will ever be, but I am far better at seeing the secrets within. Pieterzoon and those like him depend upon Kindred like me to provide the pieces with which they play. I—we, the Giovanni of Boston—may be pawns in that game, but we know that we are pawns. And a pawn that turns against the side that pushes it forward is a dangerous piece, indeed." Isabel stood straight up, arms crossed high over her chest, staring imperiously at Jacques.

Gauthier showed no sign of backing down, however. Pieterzoon had charged him with this negotiation—warned him that the Giovanni were deadly as vipers in their nest—and expected no failure. "You're speaking in metaphors, Isabel. You're occluding the issue. This is not a game, as you want to rush to conveniently reduce it to. Pawns and pieces and chess allusions are the stuff of florid fiction, and we're dealing in matters quite tangible. We need your help. In return, we are willing to leave Boston be. You will not receive such a plain or sincere offer from the Sabbat, as their dominance of the East Coast attests. It may be that you are truly prepared to weather the storm. But I have no reason to suspect that you would prefer to stand against this conflict if we offer you a chance to avoid it altogether."

"It would seem, then, Jacques, that we are at an impasse for the time being. I will take the details of your proposed alliance back and peruse them. You know where to reach me. I suggest we meet again in a few weeks to finalize the nature of the relationship—should I decide one exists."

Thursday, 15 July 1999, 1:48 AM
Seasons Restaurant, Bostonian Hotel
Boston, Massachusetts

"What the fuck were you doing in there?" Chas asked Isabel as they left the building, headed for the silver Audi coupe she had borrowed for the trip. Normally, the car had only a one-point-eight-liter four-cylinder, but Isabel had arranged to "preview" one of next year's upgrade prototypes with the six-cylinder.

"Quiet down, Chas. And don't speak to me like that or I'll have your tongue. Literally."

The pair climbed into the car, which was slung low to the ground. Isabel disdained driving, so she handed the keys to Chas. She preferred luxury cars, of course, for their amenities, but in a city that was about to be torn apart by three rival factions, speed and maneuverability were preferable to cabriolet leather.

"But there's no way you're going to cut a deal with the Sabbat, right?"

"Are you out of your mind, Chas?"

"No, but why were you busting his balls so hard?"

"Who says I have to throw in with anyone? And who says the Milliners would honor it if I agreed to it?"

"But isn't that why you're here, Isabel? To negotiate the deal?"

"I'm here because Francis Milliner asked for me. I'm here to get the most out of this little venture with the least investment on my part or the Milliners'. Why are *you* here, Chas?"

"Benito thing."

"That's right. So why don't you worry about that and I'll worry about this, okay? Have you made any progress on Benito's disappearance?"

"No," Chas had started to scowl, his hands gripping the steering wheel with a new fervor.

"Were you expecting to get something out of that meeting?"

"I figured maybe they'd offer some information about Benito as part of the deal."

"And maybe they will, Chas. Now you see? Putting Jacques over as many barrels as I can means that if he really wants this support arrangement to go through, he's got to give me what I want. Pieterzoon wouldn't suggest this unless it was necessary, so I know I've got a lot of leverage. And Pieterzoon didn't want to come himself, so he sent that little lickspittle so it would look like this is no big deal. So he thinks I think this is nothing. But that's not what I think, get it?" She smiled. Chas was playing the same game of "she thinks I think" with her and she had called him on it, if only allegorically.

The Audi swung around a corner, its wide tires grabbing the road and holding tight as the chassis rolled low to keep the turn radius tight.

"In the meantime, Chas, I've got a side project for you. It'll teach you some fundamental investigation skills."

"Whoa, hang on. I'm not here for you on this deal. I'm still working for Frankie Gee."

"Yes, well, you need the practice. I'll bill Frankie later."

Chas sighed, pointedly, as if to remind Isabel that since he didn't breathe, he meant something by it.

"That's my boy. So tomorrow night, you find out what you can about Jacques Gauthier. And tell me who calls the shots for the Sabbat in this city."

"I already know part two. It's Max Lowell."

"How do you know that?"

"Shit, my haven's in New York. Boston's just a shot up the road. Frankie's moved more stuff through Lowell than I care to think about. Fuck, if this shit comes down to a shootout, it'll probably be with Frankie's guns."

Isabel looked unwaveringly at Chas.

"See," he said with a smirk, "I'm not so stupid as I pretend."

Nope, Chas thought to himself as he boarded the T to ride back to his hotel, *I'm not so stupid at all.* And when he arrived, he dialed Frankie's number—the one with the **# area code.

Tuesday, 6 July 1999, 9:48 PM
A subterranean grotto
New York City, New York

Calebros set down the report dealing with the strange phenomenon of unusually aggressive rats. Rats hostile—to Nosferatu! What was the world coming to?

What, indeed.

He placed the report on his desk, atop one of the precarious stacks of thousands of other reports on any of hundreds of dissimilar topics. The data were flying fast and furious these nights: The Camarilla non-resistance in Washington, D.C., had finished crumbling within the past week, with the exception of the Tremere chantry which had circled the wagons and not lifted a finger to save the city. The insular warlocks had dispatched a particularly mid-level representative, one Maria Chin, to Baltimore, where Prince Garlotte was attempting to create some sort of order from the chaotic streams of refugees inundating his city. His task was made no easier by the maneuverings of Victoria Ash, Toreador ne'er-do-well, socialite, and eye candy.

But now, by the dim, flickering light of his desk lamp, Calebros pondered a matter that was considerably nearer and dearer to his heart.

6 July 1999
Re: Benito Giovanni; (Las Vegas)

Montrose reports — two East Coast Giovanni lightweights (Victor Sforza, Chas Giovanni Tello) asking questions about Benito; meet w/Milo Rothstein 6/29; return 6/30 AM, unceremoniously dispose of Rothstein. Tello flies out next night; Sforza terminated by unknown assailant(s).

Repercussions of M.R. death — few or none; already cultivated connections with other Giovanni-related elements in L.V.

Commend Emett - False pointers to L.V. successful

→ *Now that the ruckus out west has died down, Las Vegas might be the safest place to move Benito. They've already looked there.*

Saturday, 17 July 1999, 9:51 PM
Forgotten Worlds Gallery
Boston, Massachusetts

Chas Giovanni was not happy.

Whoever the fuck wanted to know where the fuck Benito Giovanni was should just leave him wherever he was and be done with it. Milo Rothstein died because of it. Victor died because of it. No telling how many of the Nosferatu shitbags who'd black-bagged Benito in the first place met the Final Death because of it. And tonight, new news. While Chas was in Boston, Frankie had heard that Benito had turned up in New Orleans. The moment he heard it, Chas knew it was bullshit—Benito had disappeared from here and then showed up in Vegas. Unless those Nosferatu were setting up a touring Benito Giovanni Petting Zoo exhibit, there was no good reason in the world for him to have surfaced in New Orleans. If he had escaped his captors, he would have gone home or called someone from the road. If he was still in someone's possession, he'd be locked down tight in either Vegas or Boston until whoever kidnapped him made whatever demand it was they planned to make. The whole thing didn't make any sense.

Who made the tip, Chas wanted to know. None of Frankie's other people could answer. Speaking of being unable to answer, Frankie hadn't picked up his phone in almost twenty-four hours, despite Chas and any number of other goombas calling him nonstop.

Then the call came in from Italy, to Isabel. Frankie Gee was dead. She told Chas, conveyed the appropriate words of condolence, and bought a plane ticket to meet some contact of hers in Atlanta.

"That's nice, Isabel. Any idea why you got the call before me, and why Italy knows but no one in New York or Boston knows yet?" Chas demanded.

"Don't take that tone, Chas. I didn't have to tell you at all. As to why I found out, it relates to something I'm doing here."

"You're here to fucking handle the Camarilla negotiation for the Milliners. What the fuck does that have to do with going to Atlanta and getting calls about my dead *capo*?"

Isabel had had enough of Chas's continually worsening attitude. "You know what, Chas? That's right. I was here to talk to Pieterzoon's people. And I did it. You, however, are here to find out where Benito Giovanni has gone, and you haven't done that. So while I have handled two separate affairs for the family, you still haven't finished your first, and you're racking up an impressive body count to accompany your failures. Victor, Frankie, and I'm sure there are more. So please, before you get all heavy-handed and indignant, just sit quietly and wait for me to get back." She knew he had become frustrated with the lack of anything leading him to Benito, but Chas was being unconscionable, and it showed no signs of abating.

"Fuck that, Isabel! I'm just supposed to sit here and wait? I'm coming with you to Atlanta to do whatever it is you're doing down there."

"No, you're not. You're going to stay here and accompany the person I've hired to handle the rest of the talk with Gauthier."

"You want me playing backup for someone else while you take your little vacation? Bullshit. Fucking bullshit. I'm not here working for you. In fact, I guess

I'm not working for anyone anymore. There's no way I'm running second man to some punk-ass Kindred you talked into doing Milliner's—"

"Oh, she's not Kindred," Isabel interrupted. She flashed him a charming smile that became insidious given the circumstances. "She's quite alive. Works for Milliner as an account executive. She knows all about our kind, though, and I've given her all the details. You're going with her to make sure she doesn't get hurt, and to let Gauthier and Pieterzoon know that we're not taking their side, or the Sabbat's."

"*What?* I'm right hand to a fucking *kine?*" It was one thing to play Victor's angle in Vegas—that was to mislead Rothstein. But backing up a mortal who was nothing more than a mouthpiece for the snot-nosed Milliners, without having it be some kind of ruse, that was inexcusable. "I'm not going to fucking do it. Fuck yourself, Isabel."

She turned around and slapped him, *hard*, across the face. "You will not speak that way to me, understood? That's fine—if that's what you want to do, you're free to leave. You don't owe me anything, you don't work for me, and you don't work for the Milliners. So crawl back to New York and let all the Giovanni and wiseguys know that not only could you not handle a simple assignment, you got one of your men and your boss killed on top of it. Go right ahead." One hand on her hip, she waved the other at the door.

That's why he wasn't happy.

Chas knew Isabel was right—in order to come out of this with any dignity at all, he had to see the matter through. If that meant attaching himself to Isabel until she was able to bring more pieces of the puzzle to the table, well, that's what he'd have to do. It was absurd that she expected him to be effectively Milliner's diplomat's retainer, but he didn't want to consider what would happen if he returned to New York with nothing but obituaries to accompany him.

It didn't help that Milliner's new go-between was a grade-A bitch. Even her name was pretentious: *Genevieve Pendleton*. Of course, she had been college-educated, which automatically made her arrogant toward the rough-edged Chas. Apparently, she'd been on the Milliner managerial staff for a few years, and they'd allowed her to be a part of the operation without making her a ghoul. That wasn't how they did things in the Old World, and it wasn't how Frankie and his ilk had adapted their racket to the New World. When you let people know what you were, it was either right before you whacked them, or right before you made them a ghoul—or a Kindred. Anything else left too many loose ends.

The net result: Chas didn't approve of his charge's being left with the opportunity to jump ship if things got ugly with this whole "Kindred" situation, and Genevieve didn't approve of having a kneebreaker present to punctuate her discussion with the other Kindred interest.

They had begun bickering only moments after Isabel left them sitting at the table. Chas had muttered a comment about Pendleton being a poor choice of negotiators—she wasn't Kindred and couldn't really represent one effectively, especially if they tried to use any of their mystical powers. She maintained that she knew Kindred inside and out, and was more than able to handle herself among them. Chas countered with a personal attack, saying that if someone sent his secretary to talk business with *him*, both the secretary and the presumptive business partner would end up dead. Pendleton, not about to suffer snubs from a pistol-whipping thug, remarked that she was sure that was how all of the less-evolved Kindred handled their affairs.

"We'll see who's less evolved when you piss off another Kindred and you need me to save your scrawny ass, Guinevere."

"Genevieve."

"Whatever. You'll just end up as someone's dinner sooner or later anyway. You think the Milliners are just going to let you grow old and trust you with the secret until you die?"

"It's in my contract," Pendleton retorted, crossing her arms and straightening her posture, as if she could hide behind the document as a shield.

Chas snorted. "Yeah, well, your contract's a load of crap. The minute the Milliners see you as more of a liability than an asset, they won't hesitate to shred that contract and you along with it. It's not like you can go to the Supreme Court and claim that you work for vampires, and they're being mean to you." His voice trailed off. "Naïve, prissy bitch."

Genevieve shook her head. "You think you're better than me because you're *dead*? Oh, that's a good one. Well, I have news for you. You can't just walk all over people because you're some secret, scary *vampire*, you know."

"I can do it because it doesn't matter to me anymore."

That was a strange reply. Genevieve cocked her head. "What do you mean?"

"I mean the code. The morals you mortals keep.

They don't matter. I'm Kindred, and all that inalienable-right bullshit you uphold doesn't mean fuck-all to me. Look at me! I fucking drink blood to survive! I kill people so I can go on...living...or whatever the fuck it's supposed to be called."

"That doesn't make any sense," Pendleton said. "It's psychologically not possible. It's not possible for vampire society to exist in a vacuum like that. That's the reason why serial killers are finally caught, and why you never hear about them until something really heinous turns up. Degenerate behavior exhibits the law of diminishing returns—the more abhorrent acts you indulge in, the more it takes you to experience the thrill of indulging in an abhorrent act. You get jaded. By way of analogy, you'd have to kill to experience even the minor emotional response you once received from, say, shoplifting. And I don't even want to think about what you do after *killing* becomes boring."

"No shit," Chas shot back. "We've got an old riddle for it: A Beast I am lest a Beast I become. We've all got the devil inside us, and we have to let him out every once in a while or he'd completely take us over. It's like fucking immunization or germ theory or something."

"That's not possible. You can't survive like that." Pendleton crossed her legs, lit a cigarette.

"Bullshit. *Bullshit*. After you've been through it all so many times, that anger—that Beast—is all you've got left, and if you fucking let it win, you're fucking done. *Done*."

"So it's a pity-fuck you're after?" Pendleton looked away, her eyes following the trail of smoke as she exhaled it.

Chas's eyes flashed red. He tasted the blood-bile rising inside him and his vision hazed with a flush of crimson. In a moment, he was on his feet, jerking Genevieve Pendleton up by the lapels of her designer jacket, lifting her so that her feet dangled above the ground, crushing the fabric of her jacket in his balled fists. Pendleton's eyes bugged wide, almost out of their sockets. "*You fucking cunt*," Chas roared, snarling lips and distended fangs barely able to form intelligible words. "Don't you fucking *ever* accuse me of playing on that shit. I don't need your fucking *pity*. I don't need your goddamn *concern* or your fucking pissant sympathy. When you're dead and gone and worm fucking food in a pine fucking box six feet under the ground, *I'm still going to be here*. Do you get it? You fucking understand? Does that make it through your fucking self-centered rational little mind? *You don't mean shit to me.* The only thing that's keeping me from pulling your fucking head off right now is the fact that Isabel's already paid you to do your fucking job and I don't want to deal with her. Does that make sense, you stupid bitch? Nothing you can say means the slightest thing to me. You're just another fucking bag of blood to me."

With that, Chas reined himself in. He threw Genevieve back into her chair, which tumbled over backward, leaving her sprawled inelegantly on the floor.

"Fuck. You see what I mean? I...You got a husband, Pendleton?"

Genevieve couldn't be sure what direction Chas was taking. "What?"

"A husband? You married? Or maybe you have a

'life partner' or some shit like that?"

"I'm, yes, married," she gulped, picking herself up off the floor and straightening her jacket.

"You love this guy?"

"I do."

"He means everything to you, right? He's 'the one,' as they say, no? The one person in the whole world who's absolutely perfect for you, right?"

"Yes. I suppose. I love him—I wouldn't want to go on without him."

"That's fucking right. Well, guess what, Pendleton? I'm going to tell you a story.

"Right after I got turned—just about a hundred years ago, maybe a little more—I met 'the one.' Perfect girl. I fell in love with her just a few months after meeting her. You see where this is fucking heading? I'm a fucking vampire *in love with a mortal woman*. I can't fucking tell her that I'm a fucking Kindred. So I play it up—the whole Masquerade thing. I try to set up this relationship with this woman in spite of the fact that *it can't happen*.

"But the thing is—she knows. She doesn't know that I'm fucking dead, but she knows that there's…*something*. And it puts her off. But it's not like I can tell her, you know? I can't break the secret because that means sooner or later I'd have to kill her *and I'm not ready to do that*. At least, not yet.

"So that's where I'm fucked. I have the absolute *perfect* person in my… life, *but I can't have her*. I can't tell her, and any time I try to just 'let it happen,' she *feels* what's wrong and it puts her off. And for all the fucking gifts that being Kindred provides—I can hit harder than anyone else, I can *make* people do what

I tell them—*I just can't fix this situation*. This woman I love, *I can't ever fucking have*. I can't make her love me, I can't have her grow to love me and I can't just be with her. It's like being a thousand fucking miles away even when I'm right next to her.

"And it makes me *sick*. Literally sick. I wake up each fucking night with a big, empty fucking *hole* in the middle of me *that I can't possibly fill. Ever*. And the worse I feel, the more I think about her, which makes me even more goddamn miserable, which makes me think about her even more.... It never fucking ends.

"And then she grows old, but I don't; I stay eternally young. And she dies. Maybe she gets married; maybe she doesn't, but it's not important because it's never fucking with *me*.

"And then there's another woman.

"And another.

"And so on and so on, every time opening the same old fucking scars that just can't heal because you can never have what you need—that person—to fix it, to make it better. Never.

"And sure, there are ways around it. You can turn the one you love—make them a Kindred—but when you do that, you kill them. You can bring them somewhat under the shadow: feed them you blood, make them your ghoul, but that's not an equitable relationship. You can force them to love you with the powers of the Blood, but that's not *real*. In the end all you can do is watch them die and feel that fucking hole inside you grow bigger every time.

"So, Genevieve fucking Pendleton, I can't ever have what you have. I can't have someone I love to come home to. I can't touch a woman's face and have her feel anything that's not touched with the natural revulsion that she's being fucking touched by *something that kills*. I can't ever have *anything* except a fucking blackness inside me that grows greater *every fucking night* and wants me to destroy everything I come in contact with.

"After a hundred fucking years of this shit, anger's all you got left. It's all you can use to keep that fucking Beast at bay—fighting fire with fire.

"Think about that next time you kiss your husband goodnight or wake up with him in the morning. Think about the fact that having him, having someone who can truly *love* you for as long as your mortal life, is something that some people just can't have. And for that, they'll never be complete men, or complete people. And then think about the only thing that can take the place of love. We can hate in abundance, and we have no more suitable subject for our hate than ourselves. So we rise each night because we *don't want to fucking hate ourselves any more than we already do*. But we're going to fail at even that."

Genevieve put out her cigarette. "I quit."

Sunday, 18 July 1999, 1:27 AM
unmarked site
Boston, Massachusetts

Chas was right. The night she appeared before him to resign, Francis Milliner had Genevieve entombed in the concrete support of a parking garage his construction company was building.

Saturday, 17 July 1999, 8:27 PM
Delta Flight 2065, Logan International Airport
Boston, Massachusetts

All the shaking shook Isabel awake, even though she wouldn't be able to rise for another forty-five minutes or so. Or rather, in another forty-five minutes she would be able to rise, if she weren't packed like cargo into an airplane-safe coffin. When the best flights departed before dark, she had found no other suitable manner of travel—moving about in daylight was a ridiculous risk, and she was always groggy before the sun fell completely.

Not that traveling cargo-class was any pleasant journey. Flying as a corpse was the only way it could be done. Airlines X-rayed the items that went into their planes' cargo holds, looking for bombs and whatnot, and if a human-shaped thing turned up in anything but a registered transportable coffin, someone was bound to notice. Even if they did need to open the transit vessel, a vampire inside would have little trouble passing for dead—just sit still and let them poke at you. This always amused Isabel. No matter how grotesque it seemed, any time her cargo-method travel had been disturbed, at least one of the people opening the casket would always *touch* her. It probably would have unsettled anyone travelling with their dear departed to know that the corpse had been molested, but Isabel knew to keep quiet. It would have been more problematic if she rose and called the baggage handlers on it, but the image entertained her nonetheless—a burly, surly bag lifter fainting dead away as the corpse whose mouth he'd just put his finger in bit it off and spit it out at him.

Such reverie was always the lightest part of the trip, however. For the entire flight, the cargo Kindred had to lie stock-still—she had no room to move. This wasn't usually a problem during the day while the Kindred slept, but flights that ended after nightfall were a different matter; the traveler simply had to rest there. Some vampires who made a habit of "deadwinging" built custom caskets that afforded them a little room for comfort, but Isabel disdained this. It was only a matter of time before someone recognized a particular coffin and grew suspicious about the same dead body that had a habit of flying around the country.

Invariably, the trouble of whatever demanded the trip bore down on the Kindred. Such was the case with Isabel's trip to Atlanta. She knew before she ever arrived in Las Vegas that some problem had arisen with the border that separated the worlds of the living and the dead. At first, the elders of Clan Giovanni had thought that only the spirits of the dead had been involved. Even the rogue sorcerer Ambrogino Giovanni had been affected, retiring to his sanctum at the loggia for two weeks to recover from the ordeal.

Then, members of the family had begun to go missing.

Elders, ancillae and neonates alike vanished, as well as a handful of their ghouls, immediate families and entourages. Across the globe, the Giovanni had fought for years to extend their influence. Across the globe, they disappeared overnight.

Then Ambrogino had called her. One of the Giovanni Kindred in the area had taken a brief trip, never to be seen again. That had been Frankie Gee,

Francis Alberto Giovanni del'Agrigento—Chas's boss. Isabel felt Chas should know that Frankie was gone, but not her suspicions why. In her opinion, he wouldn't have understood, and it was too grave to worry the Milliners with.

Ambrogino mentioned the old clan.

Isabel was too young to know exactly who the "old clan" were, but she knew that the Giovanni hadn't come by their current state honestly. Sometime in the murky past, the Giovanni had rebelled against the one who had made them vampires, destroying his brood and diablerizing him. Of course, many of the old clan escaped, never to be found. If Ambrogino was right, the problems in the lands of the dead had freed the members of the old clan who had fled there. No doubt they would be furious at their fate, and seek to exact some sort of revenge. Through his research, Ambrogino pursued that hunch, and it turned out to be true—the missing or dead Giovanni had all participated to some degree in the extirpation of their forebears, or their sires had. Don Pietro Giovanni's two childer vanished from Prague; boorish Martino della Passaglia had watched his sire snatched away by something that hid in the shadows of the ceiling in his own haven. Ludo Giovanni, the Chronicler of Bremen, left only an unfinished sentence in his notebook as his last mark on the world.

According to Ambrogino, the old clan had taken to calling itself the Harbingers of Skulls, and they would not rest until every member of the Giovanni had been culled.

Well, they certainly had ambition. The Giovanni, while not the most numerous of the clans of Caine, were neither the fewest. Such a pogrom would take decades, if not centuries. But, as Ambrogino had noted, they had waited this long, and they had nothing but time on their side.

In haste, the Giovanni elders had dispatched many able agents of the clan to learn what they could of the matter. From what information they gathered, these Kindred reasoned that the Harbingers of Skulls were few but very potent. Isabel had been among these early fact-finders, and knew the grim reality—the one she had been seeking was no doubt at least five millennia old.

Of course, this crisis affected only the Giovanni—it didn't stop the earth from spinning. Isabel had already been involved with two other important matters: monitoring the burgeoning Sabbat conquest of the American East Coast, and a prickly matter concerning the kidnapping of Benito Giovanni.

Isabel's connection to the East Coast affair was mostly a matter of consultation. She served as a liaison to members of the Sabbat and the Camarilla, intending to let both know that the Giovanni didn't care for either one of them. Giovanni-dominated Boston would *not* be the next on the menu for the Sabbat, nor would it become a haven for Camarilla refugees. More than anything, she wanted to keep the Kindred ignorant of the true nature of Giovanni business in Boston—very few among the undead knew that the Milliner family maintained Giovanni influence there, and simply assumed that the only Giovanni were those *named* Giovanni. The ignorance of others was a very powerful weapon in the Giovanni arsenal, and the Milliners had retained Isabel to ensure that they didn't lose it.

Concerning Benito, Isabel had initially chalked up his disappearance to the actions of the old clan. After researching Benito's lineage, however, she found him only distantly related to and descended from anyone who had any relation to the purge of the Giovanni progenitors. Her contacts among the Kindred informed Isabel that Benito had fallen in with some dubious characters over a recent art deal. Thereafter, a bit of mundane detective work turned up details of Benito's abduction that linked it to the Nosferatu.

Right now, all three matters weighed heavily on Isabel Giovanni's mind, and she found it difficult to sleep. Doubtless, one of these matters would have to fall by the wayside, and she saw poor Benito as having drawn the short straw. After all, he was only one Kindred—the other matters affected all of the Giovanni in one city, if not worldwide. Still, she suspected she hadn't heard the last of Benito; she didn't want to write him off, but something had to give, and his kidnapping had the greatest likelihood of righting itself if left alone.

By the same token, the reappearance of the old clan took precedence, and Isabel planned to meet a contact in Atlanta who could provide her with information on a suspected member of that group. Apparently, the thing had made its haven in New Orleans, arranged somehow for Frankie Gee to come to it, and destroyed him. Frankie had been Kindred for about four centuries—he was one of the original Sicilian robber-barons who reinvented himself as the times dictated. That someone of such advanced age could be duped into walking into his own Final Death attested to the strength of whatever it was they were dealing with. Exactly how her elders expected her to succeed where other, older Kindred had failed was beyond her, but forewarned was forearmed. Meeting the creature on her own terms, if only to observe it and make a report back to other Giovanni, gave her an edge.

Now all she had to do was maintain it.

The plane shuddered to life, lurching onto the runway and climbing slowly into the sky.

**Wednesday, 21 July 1999, 11:18 PM
Laffitte's
New Orleans, Louisiana**

Jake sat down. The bar had a low ceiling and French doors, looking—as did all of New Orleans's buildings—as if it had been there for over a hundred years.

Of course, most of them had.

But Jake hadn't come to Laffitte's to wonder at its architecture. Nor had he come to suck down prodigious amounts of tourist-grade daiquiris like the "vampires" at the other tables. No, Jake had a personal matter on his mind.

He looked around the room, which teemed with gay, frivolous, wasted life. Weekenders in for an early debauch, locals who scammed the patrons for either cash or ass, frazzled bartenders and an enormous shitsack of a man perched behind the piano, doing his best to sing songs that the bleary drunkards knew. Half of them were torch songs sped up to doubletime and the other half were what counted as "oldies." Jake smiled at that thought. An "oldie" was a song recorded in the 1950s or '60s. He'd been around for forty years before that—what did that make him?

It didn't matter. None of the drinkers saw him, or cared if they did. To them, he was simply a boozy comrade-in-arms, crawling the bars for a good time and a cheap drink. He was no threat—have a drink on us!

No one at this bar had any idea what he was. Or what the woman he was here to meet was. Marcia

Gibbert, fellow Kindred. She'd had a keen interest in New Orleans for the past few weeks, having arrived from—Anaheim?—just less than a month ago. Whenever she and Jake met, people thought they were a couple, a pair of eccentric, black, *nouveau-riche* lovers. The truth of the matter was that Marcia was looking for information on a five-thousand-year-old killer and that Jake was willing to profit from her deranged crusade. He didn't care about whatever it was that was bothering her; she had called it a family matter and left it at that. Jake understood. As a Brujah, he knew that some Kindred were quick to make judgments based upon one's lineage. He had her pegged for a Follower of Set. Maybe a Gangrel or even another Brujah. Possibly even Caitiff, but she didn't seem as grungy as most of the ones he'd met had been. Whatever; it didn't matter. She had cash, and it wasn't like Jake could hold down a day job. Maybe he could take the morbid tourists on a midnight tour of graveyards....

Marcia walked in, stooping below the low doorjamb. Peering through the smoke, she saw Jake, who waved her over to his table with an unmarked manila envelope in his hand. Suppressing the look of excitement that wanted to flash over her face, Marcia Gibbert calmly ordered a drink to keep up the charade and joined Jake at his table.

"You find something for me?" Marcia smiled. She knew Jake didn't have too much invested in her, but there was no reason not to be cordial.

Jake looked his guest over. She had broad features and fair skin, maybe even mulatto. And her eyes were blue, which was uncommon. Still, it wasn't his affair. He was here for money, so enough with the paranoia. "I found something you might like, yes. I'm afraid it's not big on facts—it sounds like it was written by a drunk or an opium addict, but you might find some of it useful."

He pushed the envelope across the table, waiting to see her reaction. If she whisked it away or made an effort to hide it, maybe it'd be worth his time to follow her later and see what she was up to. Then again, if it was really a family affair as she had said, it might be the location of one of her clan's oldest Kindred which, while interesting, was certainly not something he'd want to see firsthand.

Marcia opened the envelope deliberately, unwinding the string slowly from around the clasp, and pulled out a sheaf of yellowed papers that had torn or softened around the edges. They had been written in an even, decorative hand, the ink damaged here and there by moisture or the acids in the paper.

I don't suppose Blind Tom had always been blind. He had the look of a man who'd earned it. That left eye of his, with the milky bluewhite luster, and the right eye, vanished under a livid scar that touched his nose, made him a fright to look upon. I think I can even remember him with both eyes (or at least one), but as long as I can recall hailing him by name, I know I called him Blind Tom.

We had terribly good times, Blind Tom and I. Before I was born, he was the quartermaster or the sergeant or some such, but since losing his sight he took up living in the storm cellar underneath my mother's house. Mamma left me with him——she felt safe with him protecting me, I guess——during the day when she went to tea with her lady friends or took to town on errands. Blind Tom and I played at soldiers, or explored the patch of forest near the house. Sometimes we threw rocks at the gators from the trees, but Blind Tom never seemed to enjoy that as much as I did. He said, "Don't spit at the Devil when he's in his own house."

To be fair, I should say that I was a nervous child, always sick or worried or sleeping, and prone to spells of prodigious energy. Mamma laughed, "You see ghosts! You see the children of the woods dancing under the moon!" When she put it so fancifully, I couldn't help but laugh along, hoping our mirth would keep the…things…I saw at bay. And for the most part, it did.

But the charms of laughter couldn't last forever. 'Long about my eighth birthday, I would sometimes wake to a peculiar sound beneath my room in the wee hours. It sounded alternately like a goat's scrabbling, a mad hen, or Blind Tom singing in church. I cried out for my mother, but the sounds would stop before she could attend me.

"Lord's sake, my son, you'd think the gators were come to take you away!" I knew these sounds weren't gators, though; gators sound like hogs, or Blind Tom when he's had too much wine. Mamma would always make them end, though, and I thought nothing of it when I rose each day thereafter.

Blind Tom showed signs of being tired as I got older, and he seemed to be careless with himself. Too many times, I would find cuts on his worn face or fingers torn and bleeding.

"Why you want to be so curious, boy; ain'tcha know curiosity killed the cat?"

"I cut masself shaving," he'd answer, or, "I slammed my fingers in that demmed cellar door."

My nervousness had a certain tendency toward the clever——some might say I was precocious (though I've heard others call me fey). Before too long I noticed that the horrible sounds beneath my bed always preceded a new nick or blister on Blind Tom's frame. My interest piqued, I had to divine the truth.

"Blind Tom, was that you making all that racket under my room last night?" I asked innocently.

"Boy, you mind me and do it well," Blind Tom took a tone with me that I had never heard from him before. It was stern, demanding. It was a mode of speech I had never heard from my mother, whom Blind Tom said spoiled me, who doted or capered whimsically on my every word.

"That's Old Scratch underneath your floor, and you just keep to your covers when you hear him dancin' 'round."

I couldn't believe such a thing! I must confess it frightened me awfully. My mother lost her patience with me that night, as I refused to go to bed after numerous admonitions. She finally carried me to the bed and tucked me in herself, warning me that I'd have more to worry about than a simple spanking should I choose to flee the safety of the covers: She'd leave me for the gators in the swamps or the brownies in the woods.

She didn't have to worry. Not two minutes after she left my room, those noises started, and there was no way I was leaving my bunk. I called and called for her, but she figured I was in a spell or crying wolf and knew better than to heed my summons.

I don't know how long it went on, but after what must have been hours of bed-wetting terror, it was morning. I said nothing at breakfast that day, and my mother looked at me curiously, but went about her errands as normal.

"Blind Tom," I asked in awe, noting a pronounced limp in his gait, "what was all that commotion underneath my floor last night?"

"Demmit, boy, I told you to mind your own affairs, din't I? I said before that's Old Nick down there, and you'd best leave him to his own wickedness!"

And again that night, my mother ushered me to bed though I gave a chase like the dickens. When she finally caught me, I had exhausted myself, and helplessly collapsed in a heap she deposited in my bed.

After her shadow disappeared from the doorway, the sounds started up again, this time sounding like a mad piper playing an infernal tune. Frozen with fear, I stared at the ceiling, rigid lest I move too greatly and tumble into Lucifer's hands. Again, I wet myself that night, adamantly determined not to leave my sheets until dawn broke.

Mamma remarked that I looked sick the next morning, and that I should rest in the dayroom until she returned from Madame Poncelucard's home (upon whose newly engaged daughter she would be calling that day). She told me she would have Blind Tom check on me, to make sure I wanted for nothing at all.

The day went by in a delirious blur, and sprites cackled at me from the dayroom's long shadows, or so I thought. In the early afternoon, Blind Tom came in to inquire after my wellbeing and I observed in him a distinct favoring of his right arm. It may have been the poor light filtering past the burgundy drapes, but I thought I saw dark blood staining his coat by the dubious arm.

"Blind Tom," I begged, and a tremor colored my reedy voice, "do you know who stirred up all that ruckus last night under my floorboards?"

Blind Tom sighed before answering, tired and old. "Thet was the Devil, my boy, now never ask after him again."

The Devil! Under my mother's house! Unthinkable and yet palpably real came Blind Tom's response. Did he truly expect me to believe that with all his peculiar wounds and exhaustion, it wasn't him down there raising Cain?

Needless to say, I dreaded the bedtime looming that night, which came mercilessly early with my mother's suspicion of my impending illness.

For long hours, I peered at the ceiling, hoping to block out the sounds when they arrived.

The noises came late that night, and upon their arrival, I had steeled myself with an unyielding resolve. Terrified as I was, I could not abide this vile and mysterious wolf in sheep's clothing working his evil beneath my house. Surely he was down there, preparing some awful spell to vex me with consumption or smallpox or——blindness. How jealous was he, that he resented the vigor of a small boy so he could contrive to strip the child of his sight?

The gorge of my terror rising, it took only the tinny strains of that cursed pipe to drive me from my bed. With the white tails of my nightshirt flapping, I grabbed a candle from the hall table and lit it with the embers of the kitchen cookfire. I bolted into the night from the kitchen door, running around the house to where Blind Tom's cellar door stood. Sure enough, the dreadful piping rose from therein, and I knew that I must disturb his curse or suffer his own bitter fate.

Throwing open the door, I shrieked, "Blind Tom! Break your spell!" and leapt into the poorly lit rocky bowels of my mother's house, candle guttering and almost setting my nightshirt aflame.

There before me stood Blind Tom, shocked at my arrival. As he turned to me——an action that suggested he once had sight——I saw his lips, split and bloody around a horrid hornpipe, forcing out the tune as sweat speckled his forehead and stained the front of his jacket.

Just then I heard a deep rumbling, and Blind Tom whipped back around, too late. An invisible force racked his body and his head snapped back with violence. Blind Tom crumpled to the ground, dropping the pipe and coughing out one final gout of sticky blood, rasping, "Demn you, boy, I told you to stay back. Now he's loose."

In shock I stared down at him, but looked up as the rumbling *sound formed the ominous word: "Tomorrow."*

There, in the dim, far corner of the room, stood a dead man wearing a black robe or cowl. His vicious mouth curved into a horribly satisfied smile. He spoke to me, and his voice was like steel dragged over a rock. "Thank you, boy. I have work to do and men to see." That awful apparition faded into nothing, leaving a room swathed in shadow and heavy air.

It was then that I fled from the storm cellar, running north until I collapsed and never looking behind me. For days, every bit of energy I could muster served to propel me further and further from that hellish place. Even after I crawled out of my exhausted, starved mania and into whatever town it was, I never spoke another word. And I have never returned to my mother's house, where the dead walk and only terrible night-songs can keep them at bay.

"What is this? Where'd it come from?" Marcia asked Jake, her eyes wide and her words quick. "Who gave it to you? Did they see anything that this paper describes?"

"Damn, slow down." Jake pushed himself away from the table a bit, as if to calm the conversation with distance. "More important is, do you want it? And what can you pay me to make it worth me giving it to you?"

Marcia, no stranger to dealing with Kindred, opened the bidding low—cash was disposable, especially to the Giovanni. "I'll give you six thousand for it, as long as you answer the rest of my questions. I've got it here, in New Orleans, cash, that you can have tonight."

"Six large for some dead man's diary? Sounds pretty steep. Must be worth something. I wonder what else you have?" Doing his part to further the endless dance of the Jyhad, no matter how small the individual motion, Jake held out.

"My most immediate offer is the cash. Sixty-five hundred, tonight." Marcia countered.

"Tell you what, sister. I don't need money. I'll give you the papers. I'll even give you the background. But you owe me. I can call on you once, at any time, for a small favor. It won't necessarily require that you be here, but you'll have to help me when I need it."

Marcia pretended to mull it over for a minute. Jake wanted some sort of minor boon, the kind of promise the Camarilla thrived on. Small price to pay, if this was at least a recent and reliable record that the ancient killer she sought had once made its refuge here. "Deal," she said.

"Sweet," Jake quipped as they shook hands. "Now what else you need to know?"

"Well, first of all, what is this? Is it a piece of something larger?"

"No, it's a journal entry someone I know found in a storm cellar of one of the houses by the swamps. The rest of the papers in the satchel were just records—finances, birth certificates, deeds that had been voided and so on. It didn't sound like you were looking for any of that."

"No, I'm not. I just need locations—where was this?"

"Within twenty miles of here, I'd say. I can get you there."

"Was there anything else in the cellar? Any makeshift tombs or anything like that?"

"Jesus, keep your voice down. These people are drunk, not stupid. And no, the place was picked clean. It's been deserted for about forty years—someone bought the estate a while back for pennies on the dollar, but no one's moved in since."

Marcia looked incredulous. "How can you have a cellar in a swamp?" She raised one eyebrow, letting Jake know that she was hoping to catch him in a lie. It would be easy to fabricate this sort of thing; if she found out that it was false, he wouldn't be any worse for the effort, and if she never found out, she'd have repaid her favor for nothing.

"The house was built over a grotto. The storm cellar's a natural rock cave that's above the water table. They just built a storm door over the cave mouth and put the house right next to it. I think there's a mention of the rock walls in the journal itself."

"Okay, so how do we know that this house is the one in the journal? It says he never went back."

"Look at the back side of the last page—this thing was sent as a letter, back to the house itself. And I did a bit of research, finding the name Poncelucard on a property title for a piece of real estate about half a night's walk away. The title was dated back to 1860, which is presumably when the Poncelucards bought their house. Also, and I don't mind praising my own cleverness here, the house where this was found has a rotten set of burgundy curtains in what might have been the dayroom. That doesn't prove anything in and of itself, but it's a minor detail that matches."

"So you found this at the mansion?" Marcia continued.

"No, someone I know did. I just checked out the details afterward. I have to stand behind my merchandise, don't you know." Jake smiled, which Marcia returned demurely.

"Well, I'll respect your secrecy."

"You don't want to know if I made any copies?"

"I don't care if you did."

"And you don't want to see the house?"

"I have the address." Marcia pointed to the back of the last page.

"So, we're good on the favor." It was a statement, not a question.

"We are, indeed."

"Good luck, then," Jake remarked, without a hint of a smile. "If you need me, you know where to find me."

"Thanks, Jake. I'll be making my usual exit."

Jake rolled his eyes as Marcia rose, "accidentally" knocking over her drink so no one would see she hadn't touched it. She barked, "And I never want to see you again!" before storming out of Laffitte's, not loud enough to make a huge spectacle, but with enough drama to convince all the drunks that she and her "boyfriend" had had a falling out.

A red-faced man at the table behind him tapped Jake on the shoulder. "Aren't you going to go after her?"

Jake shook his head without looking at his commiserator. "No, we're done. I've seen her for the last time." He wondered if it would prove to be so.

Friday, 23 July 1999, 12:27 AM
The Tabernacle
Atlanta, Georgia

An addled youth in an orange shirt and oversized pants, obviously under the influence of some hallucinatory demon, staggered past the bar. He shouted something at one of his group of friends, which took the other fellow by surprise, who in turn gave an "Oh, my God" look to another member of the group before finishing what remained of his plastic bottle of beer in one enormous gulp.

Isabel Giovanni and Marcia Gibbert exchanged knowing glances—should either of them need vitae before the evening's close, it would be ready for the taking. Of course, it would also likely be laced with no end of designer chemicals and more organic substances. They had both affected the clothing styles of the assembled concert-goers: straight-legged khakis far too large for them and tiny T-shirts that clung to their torsos. Marcia had braided her kinky hair into cornrows; Isabel pulled her straight, black tresses into a pair of ponytails. They blended into the crowd perfectly.

Anyone who knew these Kindred's secrets, however, would have found it utterly incongruous—a pair of Cainites, each at least a century old, dressed in fashions that the mortal world had adopted just years ago.

Almost ironically, they looked stunning, and a seemingly ceaseless train of libidos wandered up to them and threatened to buy them drinks.

"Tell me why we're here again?" Marcia half-kidded.

"Because no one we know would come here, and

because none of these people will care what we're doing, or remember us if they do," Isabel smiled.

They climbed a set of stairs, leading them to a lounge just beyond the bathrooms, but away from the dance floor below and the stadium seats one floor above. The crowd in front of the stage surged energetically, some in states of natural exultation, others in states of drug-induced frenzy. The performer on the stage mixed a strange version of one of his signature songs, the surf-punk dance samples of the tune laid over the melody and harmony of an old Rolling Stones classic. Isabel and Marcia were simply two more guests at the raucous party.

Marcia took off her stylish-yet-functional backpack, which was all the rage among the accessory crowd currently. From it she produced the journal she had received just the night before in New Orleans. The two sat on a battered leather couch, further withdrawing from the crowd.

"Is this it?" Isabel asked.

"The whole thing. It looks like that thing you're after stayed on one of the plantations within the past hundred years. That's the most current sighting I've found. If it's as old as you think it is, it's probably fallen back into torpor since then, as no one else seems to have seen it afterward. I've checked everywhere sensible within two states around Louisiana and even with some of the offshore oil rigs in the Gulf of Mexico. Nothing. I can't imagine why a Methuselah would go to Mississippi or East Texas unless it was trying to hide, which, if it's hunting us like you say, isn't what it's trying to do."

"You're probably right—I don't think it's even considered that we're wanting to find *it*. Then again, that's moot. I'm not even going to pretend to be able to outguess it. If it's as old as we think it is, it's got to be very cunning to leave no trace of its passing."

"You really think it's one of the old clan?" Marcia asked.

"I don't know. It's impossible to say now, but it certainly seems to hate Giovanni enough to kill us specifically. Frankie Gee's only the most recent one, and when he disappeared in New Orleans, I knew it wasn't over the Milo Rothstein affair. It probably smelled him the moment he set foot in the city." Isabel was concentrating on the document before her, looking for any clue that might make certain that the monster below the journalist's home was indeed a vengeful Kindred. The journal seemed strange—a much more poetic account of the event than one might think would show up in a diary. Still, not only did she have no clue about the monster's identity, she had no idea as to the personality of the author. Still, it wasn't written in Enochian, Sanskrit or Egyptian hieroglyphics, so she hoped she could rule out being set up by the creature itself. "Did you go by the house itself?"

"No," Marcia said, "I didn't think it would be wise. If the thing was still there, I'd stand no chance against it, and the only thing you'd have to go on would be my disappearance." She shuddered a bit in spite of the intense heat of the concert hall, which was warmed beyond the normal Georgia heat by the mortals dancing around them. "I hope these pages help out. I had to promise a favor to get them."

Isabel looked up, a thin smile on her lips. "To Jake Almerson? Next time you talk to him, tell him you don't owe him any favors. And tell him he doesn't owe me one, either."

Marcia nodded whimsically and turned her own attention to the journal.

"Is there a test in the morning?" Distracted by the journal and the overwhelming music, neither Marcia nor Isabel saw the approach of the young man in the tennis visor.

"Fuck off," Marcia shot back, almost automatically, while looking up to meet his gaze. She stopped short of her attempt to chase him away verbally, though, when she felt Isabel's cold hand on her arm.

"No, wait," Isabel said. "This one's okay." Marcia turned to look at her and saw her wink; Isabel hoped the suitor saw the wink, too.

Pushing them apart with his ass, the newcomer dropped himself on the couch between them. "I'm Scott. Either of you want something to drink?"

Isabel shifted into full flirtation mode. She looked meaningfully at Marcia. "Oh, I don't know. But I guess I am kind of thirsty."

At this last remark, Marcia shook her head and smiled. "Girl, you have no shame." Then she turned to Scott. "I'm Patrice. Nice to meet you, Scott. Sorry about cutting you off like that, but your pick-up line blows."

A sheepish smirk overtook Scott's face. "Yeah, well, I didn't really expect to see anyone looking over a notebook at this show." He looked over at Isabel. "I'm sorry, beautiful; what was your name?"

"Chlöe."

"That's a really cool name. And you know what else? You have beautiful—"

"Eyes," interrupted Isabel.

"How did you know I was going to say that?" Scott said through a broadening smile.

Marcia interjected. "'Cause that's what every motherfucker says when he's trying to take home a prime piece of pussy." She made a grotesque face at Isabel, playing the part of the vapid club girl, but letting Isabel know just how stupid she though it was.

Isabel, though, was thoroughly enjoying herself by this point. She knew it wasn't any stupider than their mark. It was amazing just how often a vessel would fall into a Kindred's lap, never knowing what was in store for him. "Shut *up*, Patrice. You're going to ruin my chances with this dashing Southern gentleman."

Oh, so it's a game, now, is it, Isabel? Marcia though to herself. *Well, I'm better at this than you are. See if your old ass can keep up with someone who's young and still got it.* Isabel fought back a smile, as if reading Marcia's mind. The hunt was on.

Scott, of course, loved every minute of it. Little had he known when he selected the two women to be the recipients of his dazzling attentions that they would be so responsive to him. He didn't even have to turn on too much of his boundless charm—chalk it up to the power of natural charisma. In fact, the most difficulty these ladies gave him was in the decision between them. *What the hell*, Scott reasoned, deciding to attempt to take them both to bed. After all, life is boring without a little risk. They way things were going, the worst he'd do was to get only one of them.

The innuendo proceeded, Isabel and Marcia baiting Scott and each other and Scott responding, leaving no question at all as to his singular goal.

"Patrice" wrapped her arm around their suitor's shoulder; "Chlöe" crossed her legs so that one rested over his. Scott grinned and stretched backward, making himself comfortable and allowing the women to battle over the field of his body. Marcia leaned in to kiss his ear; Isabel pulled his head away from her and rested it on her shoulder. Scott bowed his legs away, allowing both of them greater and equal access to his libidinous bounty. Marcia tugged at his shirt and slunk one leg over his, dry-humping his thigh. Isabel locked her mouth around his, chasing his lazy tongue with hers. Certain of his impending carnal victory, Scott grew bold and slid his hand under Isabel's shirt, his hand inexpertly kneading the flesh of her small breast—which he didn't seem to mind was uncommonly cool—in half-tempo to the thundering music from the ground floor. Isabel had to fight back a spasm of laughter at his clumsy lotharian ineptitude—but blood was blood, so she persevered, shooting a grin at Marcia after breaking off her kiss.

"Why don't we take this back to the hotel?" Isabel suggested. "We're just right up the road."

Bleary-eyed, Scott acquiesced. Marcia pulled him up from the couch by his hand. Apparently, it didn't matter to him that his paramours weren't local. In fact, all that mattered to him was the recurring *I can't believe this* running through his mind.

The amorous trio stalked the five blocks to the Westin Peachtree in short order, stopping briefly in the hotel bar for a round of largely untouched vodka martinis and earning the derisive looks of the more staid guests. The drinks deterred their course only temporarily, however, and within ten minutes, they had settled their tab, taken an elevator, and stood outside Isabel's room.

"Patrice" made a grand show of fumbling with the key, though she knew it was probably unnecessary—Scott hadn't been paying attention to details since he weaseled his way onto the couch back at the Tabernacle. She pushed open the door, staggered inside and collapsed supine on the vast bed.

That was all the encouragement Scott needed. He walked deliberately over to her in a drunken attempt at sultriness and forced his knees between her legs, which Marcia had bent at the knee and left somewhat apart.

Isabel, no longer under the pretense, closed the door quietly and slid the lever over the post. She killed the light, which she had left on before leaving for the concert hall.

Meanwhile, Scott had gracelessly removed Marcia's backpack and left it by the side of the bed. He tugged her T-shirt over her head and dropped it over the pack. Marcia giggled. *Jesus, he licked his lips.*

Isabel took the opportunity to relieve Scott of his shirt in her own fashion—she tore it at the neck and split it downward, pulling it off his body like a jacket that had been donned backward. He turned around for a moment, eyes flashing in preparation for the lusty fornication that was no doubt about to ensue, only to see her appreciating his body. Scott had well-defined muscles, but not enough bulk to make him *too* big. A frisson of vain pleasure surged through him: *Yeah, I know I look good.* But Marcia distracted him back to her with a tug at the front of his pants, and her fingers quickly found their way over the top and into his waistband. Isabel took to running her hands over his back and pectorals. Not wanting to deny his lovers access to his greatest prize for a moment longer, Scott undid the button and zipper of his pants himself while Isabel threw his visor-cap aside. Marcia grabbed the elastic of his exposed boxer shorts and jerked them down, exposing his engorged sex.

He does have a reason to be so smug, after all, Marcia thought to herself before taking his girth into her mouth. And waited on the physical cue…

Marcia felt Scott's body go rigid all of a sudden. She looked up just as his hellish scream choked off, silenced by Isabel's powerful hand, which had clamped over his mouth—and broken his jaw. Isabel herself peered down at Marcia, biting down between his shoulder and neck, her eyes glazed over as the gluttonous Beast grew fatted with the young man's vitae. Marcia then distended her fangs, piercing Scott's tumescent penis and gulping in the rich blood that had traveled there in his arousal.

Scott twitched violently, held in place by Isabel, who pinned his arms in place and silenced him, and Marcia, who held his legs, preventing him from buckling or collapsing. He felt as if his body had been doused in acid—his blood turned to fire as it flowed out of his body and into the mouths of the witches who had tricked him. He kicked, shook, neither to any avail. Even as he grew tired, his blood no longer able to carry oxygen to his extremities, his exhaustion was one of anguish. *This is what it must feel like to burn to death*, Scott thought. Tears rolled down his cheeks, his nose bled and he could taste the coppery metal of blood in his mouth from where Chlöe had shattered his mandible with her bare hand. *This is how it feels to die of poison in your lungs. And these monsters are real.*

The Kindred took their time drawing Scott's precious vitae from him, prolonging his agony. Weakened by the loss of blood, Scott could no longer resist them as they broke off their kiss and moved their mouths to other parts of his body. They opened his wrists and inside his thighs, drank from his tongue and from the rippled flesh just below his left breast. For half an hour, Marcia and Isabel fed from their wretched vessel, carrying out the act as though it were mortal sex—tempting, prurient, orgasmic, base and cathartic all at once.

When the two women were done, Isabel rose and brushed stands of hair out of her eyes. "I didn't intend to finish him."

"Me, neither," said Marcia as she pulled her top back on. "But I couldn't stop once it got going."

"Help me put his clothes back on. We'll walk him out of here like he's passed out drunk and leave the body somewhere."

"He's turning blue!"

"Yeah, that happens when there's no blood in your veins. Quick—I've got makeup in the bathroom. Dust him with base and rouge while I call a cab."

Marcia did as she was told. Twenty minutes later, the Kindred and their dead companion took a taxi to the neighborhood around Fort McPherson, in the southern part of Atlanta. They broke into an abandoned box factory, surrounded the corpse with corrugated cardboard, doused it with lighter fluid, and set flame to the whole mess.

"This is fucked up," Marcia commented to no one in particular.

"Well, it's more inconvenient than anything else. Think of the time investment like you were cooking dinner as a mortal. Except as a Kindred, you get to eat *before* you prepare the meal." Isabel shrugged.

"No, I've done this before. It just never gets any easier," Marcia said.

Isabel saw blood-tears trickling down her cheeks. She resisted the urge to tell her companion that, yes, indeed, it did become easier. *Too* easy, at times.

After an hour of burning the body and reigniting the portions that remained, they swept the ashes around the factory and gathered the bones. These they pounded into unrecognizable bits of detritus and scattered them around the factory, in the trash, around the weedy outside lawn and into the sewers. One thing was sure—no one was going to find Scott.

Marcia wiped her eyes, staining her forearm with a bloody smear. The two women caught a cab and returned to their hotel.

Thursday, 29 July 1999, 3:43 AM
Seasons Restaurant, Bostonian Hotel
Boston, Massachusetts

The night could end only in disaster. That much Chas knew. Isabel expected him to accompany Genevieve Pendleton in her discussion with the Camarilla's diplomat, Jacques Gauthier. Pendleton was dead, Gauthier was pompous, Isabel hadn't made the diplomat very welcome when they last met, and Chas wanted to tear the guy in half on principle.

In the interests of keeping things from becoming a complete cluster fuck, Chas had kept his involvement fairly low-key. Isabel hadn't called him, which meant that the Milliners had assumed that she was taking care of things after they'd received Pendleton's resignation, and hadn't bothered her. The best thing for him to do was…

Well, was what? Buy time? Wing it? Tell Gauthier to fuck himself? Chas had to meet with the guy—he didn't have Gauthier's contact information to postpone the meeting—but he didn't know what the Giovanni's stance was going to be. Sure, he had an *idea* after speaking with Isabel, but he didn't know any of the finer details, and "Screw you, we're going to stay neutral" didn't seem to be the best way to handle things.

Chas had decided that the best thing to do was meet with Gauthier and tell him that the Giovanni needed a bit more time to consider what they planned to do. After that, Isabel could handle it. With any luck, Chas would get off with only minor punishment for indirectly—well, all right, directly—fucking up the situation in the first place, by preventing it from becoming any worse.

But shit never went down like that, Chas knew. Something bad was bound to happen. He felt worry gnawing behind his hunger when he woke, shaved, and dressed for the evening. To be sure, he left his pistol and brass knuckles at the Milliners' guest house where he stayed and didn't bother to take the sawed-off Louisville Slugger from the trunk of the car. If he didn't want a fight, it wouldn't work to look like he did, after all.

Jacques arrived early, which was a good sign. It showed that he took the matter seriously and cared more for the content of the meeting than he did for his own status. *Maybe this won't be such a problem after all*, Chas thought to himself. Still, Jacques and Chas hadn't exactly been pleasant to one another at their last meeting.

"Good evening, Mr. Gauthier," Chas greeted the emissary.

"Good evening, Mr. Giovanni," Gauthier replied in kind. "Where is the esteemed Miss Giovanni?"

"Something came up at the last minute and she was unable to reach you."

"I've been available all night. Every night, in fact, for the past two weeks. I even left her with information on how to leave a message for me during the day, should something strange have come up."

"I understand that, Mr. Gauthier, and I apologize." Chas wanted to go back to the name calling that had suited him when dealing with this prick earlier, but that wouldn't have made things run any smoother. "She had left another representative of the clan"—not *too* far from the truth—"to attend this meeting, but something came up that made her unable to attend, too."

"I see. So, the original negotiator with whom I had spoken about our mutual concerns left, and put someone in charge who couldn't attend our meeting, thereby leaving only the bodyguard who sat in on the first meeting to handle the follow-up. A very indelicate solution, to be sure."

"Now, settle down; I'm not Isabel's bodyguard."

"Then what are you, Mr. Giovanni?"

"We're working on something else together."

"I beg your pardon?" Gauthier looked incredulous. He raised his eyebrows in a manner that suggested he'd be quite interested in hearing what could possibly be more important than a consultation with a Camarilla dignitary in the middle of a sect conflict.

"Something different. Not related to the Camarilla interest in Boston."

"Oh, I understand perfectly. Allow me to outline the situation as I see it. A member of your clan receives me and then decides that something else demands her time more than seeing the initial concern through. In her stead, she leaves a proxy, who also has business elsewhere. And the person who finally does deign to meet me to resolve the matter doesn't actually have anything to do with the situation in the first place. I'm afraid this doesn't look very good, Mr. Giovanni. At the very best, even if I determine that Clan Giovanni has not chosen to entertain Sabbat sympathies, it certainly has no intention of forging some arrangement with the Camarilla because it won't even lend their spokesmen an ear. Am I correct?"

"Well, no, not exactly," Chas felt himself grow embarrassed, and then angry. He knew how this looked, and knew he'd have to take a few jabs for it, but there was no need to keep escalating.

"Oh, not *exactly*? Well, then, Mr. Giovanni, please tell me *exactly* what sort of impression I am to draw from the current turn of events?"

"Look, man, I'm trying to tell you—"

"Don't presume such an informal relationship, Mr. Giovanni. I can assure you that even if I chose to ignore the utter disrespect you've obviously assumed for myself—which I haven't—I still would not overlook the fact that the collective Giovanni of Boston have such a low estimation of the Camarilla that they do not choose to treat it as a serious partner even when faced with the possibility of suffering harm themselves at the hands of a mutual enemy. Whether or not you openly embrace our overtures, Mr. Giovanni, ignoring the threat posed by the Sabbat does not make it go away."

"Hey, you want to listen to me, here? I fucked up. This isn't Isabel's fault and it's not what the clan intended. I accidentally screwed up the situation with the woman who was supposed to talk to you, and I didn't know where to reach you. And rather than just no-showing or running with what I thought might be best, I just thought I'd tell you what happened."

"Ineptitude!"

"Hey, pal, sometimes things just go wrong. This is one of those times. Sorry it had to be you."

"As you should be. Do you have any idea—"

"Look, don't get all fucking sanctimonious. You don't want me to go back and tell everyone that you're getting all indignant, 'cause that might hurt your precious relationship or whatever you were just yammering on about." Chas couldn't resist the dig. Despite the fact that he had almost defused Gauthier, his temper refused to let him yield.

Gauthier once again looked shocked. He had never been spoken to so plainly—at least not to his face—by anyone, especially someone who should by rights have taken a deferential attitude. "You had best stop while you're ahead, Mr. Giovanni. Before you do any more damage to this potentially explosive arrangement, I think you should hold your tongue."

"Don't talk down to me, you stupid motherfucker, or I'll give you the beatdown of your unlife. I apologized, Isabel will fix everything, so just shut the fuck up and let everything go back to normal." *What the fuck am I doing?* Chas wondered to himself, but he couldn't stop. Gauthier had pushed him too far—with just a few words! *Chas, fucking rein it in. You know he was going to be all prissy when you came here, so just let it go.*

But the voice in Chas's mind didn't have control—something else did. He wasn't saying anything he had been actively thinking; the uncontrollable part of him had roused from its sleep and taken over.

"Threats?" It was a statement, not a question. Jacques's voice had become ominously deep and his eyes focused into a stare. "I will not have you threaten me. Do you hear me, *boy*?" This last he punctuated with a snarl and a spit, his fangs jutting out, revealing him as the monster he truly was. Jacques's hands had become talons; his face twisted into a mask of rage.

Chas, overwhelmed, shrank away from Gauthier's withering display—

—for a brief second, before his own Beast snapped the chain on which it had been tethered. Balling his hands into fists, he charged Gauthier as visions of blood and murder spun through his mind.

Jacques proved to be too nimble, however, and spun quickly out of the way. Chas barreled past, knocking over a table, scattering the settings across the room. Gauthier looked over his shoulder, his eyes slits, a reedy laugh coming from his demoniacal mouth. Almost too fast for Chas to see, he sprinted toward the kitchen. Indeed, if Chas hadn't seen the door move, he wouldn't have known Gauthier had passed through it. Like an enraged animal, he followed, bursting through the door with enough force to hurl aside anyone who had waited behind it.

Fortunately, even the staff had left the restaurant by this time, or bodies would have surely littered the kitchen floor. The room was lit in a sterile white—which suddenly became darkness. Had Chas been able to think clearly, he would have guessed that Jacques could see in less light and turned off the lights to give himself an advantage. In his frenzied state, though, reason had left him and he rushed blindly at where he guessed the light switch to be. A great row of ranges and ovens stood to one side of him; to the other loomed a tall row of shelves stocked with oversized cans of food. Chas gave this second a heavy shove, toppling it and the one behind it like a series of dominoes. One by one, the entire kitchen's worth of shelves toppled to the floor. The cans and jars likewise fell, some shattering, others clanging loudly. As the last shelf fell, Chas saw a speed-blurred shape streak from behind it. A half-second later, he found a huge metal fork protruding from his chest and he doubled over in momentary shock before jerking it out and spraying a gout of blood across the kitchen. Again the kitchen doors swung—Gauthier had bolted out of the room.

Chas roared and followed, perhaps foolishly, fork in hand. Still, Gauthier had drawn first blood, which only infuriated Chas all the more. Bursting back into the dining room, Chas saw the outline of Jacques's form, backlit by light that poured in from the outside. A pair of headlights.

Jacques Gauthier laughed once more. "You ignorant brute! You can't catch me, you know."

But Chas didn't need to be faster. Someone entered the front of the restaurant. Jacques looked over at the intruder in disbelief and Chas took full advantage of the opportunity. He dived at Gauthier with all his might, knocking over the hostess's podium. As he pinned Gauthier to the ground, he noticed another person outside, in addition to the one just beyond his peripheral vision. He could deal with them later.

Gauthier struggled beneath him, but Chas's strength was far superior. Over and over, he drove the heavy cooking fork down through Jacques's face, using the stabbing motions to punctuate his spoken hatred. "You...stupid...fuck! What...did...you...think...would...happen..."

Another voice cut him off in mid-stab and sentence.

"Don't move. Jessica! Spray him!"

A cold mist washed over Chas. He looked up in surprise, a snarl on his face. "What the fuck is wrong with you? Can't you fucking see I'm trying to kill this guy? Go away!"

The voice continued, unwavering, "Get thee behind me, Satan. Tempt not the Children of Seth, and return to the hell from which you were spawned!"

Beneath Chas, Gauthier bucked, taking his aggressor by surprise and throwing him off. Chas tumbled backward onto his haunches. Like a bolt, Gauthier was off into the night, leaving a viscous trail of blood-gobbets behind him.

"Goddamn it. God*damn* it. What is *wrong* with you? Now they're going to kick my ass over this!"

Another cold mist hit Chas in the face. "Creature of darkness! Thief of the living's blood! A walking affront to the righteousness of God!"

"Oh, for fuck's sake, give it a rest! That doesn't work! Jesus, where do you people keep coming from? First Frankie's thing in New York and now this? Who the fuck are you?" Chas peered into the darkness and saw a pale glow outlining what must have been hands. The cold mist came from the left, where he saw a slighter shape wearing some bulky backpack.

"The holy water has no effect! Jessica, switch to the other tank!"

Chas heard a click, heard the hiss that accompanied the bursts of mist and smelled gasoline. "Oh, no you fucking don't," Chas growled and leaped toward the black outline with the glowing hands. He swung the kitchen fork upward, calling upon his hellish strength to carry it through. With a sickening wet slap sound, the fork traveled upward, through the unseen man's mandible, past his mouth and into the upper part of his head, breaking through the topmost bone of his skull like a bullet punching through sheet metal. A feeble noise came from the man, who immediately slumped forward into Chas's arms. Chas dropped the man and whirled to face his other attacker—a short, thick woman holding some kind of spray gun. She must have bought it at a hardware store; it looked like the kind of thing someone would use to treat their yard with pesticides. The woman stood frozen, aghast at the death of her partner, and Chas slapped the clumsy nozzle from her hand.

"All right. What the fuck is this about?"

The woman only stammered.

"Hello? I'm talking to you, you crazy bitch. What, you can shoot me with holy water and set me on fire but you can't talk to me?" Chas shoved the woman backward, sending her asprawl over a small dinner table. The spray gun dangled uselessly aside. The woman's eyed gaped as big as saucers. She choked out some kind of simple, repetitive prayer, presumably for protection, but an answer didn't seem likely. "I'm fucking serious here. Who the fuck are you people? If you're vampire hunters, I think you need to do a little more homework next time, because that holy water crap doesn't work."

The woman kicked weakly as Chas advanced, her stout legs unable to turn back his greater strength. He slapped her on the thigh, sending her spinning sideways, and stopped her just as her head ended up before him.

"Now, are you going to give me a fucking answer or do I have to eat you?"

Still the woman protested weakly, too terrified

by being so close to such a monster to summon her strength.

"Jesus, you freak, you'd rather die? Fine. Fucking have it your way."

Chas bit down as hard as he could, not even bothering to find a large vein or artery. The woman finally found her voice and shrieked, a long, shrill wail that could have shattered glass. When he had finally drained her to the point of collapse, he licked the wound and it sealed. With any luck, when whoever found this mess tried to put two and two together, they'd assume some sort of fight between two lunatics, one with a fork through his head and the other wearing an atomizer filled with bizarre liquids. Fuck 'em—it didn't scream *vampire!* and it was probably weird enough for the police to keep it quiet from the media.

With that, Chas adjusted himself as best he could and drove back to the Milliners' guesthouse. He'd have quite a job explaining himself to them and to Isabel—but that was best accomplished on another night.

As Chas drove away, Gauthier slunk from the shadows and sated himself on the woman's remaining blood. Then he fled into the night.

Sunday, 25 July 1999, 1:18 AM
The Malecón
Havana, Cuba

"I have a proposition for you."

Anastasz di Zagreb, justicar for the sorcerous Tremere vampires, tilted his head, encouraging her to go on. "Yes, and it is...?"

"You and I, we are much alike," Isabel began. It was a thread that made the Tremere none too comfortable—he was familiar with the debased Kindred of Clan Giovanni and he was aware of a certain quirk that this one in particular indulged while feeding. He wanted nothing more at the moment than to be as little like her as possible. "And our histories share more than one sympathy." Anastasz hated this part. The Kindred and all of their petty games irritated him, and his preference was to be either "in the field" or in his own sanctum. No doubt what would follow this pretty-but-cold woman's requests would be some unpleasant request couched in the form of a favor. The Tremere was familiar with such double-bladed social engineerings—his own august position was the result of hidden favors and boons exchanged. His predecessor, the potent Karl Schrekt, had been miraculously left unconsidered for reelection to the justicar's title. Instead, at the assembly of the Camarilla's Inner Council in 1998, the Tremere had put forth the dark horse di Zagreb. Isabel's pending offer was surely some similar ruse, carefully couched in eloquence and deceit.

"Our clans have both risen from the ashes of others. We both hail from long, distinguished lines of sires who saw weakness and chose to light a candle rather than curse the darkness. I don't pretend to know the secrets of those fateful nights"—*don't patronize me, you florid bitch*, Anastasz thought—"but I do know that our clans both rose like phoenixes from the folly of others. Wouldn't you agree?"

"As much as it displeases me, I concur. Where are you headed with this, Isabel?" Such insolence! Moments like this allowed Anastasz to savor his position. To think that one as young as himself—a Kindred for only one century—could speak with such insouciance to a scion of the Giovanni! But then, Anastasz remembered, it was only the strength of the Camarilla that allowed him this luxury. Were Clan Tremere as removed from Kindred affairs as the Giovanni, his title would have meant nothing. She would have crushed him like a beetle, if only he hadn't had the ubiquitous ivory tower behind him.

"Patience, Justicar. Do not leap to judgment. Allow me to explain."

"Then be about it, Isabel. The summer nights are short and I am hungry." Masterful! Dismissive yet authoritative! Perhaps the game of politics had its benefits after all....

"Very well. Surely you are familiar with the fate of the Ravnos?"

Anastasz nodded. Earlier this very month, the Kindred world had shaken at its very foundation as one of the original, Biblical Kindred had awoken from its sleep. The founder of a clan had risen too early for the end of the world and was destroyed, dragging his childer screaming into Final Death with him. Or so the tale was told. No one who was there had been to eager to step forward—and most who had been there had been destroyed. "I am."

"Then you understand that they stand poised to retake their fallen status, much as our own sires claimed the mantle of clanhood. Once again, as the rest of the Children of Caine watch the death of their siblings, they mutter their own thanks that it was not they whom fate conspired to harm. But you Tremere know, Anastasz, as well as we Giovanni, that those who are dismissed as weak or few can turn the tables and snatch victory from the jaws of oppression."

Good Lord, thought Anastasz, *she certainly is painting this in epic strokes.*

"Many Ravnos escaped the Week of Nightmares with their unlives. The few who remain may take advantage of the weak light in which others see them. Clans have fallen before, and never without dire repercussion. Your own clan and mine came as a result, and it is whispered that the formation of the Sabbat had similar circumstances."

"Are you suggesting that the Tremere and the Sabbat—"

"Of course not. I am suggesting that we strike while the iron is hot. The Ravnos are crippled. Our work is almost done; we must simply finish the deed."

"Destroy the remaining Ravnos?" Anastasz considered this. It certainly had its merits. A line of mystics and scoundrels, the Ravnos left trouble in their wake. Many Kindred princes of Europe and the New World refused to allow Ravnos in their domains. The Ravnos had no allies, nor did they want them. They practically begged to be extinguished. Such a tactic would not only remove a lingering thorn from the Camarilla's side, it could consolidate the sect's strength and allow it to focus on larger threats. And if he played his cards right, he could prove his worth to an Inner Council that harbored doubts about his ability.

Anastasz stopped, shocked at his thoughts. Was he actually considering genocide? Did he honestly think that his reputation was worth the death of other Kindred? How blind and instinctual a creature had he become, that slaughter and murder were subjects so easily entertained? Even as a predator, he retained a sense of his own humanity—it was the only bulwark he had against the bestial urges that lurked in all Kindred. If he gave in completely, he would no longer be a conscious being; he would become wholly a monster.

"Yes." Isabel's response snapped Anastasz out of his reverie. "They offer nothing, and it is in the interests of all Kindred that we isolate and remove the threat they are still quite capable of posing." The moon shone down on Isabel's face, making her look ghoulish, and her suggestion compounded the discomfort Anastasz felt.

"This is murder, Isabel."

"No, Justicar, this is survival. Death is part of the cycle of all life—and unlife. Perhaps more so for the latter. I assure you, no Ravnos would hesitate to deliver you to your final reward."

"That's impossible to say, Isabel. We are Kindred—our motives are our own. Not all of us are murderous monsters."

"You don't think so, Justicar? You are fooling yourself. The Ravnos progenitor arose from its slumber and destroyed its own children! What more argument do you need to convince you?"

"I suggest you hold your tongue, Isabel." The discussion had taken a turn for the ugly. Anastasz whispered tersely, "Whether or not you and your clan claim membership in the Camarilla, we still claim dominion over you. Your words show little regard for the Masquerade, and we are in a public place with mortals about. I will not hesitate to take the necessary recourse—"

"Listen to what you are saying, Anastasz," Isabel returned, equally as quietly. "You apply your Masquerade and crusade selectively. The deceitful Ravnos are a far greater threat to the Masquerade than I could ever hope to be—"

"I'm not going to suggest mass murder based on your cajoling, Isabel. I won't take a stance against the Ravnos because some bigoted Kindred doesn't like them. Their witchcraft and illusion are less damning than your own behavior—we know about your little predilection, my dear. We know that you drink vitae only from your victims' severed heads. And I can assure you that not every Kindred is as jaded and callous as you. I will not be used, nor will I allow my position to be exploited by a clan that refuses to accept the responsibilities of undeath."

"I see that I have misjudged you, Justicar. You condemn me with petty, mortal conceits. This political correctness, as they call it, is not a product of the times during which either of us were Embraced. Modern does not mean better, and all your arguments crumble beneath the cold truth. For I know members of the Tzimisce, with whom your clan has struggled since your earliest nights. It is a sorcerer's war, with both of your bloodlines putting each other to death for personal power. You and the House of Tremere are far *worse* than any course of action I suggest, because my motives are utilitarian. You slaughter each other over eyes of newt and forgotten spells, and yet you claim a moral high ground when I suggest removing a problem before it becomes dire. Your hypocrisy disgusts me."

Anastasz closed his eyes and rubbed them, signaling his weariness to Isabel. Then he dropped his hands to his sides and peered out over the Atlantic Ocean, as if to encourage Isabel to make her final argument or let him go. She saw his growing frustration and played to it.

"I know all about the situation in New York, Anastasz."

The justicar turned, his eyes flashing hotly. "And what does that have to do with what you're putting before me here?"

"Pieterzoon told me everything. Well, not directly, but through his liaison, Jacques Gauthier. They asked me to convince the body of Clan Giovanni to help. That's a dangerous position to take, Justicar. The Sabbat are not pleasant enemies. We Giovanni have maintained our independence by not taking sides—at the request of your Camarilla, if my history serves me correctly—and we're now being asked to act in direct opposition to that."

"Pieterzoon is power mad and Gauthier is a buffoon."

"Yes, well, your personal opinion is secondary to the facts of the matter, Anastasz. Whatever esteem you hold for Jan and his compatriots, you have common interest in the Camarilla. That's why I've bothered to talk to you at all. I'm sure you can understand the value of knowing as much as you can about a situation before acting on it, no? I'm not willing to drag other Giovanni into your Jyhad for the sake of Pieterzoon's ego. But I am willing to strike a deal with the winning side."

"New York is part of the means. It's not the end, Isabel."

"I understand that, Justicar, but Jan has placed a tempting offer on the table. I'm sure you're no stranger to the unattainability of Boston." Isabel couldn't resist the dig. Di Zagreb, as well as anyone else who dirtied themselves in Kindred politics, knew that influence in Boston was divided into a seemingly unbreakable three-way impasse between the Camarilla, Sabbat and Giovanni.

"So then, what are you doing *here*, Isabel?"

"Talking to you, Justicar."

"No, you Giovanni. What are you doing here?"

"What everyone in Havana is doing. Waiting for Castro to die."

"And why is that?"

"Pure economics, my dear Anastasz. Once the old man goes on to his final reward, this whole country's going to become the biggest free market in the western hemisphere."

"Triangle trade, Isabel."

"What?"

"Triangle trade. It's what the Fat Man wants to do, and you're going to back it with him. When, as you say, Castro dies, this whole country's going to be the biggest black market in the New World."

"So?" Isabel smiled sweetly. "When the change to capitalism comes, greed won't be a crime anymore—it'll be standard operating procedure. It won't even *be* a black market, because Cuba will establish itself as a governmentally backed international shopping mall. Anything goes."

"But that's only part of the equation. Cuba's still going to maintain some severe antidrug legislation, because it'll be in their best interests. Half the government will be against drug trade and keep it illegal while the other half will be on the take, so keeping it illegal will make them rich on bribe money. They couldn't go too lax on drugs, anyway, because the United States would crush them politically."

"Where are you going with this, Anastasz?"

"Well, if I know you and the rest of your clan, the simple, legal investments will only wet your beaks. Sure, you'll make millions—probably billions—in the tourist boom, but it's also part of the triangle trade. You're going to run heroin from Italy to Cuba, where you'll either send it in to the U.S. through Boston or sell it and convert the profits to coke and marijuana, then move *that* through Boston, because that's where you have the customs vice in your pockets. Then, the money goes *back* to Italy, where it buys more heroin, which again goes through Cuba, etc."

Isabel's eyebrows rose and her mouth curled up a bit at the ends. "Not bad, Justicar. Not bad at all. But it won't affect you at all, will it? Boston's already a Giovanni haven, Venice has always been one, and we only need a few Kindred handling the operation here. It doesn't matter if Cuba becomes a Sabbat or Camarilla playground—both of you will shut your mouths for a few points."

"But we don't *have* to, Isabel. That's where I'm headed with this. It would be equally profitable for us to watch every import-export company that sets up in the area and shut down any that smell like Giovanni. In fact, it would be more lucrative for whoever comes out on top to run you gravediggers out of business—because they could then charge *you* whatever they wanted to keep the lanes open."

"I'm willing to play that game, Anastasz. The Kindred have long been masters of such maneuverings, and this is simply one more. Who knows—Cuba may even turn out to be Utopia, where Kindred can go about their business without that awful, artificial baggage that your ideological war seems to thrive on. The Giovanni are glad to take such risks, Justicar. It is our bread and butter, our vitae, and we have done it for *more than a thousand years*, since the nights of the crusades and before. Dealings like these are our *raison d'être*. Can you say the same? Cuba is ours—it is only a question of when."

Di Zagreb turned his shoulder away from Isabel, remaining silent.

"As I said, though, Justicar, we are willing to deal with the side that wins. We have no illusions as to your superior numbers, and in truth, we would prefer to deal with the Camarilla, as it is almost universally more civil and urbane than those cackling lunatics of the Sabbat. But don't think for a minute that you have any influence that we don't allow you to have. It would be a bitter fight between us, and one that you would almost certainly win. But at what cost?

"Keep that in mind, Justicar. For the time being,

the Giovanni side with no one, but our sympathies lie with the Camarilla. And also keep in mind that we offer our sympathies by choice."

With that, Isabel turned and walked away. The Tremere justicar thought on the meaning of her words. Perhaps he still had much to learn, after all.

Friday, 23 July 1999, 8:17 PM
Westin Peachtree Hotel
Atlanta, GA

Marcia Gibbert rose early—she knew she had to be up before Isabel to do what she needed to do. She walked over to the end table, took out a pad of paper emblazoned with the Westin logo and a pen from her bag, and prepared for Isabel a note.

I,—

I can't do this anymore. I'm sorry to leave you without any help, but the prospect of another night is too much for me.

I guess Jake Almerson still owes you a favor.
—M.

With that, Marcia covered herself as much as she could with a bathrobe, took an elevator to the top floor, climbed the access stair to the roof, and walked into the last, fading rays of the sun.

part three:
the middle of nowhere

Night unknown
The cargo hold of the *Pride of Roderigo*
Somewhere on the Atlantic Ocean

Once again, despite his wishes, the dead man woke. Trapped within the stifling box, immobilized by the hundred pounds of dirt that occupied the box with him, he nonetheless felt the stirrings of consciousness, followed by the rolling left-right-left of the ship listing at sea.

Above him, the sailors bolted back and forth across the ship's decks like trained monkeys in a carnival. The ship no doubt had a few passengers as well, but for a thirst as great as that of the dead man's, the numbers aboard might dwindle by as many as half—so he had chosen instead to weather the months-long trip under the cold aegis of torpor. But the dead man never quite reached that deathlike state; he had awakened as many as twenty times, each time closer and closer to the perilous act of rising, bursting from his rude berth and drinking his unholy fill of vitae from the oblivious kine with whom he shared the vessel.

How shameful, to be reduced to this, the dead man thought to himself. *To flee to the odious and barbaric New World. A New World, indeed! I have watched the rise and fall of a score of new worlds! This is simply another in a long line of rises and falls of mortal insects.*

Anger had consumed the dead man for nigh upon decades—while he'd once sat in the courts of kings, he had now been reduced to fleeing from a murderous coterie of usurper-merchants. His once-powerful lineage had crippled itself centuries before in atonement for its hubris, and now it suffered another, similar fate, though this time brought about by the very family that had been Embraced into its ranks.

The ignominy! With but a look, I could crumble any of their number to dust, yet they hunt even potent Cainites like me in packs, worrying us like hounds. Hate boiled in the dead man's lifeless veins, the blood within them cold with the stillness of its stasis, but burning with impotent fury. *To once have reached such heights! To have talked with God and His angels! To have held the lives of thousands in my grasp! And now, so basely to flee from a band of incestuous rogues armed with the brutality of ambition. You were vain, old one. You looked too far ahead and allowed these enemies to creep into your ranks. Why didn't they listen? Japheth and Constancia both knew. But of course, the Old One in all his martyred wisdom... We have been fools.*

The dead man, though, had not been a fool in planning his escape. Certainly, a few of his get might have fallen. Proud Elodie, her silver hair spattered with her own blood and that of the vulgar Giovanni. Jehovie, Urdra and Abelard, all burnt to ash by Giovanni torches. Even his own blood-siblings, the other childer of Matron Constancia, had met the Final Death here and again. In the filth of the sewers, the Giovanni hid, striking when even the most astute disciple of Ashur had laid his nightly fears aside and planned to sleep away the hours of the day. They streaked themselves with excrement to hide their own mortal smells; the undead among them wore heavy wools and smeared themselves with the unsavory fluids of their relations to mask their own charnel odors. They crawled up from waste tunnels, hid beneath previously unmolested bones in sarcophagi and scuttled out like malicious spiders from cenotaphs and gravestones. Like houndsmen, they rode up to their sires' loggias and sanctums, waving torches, brandishing knives and blackened stakes. They licked their lips as they put the childer of Ashur to the flame or into the recesses of torpor. They did it with a ruthless resolve, catching the fleeing spirits of those who made a desperate bid to escape their bodies and binding them into the glistening bones of freshly dead cadavers, or the fiendishly aborted corpses they ripped from their own sisters' wombs. Steeped with their own blood and the vitae of their elders, the Giovanni devoured the Cainites who had made them from within—and atop it all, they dared to call themselves Kindred, after the wishes of those selfish bastards who convened in England! Of all places to set precedent, why would anyone choose a land where Scots were considered people and men knew their ewes carnally!

Can you hear me now, God? Can you hear me beneath these decks? From under this layer of pine and the shit of worms? Damn them all for not lifting a finger as their precious Kindred drowned in their own vitae before them!

The dead man knew, though, that revenge was a dish best served with the spice of age. Flight was his only choice—flight to stab at the vile Giovanni during some night yet to be seen. With money obtained by selling the fingers of saints almost four centuries before, he booked freight "passage" on the *Pride of Roderigo*. When the ship arrived at its Cuban port, a family of exiled Waldensian descendants would transport the precious cargo to the North American mainland. From there, the wooden vessel would travel by cart to the swamps of the Creoles, who knew better than to ask questions of the dead or those associated with them. If nothing else, the dead man would be dumped in the swamp, rising only when the time was right and the rays of the sun could not scorch him. From there, he would gather around him the stupid denizens of the New World, taking their blood as he wished and sharpening his knife for use against the throats of the Giovanni once they had hunted the rest of his kind to extinction. The plans for travel had no flaws—he had corresponded with the Waldensians for generations through his spirit messengers and knew he could depend utterly on them. The Creoles were French Catholics, or black and Spanish mutts with their own barbaric customs, among whom few would dare to provoke an obvious vessel of the dead. The simple coffin itself had been rubbed with a great quantity of oil and then beeswax, to prevent the salty ocean air or humid New World climes from rotting it away. Yes, all the plans lay in place. Even if disaster befell, provided the dead man could move and speak a few words, he could transfer his own soul into the secret dark of the Underworld, and from there plan how to return to the world of the living kine.

The plan abounded with safety measures and surety. The only thing left to do was weather the remaining nights until his arrival. And from there, the dead man could bring the full weight of his eons of hatred to bear on the jackals who so desperately deserved it. And to a creature who had walked in Adam's shadow, who had kissed the face of God, what cost was a few more nights?

A tiny cost. An infinitesimal cost. A few more nights seemed a minuscule price to pay for the vindication of millennia.

Sunday, 22 August 1999, 12:32 AM
Margaret Reilly's haven
Manhattan, New York

"You look tired, Isabel."

Isabel stopped in the middle of removing her jacket. "Does that strike you as a pleasant thing to say, Margaret?" She looked at her host with large, brown eyes, trying to read the other woman's intent. Did she plan to put Isabel off with insults and aggravate her into making a mistake? Or was she just boorish, selfish, and so far withdrawn from polite society like most Sabbat that she spared no effort on civility?

Margaret, the leader and priest of a pack of rabid Cainites that reported directly to Sascha Vykos, shrugged her shoulders. "You're not here for me to flatter you."

"No, I'm not, but a bit of decorum would certainly be appropriate."

"Fine. You look simply ravishing. If I wasn't dead, I'd want to fuck the hell out of you."

"How sweet. If you weren't dead, though, I wouldn't give you the time of night, especially in that outfit. Now, do you just want to exchange *bon mots* or did this invitation have some sort of purpose behind it?"

Isabel looked at herself as she passed a mirror in the foyer of Margaret's haven. The witch was right— she *did* look tired. Unconsciously, Isabel drew in a breath. The events of the past few months had worn on her, and she didn't intend to let this negotiation go sour as had the one Chas accidentally bungled with Pieterzoon's flunky. If she had any luck at all, Isabel would find out that Gauthier had been unceremoniously discharged from Pieterzoon's entourage, so bad a showing had he made, himself. Still, despite the fact that she had no intention of forging any kind of alliance with either the Sabbat or the Camarilla, she did her best to entertain their courtship. If either of them perceived the Giovanni as a threat, either of them could forestall their efforts against the opposite sect and turn their attentions to the necromancers.

"You're not going to like the purpose; I can guarantee that. But I've never been one to soften the blow, so I'm not going to song-and-dance you with such fruitless consideration." Margaret's diplomacy style differed a great deal from Gauthier's.

Isabel once again stood stock still. "Then why bother with the pretense of proposal at all? I know what this is about. It's about the Sabbat and the Camarilla lined up on either side of Boston and laying claim to it."

"Smart girl."

"Well, it doesn't take a genius. You're forgetting something, though."

"And what's that?"

"Not every city *needs* to be under the thumb of the Sabbat or Camarilla."

"Isabel, I think you're being a bit naïve, no? You know that we're fighting a war, and if a city's not with us, it's against us."

"But what does that mean? I'll tell you plainly, the Giovanni have no interest in pursuing an alliance with the Sabbat. Now, wait; nor do we have an interest in leaguing with the Camarilla."

"Yes, I heard about how your dialogue with Pieterzoon's man went. And for the record, the Giovanni have indeed formed relationships with the Sabbat, albeit on an individual level."

"You mean Genevra? She's dead, you know."

"Aren't we all?"

"That's not what I meant."

"Me neither." Margaret smiled wickedly. "Sooner or later, even the eldest among us has to fall. Genevra's not the only necromancer to negotiate with the Sabbat."

"Well, she's the only one dealing with the Sabbat who was in Boston. I know Francis Giovanni sold guns to Max Lowell, but that's a commercial arrangement, not some high-handed philosophical alliance in your religious war."

"Such a smug tone! You know that we could just focus on the Giovanni in Boston and turn our attentions back to the Camarilla later, don't you, Isabel?"

"I know you could, but you won't. The very night you make Giovanni enmity a priority, the Camarilla will crawl into Boston from the woodwork. You *might*—emphasis on the possibility—rout the Giovanni from Boston, but in doing so you'll double the effort it takes to infest it completely."

"Infest, eh?"

"Yes, like vermin. You and I both know your resources would be better used either against the Camarilla or—and I know sensibility is a stretch for you zealot-types—more sensibly by taking from Boston what you want and not worrying about the nebulous sect affiliation of the city, which isn't quantifiable anyway. At least, we Giovanni see it that way. We know you have people in Boston; so does the Camarilla. And it doesn't affect us in the least. Kindred…excuse me, Cainites battling in the streets, however, doesn't do any of us any good." Isabel took a seat on what she assumed to be a leather chair and crossed her hands in her lap.

Margaret followed suit. "Moderation is not diplomacy, Isabel. But we should take refreshment before we continue further. Jonathan!"

From the shadows beyond the room emerged a thin, pale young man, perhaps in his early twenties or late teens. He wore no clothes, and all external evidence of his gender had been removed—he displayed no phallus, nor pubic hair, and the only reason Isabel guessed him to be male at all was a suggestion in the tone of his musculature. His head and face were likewise hairless. And most unsettling of all was the fact that Margaret had removed all traces of Jonathan's mouth and nose from his face; his sorrowful eyes peered out from the otherwise featureless alabaster expanse of his countenance.

Isabel kept her revulsion in check—of all the things she'd done in life and unlife of which others might have disapproved, at least they were basically human in nature. What some might have considered sexual perversion, acts of brutality or even depraved indifference all had their origin in the original humanity of their perpetrator or, more often, the mortality of their victims or subjects. With members of the Sabbat, like Margaret, viciousness often had no relation to humanity. Jonathan, for example, had been remade in the image of some androgynous ideal

Margaret at some point had found aesthetically pleasant. Or perhaps she had so little sympathy with or empathy for the kine that Jonathan existed to serve her needs and deny his own. Surely, though, if he was a ghoul, he would need to take blood from her in some way. Were he not a ghoul, he would still need to eat. Perhaps he was some sort of Tzimisce "performance," which Margaret fleshcrafted again and again as his needs arose, only to revert him to his present state afterward. Isabel dropped the train of thought entirely; there was no telling with someone so completely outside of normal thought as Margaret.

"Oh, don't be so particular. I sealed his mouth as a service to you, so you wouldn't have to hear him scream when you took blood from him. I know how agonizing the Giovanni Kiss is for its victims. I must also confess that I'm interested in seeing your feeding peculiarity in practice. You don't mind, do you Jonathan, that my friend Isabel will be removing your head."

"Don't tell me you believe that rubbish, Margaret? That I can drink only from severed heads? Why, if that were true, wouldn't I have sunk to your level of depravity long ago? After all, if we're to believe everything we hear, I should suspect your Sabbat of mindless, destructive, cackling Satanism. And the simple fact that I'm here and willing to discuss your plans about Boston proves that rumors are sometimes unfounded, does it not? Would I bargain with such a fool?"

"You disappoint me, Isabel. By all means, though, feed. I was hoping for a display of madness or excess, and instead you tell me that I've placed too much stock in urban legend."

Isabel took the opportunity to feed. Jonathan buckled beneath her, falling to his knees as she supped his life's blood from his throat. As she drank, Isabel heard a reedy whine punctuated by incomprehensible clicks. She looked down, lost in the burning thrill of the vitae, to see two opening and closing scolices on the insides of Jonathan's palms. Apparently Margaret had not bestowed voice boxes upon them, and the thin whine was just air drawn in and expelled from them. The clicks came from the tiny needle-fangs that surrounded the openings, grinding and clashing as the hand-mouths writhed. Disgusted, she pushed him away.

Margaret met her eyes with a grin. "Well, the boy must eat somehow, must he not? Here, Jonathan, my poor child; take back some of what our judgmental saint Isabel has taken from you." She opened the front of her sheer silk shirt, exposing a flawless ivory breast, the peak of which had been fleshcrafted smooth and unnippled. Jonathan reached out his hand and caressed his domitor's skin, piercing the flesh ever so shallowly and no doubt drawing out savory trickles of her rich blood. "You should be glad, Isabel. Surely you would suspect me of attempting to forge a blood bond, had I given Jonathan his nightly due first."

"I've had enough of this." Isabel broke off the conversation. She rose, returned to the foyer and collected her jacket. Without even attempting to make eye contact with Margaret, she shouted into the other room, "And I'm sure you can see that we have nothing in common, and therefore nothing to gain with even an empty alliance. Don't be so foolish as to think you can pluck Boston like a ripe plum. Neither of the groups of Kindred who stand against you would permit it."

"Ah, simple Isabel. Permission is not part of the problem. Within the week, Buffalo will fall to us. Hartford will be ours before year's end. Already, a war party of archbishops has gathered a group of Cainites to dominate precious Boston by force or fortune. Take my advice, Isabel. Pay tribute, or crumble like the rest of the East Coast."

But Isabel never heard this last; she had left Margaret's wretched haven and summoned a private car to take her to Grand Central Station.

Friday, 27 August 1999, 12:03 AM
Wisconsin Avenue
Washington, D.C.

Polonia and Borges shared grave looks, which gave way to avaricious, vulpine smiles. Polonia cocked an eyebrow and closed his eyes in concentration.

Hundreds of miles away, a mortal, animated like a puppet by Polonia's formidable will, rose from her prone pose and raised her arms above her head. Around her, in a circle, loomed a pack of ravenous Sabbat, waiting for just this signal.

Polonia released his control of the subject, whose last conscious thought was, "What am I doing here?" before the frenzied Cainites tore her to dripping shreds in their excitement. An expressionless vampire touched each of the howling Cainites on the forehead before turning them loose into the night.

Like rabid wolves, the pack descended upon Boston.

Monday, 25 October 1999, 12:15 AM
The Mausoleum loggia
Venice, Italy

"My Uncle Martino sends his regards."

Isabel Giovanni stood in her dressing gown, a half-smile gracing her fair skin, the door to her chamber open to receive this guest. Young Kwei della Passaglia, "nephew" to one of the most prominent Giovanni vampires of that family, stood before her. In his hands, he held a small, wrapped box: a gift.

"Welcome, Kwei. Please, come in. May I offer you anything?" A test, thought Isabel. If Martino has his nephew—practically a boy!—ghouled, he would perhaps ask for a draught of vitae. Isabel closed her gown around her and pulled a heavy robe over her shoulders.

Kwei placed the gift box on the vanity table and looked around the room. Like a few of the other rooms he had seen in the loggia, Isabel's seemed more like a temporary apartment or a guest house than a true bedroom. Isabel had a few personal effects scattered around, but the room certainly didn't look lived-in. He noted a decanter on a cart on the far side of the room. "I'll take a brandy, if you don't mind. It's uncommonly cool tonight."

"Help yourself. And how is your uncle?" Isabel smiled. Martino had been Kindred for at least two centuries and probably more. Unless Kwei was a very well-preserved ghoul, Martino was more likely his great uncle ten times over, if they were related at all.

"Fine, very well, thank you. This season has given a very good bounty of the silk." Kwei's Italian was obviously more scholastic than conversational. "He knows you are very fond of silk, so he sent you the present. I hope I haven't spoiled the surprise. Forgive my ignorance, but you are his sister?"

"Something like that." Isabel brushed her hair as Kwei poured a shallow glass of brandy. Martino was an acquaintance of her sire, actually. Long ago, he had married his way into the Giovanni family and shortly thereafter become a member of the Giovanni clan. He and Isabel had no love lost between them—she considered him a yellow-fevered pimp and he thought she was a symbol of everything that was wrong with the clan, from vice to indulgence and everything in between. "It's...hard to keep track of. The family is very old."

Kwei smiled, sipping from his snifter.

"But please, Kwei, take a seat." Isabel took a dress from the back of a chair and hung it, making a place for her guest to relax. "Did your Uncle Martino have anything else he wished me to know? I heard about the unfortunate demise of his father." She could practically hear the quotation marks around this last. If Kwei knew anything about the unnatural aspects of the family, this would be his opportunity to impart that graciously.

"It is the greatest tragedy, thank you for your condolences," Kwei replied. Probably not even a ghoul, Isabel reasoned. "Such is the danger of my uncle's occupation. Many from the East would have him fail."

"Yes, well, many in the West would have him fail, too. Your uncle is a bold man, Kwei, as I'm sure you know."

Kwei raised an eyebrow. "What do you mean by this?" He inflected the question incorrectly, the emphasis falling on *this* and not *mean*.

"Surely you know that he and I are not the most cordial of relations?" Isabel replied. "He would have told you that in preparation for the journey."

"No, he did not. I am sorry to hear this."

"It's not your fault. I won't punish you unless he goes out of his way to offend me. Now let me see that gift." Isabel's smile was barbed.

With a nervous look, Kwei handed Isabel the package. It was heavy. Isabel wondered to herself if Martino was unhappy with Kwei, or whether the boy had done something to upset his "uncle." The gift inside would tell the truth of the tale. Certainly, the trip itself would have been exciting for the boy, who had probably never left Hong Kong. Martino knew, however, that he and Isabel had an unsettled score between them. Years ago, she had sent one of her own ghouls to deliver a wedding gift to one of the members of his mortal family. Martino considered the gift, delivered by proxy, to be a great slight—not only had Isabel refused to deliver the gift in person, she had sent a censer stoked with an incense to which the bride was terribly allergic. The poor girl had taken a great whiff and immediately fallen into a reactive coma. Martino dismissed the embarrassed ghoul, only to have the young man's throat slit several hours later. A terse note in della Passaglia's hand informed Isabel of her gaffe. Not that she had ever liked him anyway, or would have considered attending the wedding. Still, it looked either spiteful or amateur on Isabel's part, depending upon which way one viewed the accident.

With this on her mind, Isabel opened the box. Inside rested a dense, rectangular object wrapped in an opaque tissue paper. A piece of folded rice paper sat atop the gift. Isabel opened the note and read:

I.—

Enclosed find something that I hope will help you with your current charge. I hope turning the pages doesn't irritate your delicate skin.

—M.

She unwrapped the gift: a book bound in a silk cover. Martino knew Isabel hated his silks. She considered them as coarse as him and marred by numerous flaws. This was his revenge for the incense—a subtle yet unmistakable flouting of Isabel's tastes. In the world of the Kindred, such subtleties carried great weight; it was how the race of Caine balanced their intricate scores of status, how they tallied points at various stages of the game of Jyhad. Martino had, from his point of view, evened the score by murdering Isabel's ghoul so many years ago. Now that he had the opportunity, Isabel saw, he took the chance to place himself in the lead by not only acknowledging her tastes, but forcing her to put them aside for the sake of his assistance.

Still, she had recourse. Martino's "gift" no doubt related to the ancient vampire she tracked—perhaps a geomancer's matrix that revealed the location of its crypt or an Eastern necromantic ritual that could counter one of its potent abilities.

On this, Isabel gambled. The journal Marcia had

found pointed out the likely location—or at least a *recent* location—of the creature she sought. By returning Martino's gift to him, she could prevent him from achieving his petty victory over her. Such was the nature of the gamble. Could she afford to turn away this information, knowing that it might possibly forfeit whatever advantage she could glean from it? Or should she avoid allowing Martino to take the lead in their private war, a war that paled in comparison to the larger stakes at hand concerning the matter of the old clan's return?

In the end, though, Kindred are proud creatures. Isabel had made her decision as immediately as it had been presented to her.

"Why, Kwei, I'm afraid your uncle's distance from the loggia has put him regrettably out of touch. This isn't the book I was looking for. I couldn't possibly allow him to give it to me—it belongs in his own library, where someone might be able to make better use of it than I." She carefully handed the book back to him, making an elaborate production out of not opening it at all. "Please, return it to him and let him know that I appreciate the gesture, but that I just can't allow him to sacrifice his own resources so greatly for my benefit."

With that, she hurried Kwei della Passaglia from her chamber and into the hallway, smiling good night to him as she closed the door.

Kwei, no fool, had some inkling of what had just occurred. Many times, he had seen the Byzantine and decidedly Western minutiae of this social drama unfold before him, as it related to his uncle or one of the other Europeans or Americans in his uncle's employ. He breathed a sigh of relief, knowing as he was excused from Isabel Giovanni's room that, for a brief moment, his life had been at stake. With another sigh, he turned and walked to his own guestroom, knowing that when he returned to deliver the news to his uncle, his life would once again be on the line.

Tuesday, 26 October 1999, 4:02 AM
The Mausoleum loggia
Venice, Italy

"This doesn't make any sense." Chas furrowed his brow and looked at the other Kindred in the room.

"An unfortunate fact, but one to which I can offer no better answer. This is simply how things *are*, and I can't give you any better rationale without delving into the finer details of our spirit magic, which I'm not sure you'd want anyway," replied Ambrogino Giovanni. "Isabel understands as much as she does only because she has a grounding in our necromantic practice. To be honest, it shouldn't really matter to you anyway. You're just muscle."

Chas didn't know whether that was an insult or a simple declaration. Sometimes these old vampires hadn't had contact with others in so long, their graces atrophied.

"Don't worry, Chas. Here's how it works." Isabel reclined in her chair rubbing her eyes, seemingly grateful for the chance to step back from what had been an intense conversation with Ambrogino. "We talked before about the ghosts, remember? Well, as it turns out, a huge shockwave of spiritual energy just devastated their world. Think of it like a hurricane, blowing through a city and destroying everything it touches. In the aftermath of this spiritual storm, the boundaries between the worlds of the living and the dead blurred a bit. In some places they were so weak, any spirit could force its way through. In other places, they didn't have to force their way through—the storm left gaping holes in the veil between the worlds."

Chas chimed in, wanting to make sure he understood. "Okay, so, that means what? There are ghosts out and about? Wandering through the world? What the fuck does that mean? Unless we have something specific to do with them, why should that matter at all?"

"It matters because of the consequences," Ambrogino added. "Know primarily that necromantic magic is a science, not an art. When creating the effects of death magic, quantifiable results are almost always reliably produced. If the desired result does not occur, something has failed somewhere in the chain of events required to bring it about. This may be something uncontrollable, such as great force of will on the part of a given ghost. It may have been a formulaic step the necromancer has omitted. It may have been something so minor as a brief lapse of concentration, or a mispronunciation of a spoken word. Whatever the case, some requirement has not been satisfied."

"Okay," Chas said, incredulous again, his eyes becoming slits.

"All that, we've established. In the case of the spirit storm's aftermath, however, something *else* has become a part of the equation—something unquantifiable. It might be a very potent Kindred, or an unthinkably powerful spirit," Ambrogino continued.

"Or, as some Kindred have guessed," Isabel interrupted, "it might be the hand of God Himself."

Chas snorted. "God? You think God came down from heaven and started slapping vampires and ghosts around? Wouldn't it have been a bit more...oh, I don't know…fucking obvious? Wouldn't He just cast lightning bolts down from the heavens or make the sun shine all day and night?"

Ambrogino stood, directing a scornful finger at Chas. "Do not presume to understand God, whelp. Before Him, you are nothing but a mote of dust in the cloud that circles the world. You've heard it before: 'He works in mysterious ways.' The simple fact that we can't empirically find a cause for the storm or its results suggests something far beyond our capacity to understand, let alone master. Something more powerful than our magic, or indeed, the magic of anyone else who has come forth to offer a less mystical reason."

Isabel cut in, hoping to defuse Ambrogino's ire and bring them back to the subject. "But the situation with the ghosts is not the gravest matter, even though it does present us with the most immediate inconvenience. I mentioned God because it seems that the storm was not His intention. In fact, He seems to have taken steps to clean up the detritus left by the storm. The agents of God now want to take back the night—they want to destroy the ghosts who have forced their way back from their rightful deaths. Sometimes, they run afoul of vampires, whom they also consider monsters to be exterminated. This is what you ran into after your inexpert handling of the Camarilla negotiation in Boston."

Chas blushed inadvertently and felt a quick flash of red anger.

"The death of your attendant Victor also matches the *modus operandi* of these new hunters. A team of them has made its home in Las Vegas. We think they believed *he* was a vampire—you were sleeping in the bathroom to avoid the sun, and it didn't even occur to them to check there. Uncertain of the best way to destroy a 'vampire,' they experimented and poisoned him. That was the almond smell you remember—don't look so shocked; you know I can perceive your thoughts. Cyanide."

"Okay," Chas found his way back into the conversation, "then how does that relate to the other two things we've been chasing around? What does it have to do with the 'old clan' or whatever, and how does Benito fit into the picture?"

"Well, Chas, to be honest, Benito doesn't directly fit into the immediate crisis. His disappearance those four months ago just coincidentally took place at the same time that we found out about the problem in the Underworld. Now, I'm sure Benito *knew* about what was going on, at least in some capacity, because he practices the black art himself, but he's not an instrumental player in that particular chapter of the Giovanni drama," Isabel confided. "I'm the first to admit that I've not pursued his disappearance with my full attentions because one missing Giovanni isn't as important to the wellbeing of the entire clan as is the return of the clan we thought we'd exterminated in the past."

Ambrogino interjected, "Which leads us to the second part of your question: the old clan itself. When the Giovanni first claimed the mantle of clanship, we had to make sure that no threat to our claim would surface. The Kindred who Embraced us had become an obstacle to us, rather than a benefactor. We destroyed his brood to the best of our abilities. I myself hunted what we thought to be the last surviving member of that bloodline to a castle in Eastern Europe, where I discussed the ethics of the matter with the legendary Dracula.

"It would seem, however, that our efforts were incomplete. We underestimated our progenitors—they had learned much from the necromancy we taught them. Several of the more potent childer of Ashur managed to escape into the Underworld, where they could easily hide from us as they had not become true ghosts—we had no power over them while they cowered in the lands of the dead. We could not compel them to heed our call; we could not force them to serve us as they were still Kindred, albeit Kindred trapped in the world of spirits.

"After centuries, we became overconfident. We hadn't heard anything from these Kindred for a very long time, and we just assumed that the Underworld had overwhelmed them, as it is an inhospitable place for any Kindred who stays there for a protracted period.

"We were wrong. The truth of the matter is that the old clan Kindred who escaped thrived in that hellish realm. They practiced their *nigromancy* unimpeded by the boundary between the worlds. The same veil that trapped them on the far side of the spirit world no longer separated them from the place where their mystic powers originated. Although the Giovanni created the magic that became the Kindred practice of necromancy, the old clan mastered it in the hundreds of years they spent beyond the Shroud.

"Finally, when the spirit storm withered the veil, the old clan took the chance to burst back through to the realm of the living—this world. Now, there aren't many of these Kindred. I estimate perhaps twenty of them in all. But the old clan who managed to escape and grow are very powerful. The childe of the Kindred who Embraced Augustus Giovanni may even be among them. Only the most skilled at the time of our purge could have managed to flee to the Underworld, and they have since grown tremendously stronger."

"So, just kicking their asses is out of the question," Chas commented.

"Well, yes, to put it bluntly," Ambrogino replied. "With creatures of that age and wile, the only hope one has is trickery. Something so old might be cunning indeed, but a physical confrontation is suicide. Some magical recourse must exist—such are the ends to which the foremost Giovanni necromancers have been researching."

"Um, can I ask a question, then?" Chas ventured.

"Of course."

"If we can't beat this thing, and it's far more powerful than us magically, why the fuck is Isabel chasing it? No offense, Isabel, I know you're good at what you do, but you're not as old as these things are and they're probably a damn sight better with the death magic, too. I mean, I know I don't have to go along with you, but I'm choosing to, at this point, but if it's just going to get me killed, I'd like to know so I can seek some other opportunities, you know?"

Isabel smiled. "Ah, Chas; always able to add a sense of levity. What Ambrogino's talking about is just conjecture. No one from our clan has verifiably seen one of these creatures and survived. Even

Martino in Hong Kong saw only the briefest blur, which could have been anything, before fleeing his sire's demise. We need to see this, to know it exists and to take from it what we can. If it doesn't perceive me as a threat, I might be able to report back on the matter. Intelligence is a valuable resource."

"But if it's killing Giovanni…" Chas trailed off, unable to reason through the thought.

"Not all Giovanni—the old clan seem to be starting with the ones personally responsible for their decimation, and then moving down the bloodlines," Isabel added.

"So then why haven't any of them come after you, Ambrogino?"

Ambrogino looked at Isabel, then back at Chas. "I'm not sure. My own abilities are quite potent, and perhaps they want to remove the lesser threats before focusing on a greater one such as myself."

"I still don't get it," Chas spoke to the world in general.

"No one does, except the old clan," Isabel confided in him. "Until we find out exactly what they want to do, all we can do is cover ourselves."

"And I have a Kindred who can help you do just that," Ambrogino added.

Thursday, 28 October 1999, 1:17 AM
The French Quarter
New Orleans, Louisiana

"Ladies and gentlemen, I am proud to present to you...Natasia!"

The dull but heavy roar of the partygoers' conversations briefly turned into a cheer before once again becoming a monotonous din. Not many people here even knew Natasia, but they had come to the dilapidated house just off the main drag because the party had been underway nonstop for the better part of a day. The abandoned townhouse was filled to capacity with party guests. People of all stripes had come, having heard through the grapevine that Jake Almerson was adopting a child or something, and, hey, why not help this Jake character celebrate. Of course, some people knew Jake—knew that he was indeed celebrating with his childe, but that the word had a terribly different meaning from the homonym that most of the guests assumed was intended.

Indeed, Jake Almerson had thrown quite a party to commemorate the release of his childe, a Kindred Embraced just over a year ago. Natasia's Brujah sire had let every carouser in town hear about the impending bash—even at this very moment, some of Jake's contacts were prowling Bourbon Street, directing drunken tourists and smarmy locals to the epic debauch taking place only a few blocks away.

Six hours ago, a pair of police cruisers had arrived. Two officers walked up the sidewalk to the house, shaking their heads and smiling at one another. After a cursory effort at finding someone—anyone—who was at all related to the organization of this thing, they gave up. Better to let the neighbors make a few complaints about the noise and let the party die down by itself than to turn this thing into a police riot. Besides, a few ambulances had already been called to cart away exhausted or intoxicated celebrants. The sight of one of those always served to briefly turn the excess down by a few notches. With a shrug, the police returned to their cars, with to-go cups, and went on their way.

Upstairs, someone had fallen through the floor of what was once a small library, but he was all right, having broken his fall on a pair of E-rolling teenagers groping each other in the rudely converted laundry room. The toilet resided as a transplanted throne in the middle of the living room, occupied currently by "King Bacchus," a drunken Hell's Angel of unknown origin. A fight had broken out briefly, but the winner had put down his foe by crashing his victim's head through a window and raking the shattered glass across his forehead. For the most part, though, the party was just that—a celebration.

Chas escorted Isabel up the cracked pathway and stepped over the unconscious body of a visiting baseball player from the University of Texas.

"Nice place, but I wouldn't think it was your sort of crowd," Chas smirked at Isabel.

"I've known Jake for a long time," Isabel replied lamely. "Everyone has their hobby. His is throwing parties."

"You said he wasn't the most amiable person in the world."

"Look around. Does he need to be?"

As they entered the house, a small group seemed

to be hopping up and down in the corner. Chas grabbed an addled partygoer who just happened to be walking by.

"The fuck happened over there?"

The bloodshot eyes of the other guest briefly focused. "They put out the goddamn fire. It's Natasia's birthday, you know. Hey, do you know who Natasia *is*?"

"No." Chas let the poor guy go. "Fire, huh? Sounds like one hell of a party!"

Isabel made no comment, instead taking Chas by the hand and beginning the arduous process of climbing the stairs, which entailed shoving a score of people out of the way.

The reek of marijuana hung over the hallway at the top of the stairs, as did a less prevalent but powerful chemical tang of cocaine smoke. The scents of mortal sweat and dry rot also clashed, flavored with the slightest hint of vomit.

Isabel pressed on, but Chas shook himself free from her grasp. The crowd had more than begun to get on his nerves. It was one thing to throw a party, but it was another altogether to corral a circus of freaks like this. Chas sucked in an unnecessary breath, hulking his body up and looking for any excuse to hammer one of these drunks in the face. To his surprise, the crowd seemed to swell around him, rolling over and off him as he passed, almost as if they felt the presence of his hostility on some subconscious level and equally subconsciously moved to avoid him.

A few hands brushed against him, the advances of women too drunk to feel his tangible menace, looking for a quick amorous relation with, well, anyone, but Chas ignored them. If he was going to get into a fight here, it wasn't going to be with some drunk slut he could break in half by slapping her. Still, maybe one of these skanks had a boyfriend who'd be up for some freelance dental work….

The sight of Isabel in the hallway shook him from his violent fantasy. She closed one door, turned around, and saw him before opening the other door in front of her. She waved him forward.

"You wanna fuckin' drink, man?" The guy Chas had stopped downstairs stood before him, having just climbed the stairs himself and seen a familiar face. "You don' hafta go back downstairs. I think there's some booze in the…I know there's beers in the bathtub."

"No, thanks." Chas reined in the urge to snap this punk like a twig. Isabel was waving for him, which probably meant she'd found Jake and they could get the fuck out of here. "I, uh, I don't like beer."

"Suit yourself, brother. You looking for something more serious? I know a guy here's got tabs, some rolls…."

"No, man, I'm just going over there to see my…" Chas walked past his new acquaintance and let the conversation drop. He didn't know how he would have finished the sentence anyway.

He joined Isabel, who shook her head in mock disapproval and opened the door.

"Goddammit, that fucking door's closed for a reason," boomed a voice from within the darkness of the room, a solid baritone, with more than a hint that someone had interrupted its owner before. A heavy musk hung in the air.

"I'm sorry for interrupting, Jake, but we really should talk."

Reclining bodies populated the room, perhaps a dozen in number. Some leaned haphazardly over the sides of broken chairs; others lay on the floor or on the tattered couch propped up against the wall. The room itself had its windows blocked, papered over with duct tape and stained sheets of corrugated cardboard. None of the light from the street made it into the room; only the tired glow of a single candle illuminated the place. The air was heavy with haze.

"Well, who's fucking asking?" One of the forms, the darkest, moved, like a shadow becoming a solid man. "Oh. I fucking should have figured."

"Such rude talk." Isabel noticed that all of the other occupants in the room were women. "What is it this time? I don't smell any dope in here. Are they drunk?"

"They're fucked on absinthe. Make it myself."

"Is that your idea of a joke?"

"Hey, pretty Isabel, this is New Orleans. It's what Lestat would do," Jake smiled. Isabel saw his eyes had become bloodshot—she hoped he was still sensible enough to help her.

"That's lovely, Jake. Are any of them dead? I don't want someone to remember me in the house when the police turn up a room full of dead hookers."

"They're not hookers. They're Zetas from Georgia State, I think. Or maybe it was Sam Houston State. I don't remember. Who the fuck cares?"

"That wasn't the important part. I asked if they were dead."

"This one's dead," Chas interjected, lifting one of the smaller girls, who hung like a broken doll from his arm.

"They're not dead. Least I don't think so. I think she's just cold. Absinthe turns on you, man. Don't trust it. Don't fucking drink that shit." Jake smiled. "Hey, have you met Natasia? She's around here somewhere. My pride and joy, baby—a childe of my own."

"Did she used to be a Zeta?" Isabel asked demurely, which came across as all the more grotesque as she pushed an unresisting girl aside to make room for herself on the ruined couch. Chas walked over to the door, putting his broad back against it.

"No, shit, Isabel. I think she was a…she was some kind of flight attendant. No, wait, she was…fuck, I don't remember. But she's mine now." He turned to look at Chas. "What, motherfucker, you think someone's goin' to try bustin' out of here?"

Chas looked down at Jake, who lay on his side on the floor, using one of the girls as a pillow, resting his head on her exposed belly. "No, I'm worried about someone else coming in. You I can take care of, but I don't want to kill someone I don't have to."

"Fuck, Isabel, what you bring this punk motherfucker here for? Is he your toy?"

"He's looking out for me, Jake. He's helping me out with something. I need your help, too."

"Fuck that shit. I can't leave. I'm the fucking host of this little get-to-motherfucking-gether. I don't like your boy, anyway. We'd scrap."

Chas laughed. "You don't think I could waste some stoned nigger? Let's see, huh? What is it you spooks say to each other? Let's throw down, yo."

Jake turned to Isabel. "Oh, you got a real winner here, baby."

"Chas, can't you please keep a handle on it?" Isabel looked to Chas, shaking her head and holding her hand up, hoping that Chas would take the cue and let it rest.

"Well, let's hurry it up, Isabel. Get this fucking monkey to sing and let's go." Chas crossed his arms over his chest.

Jake laughed aloud and raised his hand to rub his eyes. "What do you want, Isabel? What do you and Robert de Niro here want? Let me get back to my harem, huh?"

"We need to find Oliver Prudhomme," Chas said. No sense in letting Isabel turn this into something even more protracted than it already was.

"Prudhomme? That motherfucker's out of his mind. He don't have nothing you need."

Indeed, Ambrogino had warned Isabel about Prudhomme's precarious state of mind. Apparently, the weight of being a Kindred bore heavily upon him. Still, Ambrogino was a better necromancer than Isabel was, and she had never been led astray by his information before. If Ambrogino said Prudhomme was key, nothing Jake knew was likely to convince her otherwise. "Let us decide that for ourselves, Jake," she said.

"Well, fuck it anyway, because I don't know where the motherfucker stays."

"Oh, now Jake, that can't be true. Are you telling me there's something the would-be prince of New Orleans doesn't know?"

"Fuck you, Isabel. I never claimed to be prince. And fuck you, too, bitch." He waved a hand over his shoulder at Chas.

"So you *don't* know then. You're useless." Isabel put her hands on the cushions at her side, as if to push herself up.

"Useless? I'm not the motherfucker who comes to a party and fucking sweats a brother who's just trying to have a good time. You want to find Oliver fucking Prudhomme, you try looking in the dumpsters behind Emeril's or maybe in the parking lot over at the Hotel Inter-Continental. He got a few problems."

"That's no good, Jake, and you know it. I guess you'll have to pay me back that favor sometime when you're actually capable of fulfilling it. I'm sure the Kindred of New Orleans will be able to sleep well during the day knowing that Jake Almerson can't find them. They might even think it's funny."

"Oh, it's like that now, is it? That's fine," Jake rolled onto his back again. "I just wanted to hear you say it. That just about makes us even, right? I mean, I'd hate for you to think you can't trust old Jake to keep his word."

Isabel shook her head. "That's right, Jake. It's all even."

"Now *that's* what the brother wants to hear. Your Oliver Prudhomme, he stays in an old school about twenty minutes up the state highway. It's one of the old towns, been dried up for a while. You'll know when you get there."

"Thank you, Jake; you've been a very gracious host."

"Oh, the pleasure was all mine. Make sure you

come back and see me sometime. You can even bring your smart friend, there."

"Fuck you, eggplant."

"Bye, now." Jake waved good-bye with the limp hand of the girl beneath him.

Isabel and Chas waded through the motley crowd of partygoers at the top of the stairs, stopping only to push aside a sailor stuffing a huge wad of weed into a pipe made from a fresh apple.

"Wanna take a hit off the apple?"

"No, that's all right," Chas brushed the sailor off.

In the front, on the lawn, the two Giovanni Kindred saw another pair of police cruisers pull up just as they made it to the gate that let them out on the street.

"Pretty rowdy in there, no?" One of the police called to the pair as he climbed out of his vehicle and tucked his baton and flashlight into their loops at his belt. As if to punctuate the question, something on fire tumbled out of a hole in what must have been the house's attic, and a bum leaning against the fence issued forth a gout of vomit.

"Yeah, it's a circus in there," Chas muttered offhandedly. "Oh, yeah, officer; one more thing. There are absolutely no drugs in the room on the left at the top of the stairs."

Isabel slapped Chas and shot him a look that the cop and his tardy partner noticed.

"Mm-hmm. You two have a fine evening," the officer replied, checking his holster and pepper spray.

"Oh, we will, sir. You, too." With that, Chas swung the Audi into the lane and through the darkness that pressed in from the edges of the city's border.

Friday, 29 October 1999, 2:02 AM
The Ponchartrain School
La Lac Blanc, Louisiana

Chas parked the Audi curbside, where a decrepit staircase began its ascent and climbed upward for a good twenty feet. At the top of the stairs loomed an abandoned school. Because local government worked differently in Louisiana—the state had no counties, being instead divided into dioceses managed by the Church—the school had simply fallen into disuse after the community around it had been swallowed by the swamp over sixty years ago. The town had just vanished, leaving behind only a few legacies of its existence, which themselves now lay beneath layers and layers of vines and calcium deposits. The rain had left the six buildings that still stood streaked with mildew and rot. The whole area looked sick, like a pile of chalky bones slowly, inevitably crumbling into the ground where they had been left. Even the road had been overgrown, the dirt of its surface providing ample soil for malicious new vegetation to take root. The car's all-wheel drive had slipped a few times when Chas had guided the Audi too quickly into an easy curve.

It didn't help that the trees grew into an unnatural canopy, shielding much of the moon's light from the area and casting skeletal shadows where illumination managed to fight its way through the web of branches. Even the air was still, dead. Heavy and wet, like the still waters of the swamp itself, beneath the surface of which untold horrors slid effortlessly through the murk.

"How the fuck is anyone supposed to find this place, out here in the middle of fucking nowhere?" Chas wondered aloud.

"I think that's the point," Isabel replied. She shifted the shoulder bag she carried, which held the strange manuscript Marcia Gibbert had given her.

They climbed the stair, fumbling inelegantly in the darkness, but making it to the top without any grievous injury. Chas's small electric flashlight did little to light their environment. Its beam seemed to vanish into the gloom only a few feet before them, and faded completely by the time they stood before the front door of the building.

Isabel heard a wheezing, hissing sound as she reached toward the door. "Do you hear that, Chas?"

"Sorry. That's me," Chas answered, and Isabel could hear the smile on his face in his tone of voice.

"Is something funny?" She looked at him as best she could, the ivory of his teeth and his sunken eyes making his face a demonic apparition floating in the darkness before her.

"It's not really funny so much as it is strange," he said. "I've done this sort of thing a million times, but never in this sort of situation, you know? I've done whatever it was that Frankie Gee told me, walking into weird shit and talking to people who made their havens in fucked-up places. I've talked to Nosferatu who set up their nests beneath the fucking Chelsea Hotel. I've talked to Kindred in the basements of St. Mark's and spent the day hiding in access tunnels of the New York subway. It's not like this—that shit is all paved. No trees. No nothing, but concrete. Even Central Park feels, I don't know, *made* instead of natural. This shit—I'd never have thought you'd catch me out here. I don't even care that it's not the city. What bugs me is that it's not under control. It's basically just this fucked-up place that some Kindred found and decided to stay here. Like the rest of the world didn't want him. Like the other Kindred didn't have any use for him, and forced him to just go somewhere."

"Isn't that always the case, though?" Isabel asked, growing nervous that something was unsettling Chas this much. She had watched his decline dispassionately for several months now; it wasn't her place to steer him toward some moral end. Maybe it was a product of him becoming more Beast than man—perhaps he was growing more in tune with the nebulous stimuli that animals seemed to be able to feel, to which men and women were oblivious. "Don't we always have to go where we can? I have a feeling our friend here is more than a little unsettled, and this is as close as he can come to everyone else without them feeling completely overtaken by what he is. Come on, Chas; you know we're predators. You know we can only stay among the sheep for so long. This fellow probably can't do it for any length of time at all."

"I'm not pretending to know what the fuck it is, Isabel. It just feels...*dead*."

Isabel opened the door, which Chas held, motioning her inside. *He really has become an animal*, Isabel thought to herself. *It's not even unchivalrous—he just feels something dreadful inside and his instincts have him sending me in first.* Instinctively, she called upon her occult abilities to enable her to look through the veil between worlds. Sure enough, the halls of the school looked even more ghastly in the world of the dead. Thin layers of gossamer wafted in a sickly ghost-breeze and scores of tiny blackish handprints dotted the walls. All of the windows in the ghost-hall were broken, peering into vacant offices strewn with papers or classrooms in which spectral jackets hung from hooks on the walls.

A tinny music echoed down the empty hallways. Chas and Isabel shared a silent look before moving toward it. As they rounded a corner, the music grew louder and they both saw a flickering orange light emanating from one of the classrooms ahead. It must not have had any windows facing the front of the building; surely they would have seen even the faintest firelight from the outside.

At their approach, they discerned a voice just below the strains of the music, which had itself become clearer. The doleful music was Hank Williams, his lonely guitar notes traveling across the still air and sounding a million miles away. Over the lyrics of the song, the voice lectured.

"And what can we do when we can find no hope inside ourselves, children? What do we do when it seems that the world would be better off without us? We must not give in to the loss of our hope—the Lord says despair is a sin, for it denies the faith He wants us to have in Him. Trust in the Lord; He is our shepherd and our salvation. That's what we must do, children. We must ask God for His help. We must pray. He loves us, and asks only that we give ourselves to Him. Remember that His son, Jesus, died for all of us—he took all of our sins and made it possible for God to excuse them for us. God's love is infinite; God's love is unconditional. But we must allow Him to give it to us. He doesn't want us to have it if we must take it against our will—God allows us to choose.

"You children know better than I. You are with God. You *know*. I am still here—I don't yet know what you do, and all I have is faith. He has heard your prayers, and sent me to let you meet Him, hasn't He? It's not as complex as it sounds. I'm not a cruel man. Although there are some among you whose parents would say that I am a tool of the Devil—or even that I am the Devil himself—you know better than that. You know that God has His own designs and that I serve them, not the will of the Devil. Could it possibly be said that the Devil's tool has God in his heart? How can a man like me, who places his faith and fate in the hands of God, conceivably do the work of the Devil? Am I deluded, children? I don't think so. I pray. I have spoken to God and He has let me know that even one so far from Him as I am is still not outside the boundaries of His love.

"Pray, children. Pray to see another sunrise. Pray that all of God's creation remain open to you. Pray that God shows you how to avoid the jaws of Hell— Hell is this world, children, and I have saved you from it. I am in Hell, and I have delivered you unto the eaves of the Lord God's house. Children, listen! Don't hate me! I have given you the greatest gift of all! I have given you heaven! Were you to have done this yourself, you would reside here still, or on a circle below. Children! Answer me! Tell me that you have no hatred for me; that you have only the Lord's love!

God! God, I have given these children back to You. I have returned them to Your table! They have died where their names do not matter. I have cut the thin, silver tether that bound them to this Hell. They are Yours once again!

"God?

"Children?"

Isabel knocked on the door frame. "Mr. Prudhomme?"

The man betrayed no sign of being startled. He looked to be of about fifty mortal years, a compact, white-haired man with a strangely clean-cut beard and mustache. He wore pleated pants, a white shirt and a cardigan sweater, all of which were curiously free of the vegetative filth of the forsaken swamp-town.

"Yes? I beg your pardon, children; I have a guest. It is Miss Isabel from the Father Superior's office. Say hello to Miss Isabel, children!"

Silence.

Isabel looked into the room, beyond the man she assumed to be Ambrogino's contact Oliver Prudhomme. Rows and columns of small, wooden desks occupied the center of the room, each occupied by the still body of a small child. Some had obviously been there longer than others, having decomposed to the point that the only thing human about them was their vague shape. Others had joined the class only recently, their cool skin and blue lips not yet showing any signs of putrefaction. All had their eyes closed, their tiny hands clasped in a rude approximation of the prayer pose. Boys and girls both occupied the class, roughly two dozen in number, some wearing blue jeans and T-shirts like modern children, others in more formal clothes and even uniforms that suggested decades long past.

The Hank Williams songs twanged along softly, the only sound that broke the quiet.

"Mr. Prudhomme, I was referred to you by Ambrogino Giovanni," Isabel began.

"I know, Isabel. I know you. I know what you want." Prudhomme suddenly seemed very tired, as if being interrupted in his fervor had drained him. He removed a pair of pince-nez from the bridge of his nose and rubbed his eyes between pinched fingers. "Children, I beg your pardon. Please begin your prayers, and I shall return presently." Prudhomme moved to step out of the room, looking expectantly to Isabel and Chas to precede him.

"What the fuck is this, anyway?" Chas reached out his hand, halting Prudhomme at the shoulder. "What the hell is up with these kids? Are you some kind of sick fuck?"

Prudhomme stepped back from Chas's hand, aghast. "Miss Isabel, does this insolent youth travel with you?" He shrank from Chas's gesture as if admonished rather than challenged.

For her part, Isabel was shocked, as well. "Chas, what do you think you're doing?"

"It's this guy, Isabel. He's the one who's responsible for the fucked-up *feel* this place has. Aren't you, you freak? You know exactly where those kids are."

"Chas, what are you—"

"Don't fuck with me, Isabel. You know I'm right. I'm right, ain't that so, Prudhomme? You've got all these fucking kids bottled up somewhere. You're doing some of that death-magic shit to keep these fucking kids around." Chas stepped forward, grabbing handfuls of Prudhomme's sweater, lifting him up to his own snarling face. "You fucking pig."

Isabel grabbed Chas by the shoulder and forced him to turn about, looking her in the face. *"Let him go, Chas. Now."*

Chas's eyes clouded over. He hissed and his eyes squinted as he dropped Prudhomme to the floor. Oliver crawled backward across the ground, away from his tormentor as Isabel looked upward at her companion.

"Don't try that shit on me. Don't fucking try it. I'll break you in half, whore." Chas loomed over Isabel, but she refused to shrink, placing one hand on his sternum to prevent him from leaning into her any more.

"Please, watch your mouth around the children," Prudhomme protested.

Isabel reasserted herself, gently pressing Chas away from her and staring into his eyes unfalteringly. *"You will stand down."*

And Chas did, unable to resist. He continued to snarl, a veil of crimson cast over his vision. Isabel saw him on the verge of frenzy and moved away from him herself. "Relax, Chas," she whispered. "He's not even one of us. One of the family. He can't do that."

Chas shook, waking from a dream. A scowl still lay etched across his face but the red rage subsided. "I...oh, fuck. I...I'm sorry. I don't know what happened."

"You're not well, Chas. You're too close to the Beast," Isabel said.

"She's right. You've spent too much time with the wrong half of you," Prudhomme conjectured, rising to his feet. Still a bit tentative, he approached. "Let me see—look at me." Prudhomme held his hands out before him to show Chas he had no ill intent. "Just let me look. Yes, you are not far at all. The Man has been overcome."

"The fuck does that mean, old man? That I'm trouble? Fuck, yeah, I'm trouble. Trouble for someone like you."

"Chas, I'm warning you. Calm down," Isabel's voice rose.

It was Chas's turn to be wearied. His posture slumped and he leaned back against the wall. "Oh, fuck. What's wrong with me?" he asked no one in particular. He caught his head in his hands as it tilted forward. Isabel eased him down to sit on the floor. "What's going on in there, Prudhomme? You're the teacher?"

"I'm as much student as teacher, I'm afraid."

"What was all that shit in there about God and returning the children to Him?"

"It's as I spoke it. Those children have all died. Someone needs to take care of them."

"You sent them all back to God? You killed them all?"

Oliver Prudhomme looked sheepishly at Isabel, who intervened. "Chas, would you wait in the car, please. Everything is all right here; thank you for making sure I arrived safely."

Chas rose, giving a wary glance to Prudhomme before turning and taking his brooding leave. His shoes left cold echoes in the hall as he stalked away.

"I apologize for that. He's not been the same since…" Isabel's voice trailed off. She couldn't make excuses for him. Not only was it not her place, she'd watched as Chas had slowly allowed the Beast to erode what had been left of him after the Embrace.

"Don't mind it, my dear," Oliver Prudhomme rubbed his forehead with the arch of his thumb and forefinger. "Please, just let me see the papers. I knew to expect you."

Isabel looked skeptical. "Ambrogino told you?"

"Ambrogino? I don't know who you're talking about. I saw that you would come. The children were very excited; they've been whispering about you all night. Young Cleveland Thibodeaux has quite the crush on you. You have something you need me for."

Isabel thought it best not to ask any unnecessary questions. She opened her bag and handed Oliver the journal. "I need your keen powers of memory, Mr. Prudhomme. You've been here for as long as Ambro— as long as the man who told me to seek you can remember. A while ago, an acquaintance of mine found this and I was hoping you could tell me anything about the place. Any strange occurrences, anything out of the ordinary you remember. We know where the place is, but it seems to have once held something decidedly unpleasant, and we though we should consult with an expert on the matter before opening it up ourselves."

Prudhomme looked over the sheaf of paper, placing his pince-nez back on his nose and shuffling the individual sheets. Slowly, a look of recognition crossed his face, which gave way to a look of horror. In the darkness, he became even paler than his

Cainite complexion normally allowed for. "Oh, my God," he stammered.

"What? What? You remember something about this? You know what it's talking about?"

"I certainly do. I know exactly what it's talking about. I remember this as vividly as if it were last night. It's talking about the monster that made its haven not far from here—the dead thing that slept beneath the cold water and ate everything it could lure down there."

"Yes, yes!" Isabel grew excited as a tremor of excited terror ran through her. "You remember it! What do you know? What do you know for certain about this thing?"

"Why, I know everything about it. You see, over a century and a half ago, I wrote this."

Wednesday, 27 October 1999, 11:24 PM
Highway 95
Outside Las Vegas, Nevada

Benito heard the thrum of an automobile's engine and felt the air vibrate around him. He could see nothing; the black bag over his head had been tied tightly around his neck and he found himself swallowing blindly, involuntarily. He could smell the dried blood caked on the side of his face, feel it crusted beneath his right eye. He could also smell the reek that had accompanied his captors for the past—God only knew how long. Nights? Weeks? Jesus; *months*? He had no idea. His odoriferous hijackers had fed him enough blood to keep him cognizant but not enough to risk his breaking free. They were as strong as he—perhaps they were Brujah, or maybe Nosferatu. They might even be rival Giovanni, but he couldn't imagine that overbearing Nickolai having enough sense to play two factions of Giovanni against each other.

No, all the evidence pointed to the Nosferatu. Benito imagined that plucked fiend Montrose being involved somehow, and he had certainly been pumped for information during his stay with his captors. But now it seemed they were done with him.

"What's going on?" Benito shouted to anyone who might be bothered to answer or might be sympathetic enough to reply. None of that here, though; his outburst only earned him a slap to the head and a gravelly, "Shut the fuck up."

Then the acoustics changed. Benito felt himself shoved upward and over, and the sound of the engine changed to a dull roar—he had been put into a vehicle of some sort. A sliding door slammed right next to his head.

Keep calm, old boy, Benito told himself. *If they needed you dead, they wouldn't bother taking you somewhere first.*

His captors were quiet from that point onward. Benito didn't even know if the plural was appropriate; it could have simply been one person charged with delivering this relatively passive cargo to wherever he was headed. Or, the group could have just been operating with the efficiency they had exhibited all along—these were professionals.

Now that he was close to the outside world again, Benito felt a coolness to the air. The air also felt relatively dry—this wasn't Boston, to be sure. He couldn't smell the faint tang of the salt on the breeze or hear the dim rush of traffic from the nearby city. No, Benito knew he was probably in the middle of nowhere, where whoever these fucks were who had him could do what they pleased even in disposing of him, and nobody would be any wiser.

The vehicle rumbled on for an indeterminate amount of time—Benito hadn't had access to his watch or even a calendar for so long that he was unable to gauge the period he had been on the road for this little jaunt. To his best guess, it was perhaps ten minutes.

As if in response to his thoughts, the van slowed, moved a bit laterally (Benito's weight shifted greatly to the left and then overcompensated to the right), and finally came to a stop. Two doors opened and closed, then the sliding door opened. Benito was jerked out of the back of the vehicle, where he once again felt the outside air—very cool.

The two unknown captors then hurled Benito to the ground. Delivered a few unavoidable and brutal kicks to his ribs, and drove away, the sound of the transport vehicle dopplering away into the distance.

Cool, still air. Cool, loose earth below him. Sand? A coyote howling in the distance. Coyotes? Sand? He was in the fucking desert?

Fine. Just fine and dandy. When he had waited a suitable time to make sure no one had stayed with him, to watch, for whatever reason, that he remained bound and motionless, Benito Giovanni summoned the last reserves of his fading strength to burst the bonds that held his hands. He stripped the bag from his head and looked over the vast expanse of the Nevada sandscape.

Friday, 29 October 1999, 11:59 PM
The Mausoleum loggia
Venice, Italy

Ambrogino Giovanni laid out his implements before him: a solitary black candle, a length of rough rope knotted into a noose, a strip of burgundy velvet. Putting out the rest of the lights in the room, he struck a match, lit the candle, and waited for the taper to generate a thick column of smoke.

As the wick guttered and the smoke rose, Ambrogino raised the candle over the noose and spilled a few heavy drops of dark wax over it. He then passed the candle's flame under his left index finger, slowly moving it back and forth. The skin smoldered, caught fire, blackened, and finally split open, loosing a coarse spatter of blood over the rope, which Ambrogino, wincing in pain, blotted with the velvet.

Willing his deathless vitae to close the wound, Ambrogino spoke aloud. "By the ferryman's rede, by the song of Charon, I command thee, William Burke, to appear before me."

The candle's flame blew out as a gust of cold air wisped through the room. "Wot the bloody fuck is it, then?" came a hoarse voice that had no body. "Wot, another trip for me? You have another thing wot needs said?"

"I do indeed, my malicious lad," Ambrogino returned. "To the New World again—all the way across the sea."

"That's a load of rot. Oi won't do it, oi won't. Yeh cain't tell Billy Burke wot to do. He's his own man, he is. Billy Burke takes to none but his own counsel, that's roight."

"Ah, Mr. Burke, I'm afraid you're mistaken. You will indeed do as I ask. You're no longer your own man, as you can see, and I am a master of your dead ilk." Ambrogino took great pleasure in summoning the ghosts of murderers, thieves and the like. He found it to be a great source of irony that he should send these selfish ghosts out to run his errands, deliver his messages, and bully his enemies. William Burke had been a resurrectionist in life, a graverobber who sold purloined corpses to doctors, anatomists and the like who needed fresh specimens upon which to experiment or study. Burke had done such brisk business in Scotland that he soon exhausted the natural supply of cadavers and had turned to murder in order to keep himself in goods.

"Toss off and the Devil kin tehk you. I've run moi last for you."

Ambrogino smiled. He sang out to his wraithly guest: "Up the cellar, down the stair; But and ben with Burke and Hare; Burke's the butcher, Hare's the thief; Knox the boy what buys the beef."

"Cut that drivel out!" roared Burke's ghost. His partner, William Hare, had committed the grave-robberies and murders with him, in order to keep a doctor named Knox supplied with specimens during the first half of the nineteenth century. Before long, Hare confessed when questioned by police and gave up his accomplice. Burke hung and was publicly dissected, but his vengeful spirit refused to go to its final resting place. The whole incident had survived in infamy as a morbid children's song, which caused Burke's specter no end of anguish. "Yeh cocker, wot is it, then? Wot is it? I'll go an' do it jess to be awey from you!"

"That's a good boy, Burke. I want you to talk to the same Kindred you talked to last time. He's in the same place. You tell him the one who's coming to see him—Isabel—she's to survive the encounter and make it back to me. Let him know that if anything should happen to her, I'll be quite upset. Understood, William Burke? Do you have it all clear?"

"This the one with the crown of skulls, then?"

"It is indeed, William Burke."

"Ooh, he's a cold one, roight. I don' ken wot truck you have but if it keeps me awey from you *an'* him, oi'll do it and be off."

"That's a good lad, William Burke. Good for you."

Friday, 29 October 1999, 10:11 PM
Highway 95
Outside Las Vegas, Nevada

Benito had spent the previous two days under an outcropping of rock. He slumbered fitfully, never sure whether the sun's movement through the sky would push the shadow of his makeshift haven back and expose him to its rays. Many times during the day he woke, amid a sweat of precious blood which he licked from his fingers, and sluggishly rearranged himself out of the reach of the encroaching light.

By the time Friday night fell, Benito had recovered as much as possible, given the circumstances. He had fed surreptitiously during the past two days as the opportunities presented themselves, a bit from a lizard at one time, the cold, thick blood of a snake at another. He remembered the lizard whipping its tail in pain, its body holding little more than a mortal's shot-glass worth of blood. Not enough to subsist on, granted, but enough to keep from starving utterly. He was hungry, that was true, but not so hungry that he needed to devote all his will and attention to fighting back the Beast. Benito had no doubt, however, that such would not be the case tomorrow night. He needed to feed as quickly as possible.

He walked for a while, and finally got his bearings. The Nosferatu (he assumed) had dumped him about thirty miles out of Las Vegas, so said the mile markers and highway signs. Traffic on the highway—U.S. 95—was still fairly heavy, but he didn't want to try to hitchhike just yet. Benito knew that he must look like all hell and didn't want to work some vacationing orthodontist into a berserk lather and find himself facing down highway patrolmen following an APB for the "madman of the desert!" Surely a gas station would come up before long, where he could use the bathroom to make himself presentable and maybe even catch a bus into the city. Benito knew the Vegas Rothsteins didn't like him much, but it wasn't like he planned to stay there and set up shop. Just one night, maybe two, and he could get his act together and head back to Boston, where he belonged.

Sure enough, just over the next dune, Benito could see the buggy white lights of a gas station. He double-timed as best as he could without exerting himself. It wouldn't do to show up having sweated out his last reserves of vitae and either frenzy or have those highway patrol cops looking this time for a blood-soaked "madman of the desert!" About a tenth of a mile away from the gas station, he slowed down and walked the rest of the distance.

It was one of those ramshackle affairs—an old single-proprietorship that was supposed to have vanished in the late '50s when all of the oil conglomerates either bought them or drove them into bankruptcy. The place looked like the guy who ran it—"Dan," his nametag said—probably lived there, sleeping in the office and watching Springer during the day while business was slow.

Benito made the store rounds quickly, picking up a bar of soap, a razor (he had been Embraced with a five-o'clock shadow and shaved each night after rising—that is, each night after rising when he wasn't detained by a thug squad of Nosferatu vampires), and a touristy T-shirt, which had the distinction of not being covered with who-knows-how-long's worth of desert grime and blood. Then he brought his bounty to the cashier, who eyed him with a kind of wary mirth.

"You a vampire or a hitman?" asked "Dan" from behind the counter.

"I beg your pardon?" Benito looked incredulously at the attendant.

"Vampire or hitman?"

"I'm afraid I don't know what you mean."

"Aw, never mind. It's just that I get some weirdoes in here sometimes. You wouldn't believe the crazy crapola they tell me."

"Well, I can assure you, I am neither a vampire nor a hitman. I ran into some rough company and they dumped me in the desert, but with just a little attention to hygiene, I'll be on my way and better off without them."

"Hell, mister, you want I should call the cops?"

Oh, no you don't. I am not the madman of the desert. "No, that won't be necessary. I don't want to push my luck." Benito couldn't help but smile, however ironically.

"Okay, then. That'll be twenty-four ninety-seven."

Shit.

"Um..." Benito fumbled about himself. Money! Heaven forbid the goddamn Nosferatu should leave him in the desert with any semblance of dignity.

"Twenty-four ninety-seven," "Dan" repeated.

"Yes, I heard you. It's just that..." Benito cut himself off. No sense adding insult to injury.

"Oh, yeah; the 'rough company.' I forgot."

Benito winced.

"Look, pal. You got an honest face. I'll tell you what. You leave me your driver's license and I'll let you come back in the morning and pay me back."

"I, uh… They didn't even leave me with my driver's license."

"You wanna make a phone call? Have your wife or your buddies come out and give you a hand?"

"Dan" sure wanted this sale. Still, using the phone couldn't hurt. Not that he knew anyone's number in Las Vegas, but he could call back to Francis Giovanni in New York or even have his secretary, Ms. Windham, dig up one of the Rothsteins' numbers. "Er…okay." "Dan" handed the phone over to him and Benito dialed his Boston office.

"Good evening; Boston Financial; may I help you?" Ms. Windham, thank God.

"Ms Windham! A pleasure to hear your voice!"

"Mr. Giovanni?"

"The same! I apologize for my absence. Things must certainly have taken a turn for the strange there, am I correct?" Benito turned to "Dan," who wore a look of sympathy crossed with a shit-eating grin. He tucked the phone away from his mouth and asked, "Can I get Western Union here?" "Dan" nodded.

"Oh, things have been just crazy since you were called away, sir! Mr. Lorenzo has been beside himself for the past four months and none of us knew if you were ever coming back." *Four months? Jesus.* "Is everything all right?"

"I suppose, Ms. Windham, that everything is as all right as it can be, given the circumstances. Now, can you do me a favor?"

"Yes, Mr. Giovanni. What is it?"

"I need you to wire money to me. I'm at—say, 'Dan,' what is this place?"

"Nussbaum Fuel," "Dan" beamed proudly.

"You hear that, Ms. Windham? Nussbaum Fuel outside Las Vegas. Please wire me one hundred twenty-four dollars and ninety-seven cents. Thank you."

"Yes, Mr. Giovanni. I'll take it out of petty cash and have it there in half an hour."

"Thank you again, Ms. Windham." That should get Benito cleaned up, into a cab, and into the city, where he could call upon either his credit-card company or local hospitality in order to procure a room.

True to her word, Ms. Windham had the money wired within thirty minutes. Benito paid "Dan" and borrowed the key to the restroom.

Saturday, 30 October 1999, 10:54 PM
Outside New Orleans
New Orleans, Louisiana

"I have a question for you." Isabel came out of the blue with her statement. For almost fifteen minutes, neither she nor Chas had said anything, preoccupied as they were with the monumental task facing them. The time for planning was over—the two of them, sorely outmatched if things became anything other than observational or conversational, were knowingly, consciously headed into the lair of what might very well be a Methuselah. Few vampires would undertake such a thing lightly, and the gravity of the situation cast a pall over the mood in the car. Quite possibly, they were driving to their Final Deaths. Equally as possibly, the ancient Kindred, which had secreted itself in the ghostly Underworld that co-located to the desolate swamps of Louisiana (which might have still been unexplored territory at the time of its self-imposed exile), could have something utterly incomprehensible in mind for them. Would it bat them around as playthings? Turn them into pawns for one of its next maneuvers in the Jyhad? Destroy their bodies and enslave their souls? It was impossible to tell—until they arrived.

"I guess you'd better ask, then. Never know if you'll have a chance after this," Chas replied, his mood of fatalism evident in his voice.

"You've been having some trouble of late, no?"

"That's your fucking question?" Chas shot Isabel a cross look over his shoulder. She noticed his hands tensed around the steering wheel, his knuckles whitening and his arm twitching beneath his jacket.

"Don't be a bastard. You know you don't have to come along for this. As a matter of fact, I'm not exactly sure *why* you're coming along. Don't misunderstand me—I certainly appreciate your being here—but what is it?"

"Okay, is *that* your question?"

"No, but go ahead and answer it anyway. It might give me a little background when I finally get around to asking." Isabel smiled, hoping to set her companion at ease.

"Well, if this were a movie, now would be the part where I tell you I love you."

"Oh, Chas, don't—"

"Relax, relax; I'm just fucking kidding. It's all I can do anymore, freak out and screw around."

"Well, that's my second question. Or my first, really. What made you lose control back at Prudhomme's school?"

"Oh, that. Nothing. Just some fucked-up shit from when I was younger."

"Well…?"

Chas licked his lips and paused a bit before continuing. "It's this fucking family. When you're part of the Giovanni, some decisions get made for you. You don't always have the chance to control your own destiny. One night, some crazy guinea—no offense—on high gets a wild hair up his ass and someone completely uninvolved ends up paying for it."

"I don't know what you're saying. Well, I have an idea, but what do you mean specifically?"

"Okay, but you have to keep this quiet. It's not common knowledge."

"Please," Isabel rolled her eyes.

"All right. Back before they decided to Embrace me, I had already started a mortal family. Pretty wife, house in Jersey, everything I own registered in someone else's name, church on Sundays, couple of kids—the regular Mafia-guy package, you know? Then, all of the sudden, Frankie Gee shows up—I've been working for him off and on, more cowboy shit than him being my *capo*. He says he wants to bring me in full-time, make me part of the crew. Now, I know I'll never be made because I'm one-sixteenth Spanish or something and those Lagos want you to be one-hundred-percent Italian, but getting into a crew is getting close. It means I don't have to do any day-job bullshit anymore—I'll get a piece of any racket that comes up and I'll be more than a mook. People will come to me when they have capers they need pulled and I'll get to pull my own. It's being with someone; it's being protected from all the other motherfuckers out there who want to rip off the small guys, you know? I mean, I did some little bookie shit every now and then, back in the day, and if one of the connected guys, made or not, decides not to pay you for six grand he owes you, tough shit. He's with the crew and someone like Frankie Gee will whack you if you get lippy about it—he's got to protect *his* guys, see?

"So part of Frankie Gee's pitch to me was sacrifice. You give up the security of your day job for the big scores. You give up the insurance unions and pension funds and all that old-school shit—I don't even know if people in the modern world even get that shit anymore, it's been so long. You sacrifice, and you live a better life for it, or you make a better unlife for it; whatever. In this case, since I was part of the family, they wanted to proxy me; make me a ghoul, you know? Give me a test to see if I was worth a damn, and then they could make me Kindred. So I pass that test with flying colors and all. It was something simple, some bullshit truck hijacking and then running around afterward making sure the goods went where they wouldn't cause any trouble from the people who bought them, and getting paid on them. The heist was my trial for the mob shit as well as seeing if I deserved to be part of the Kindred. Pretty easy if you ask me.

"They turned me later that year. I don't know how your Embrace went, but the first part of mine was fairly run-of-the-mill. They had one of the guys drain me—which was another tough-guy part of the test, because I'm sure you know how fucking bad it hurts when one of us drinks from some poor slob—and then finish the job with a splash of blood across my lips. I remember thinking it was a pretty strange situation because we were in the cellar of a butcher's shop in New York. This is, like, about a hundred years ago, and it's all very new to me—you know what I mean. It's not like tonight, when every fucking punk who's ever seen a movie or black-wearing spooky kid knows what to expect. I mean, our family keeps things kinda fucked-up intentionally, you know? I mean, the whole time I'm a ghoul and drinking blood, I'm thinking it's some kind of Roman Catholic guinea communion thing, and that this is how everybody out there does it. I never read *Dracula* and I never had none of this Anne Rice shit to tell me what the whole vampire thing is about, you know? I mean, vampires fucking *get off* on all that sort of bent psychological shit—keeping you in the dark, never letting you know what they plan to do with you. I'm guilty of it, too. I guess it keeps you from being bored with fucking having to live forever. It's a nasty game."

"You're changing the subject a bit, aren't you, Chas?" Isabel interrupted.

This silenced him for a moment. "Yeah, I guess I am."

"What happened, then? You worked yourself off track after being Embraced."

"Well, that's it, you see. Fucking Frankie, and all that talk about sacrifice. He wasn't fucking talking about me having to sacrifice some bullshit attachment. He wanted me to fucking *make* a sacrifice—prove that what I was becoming was more important than what I had been. Those fucks—once they turned me, they left the cellar and locked the fucking door. I'm all freaking out in the hunger, running all over the room, looking for anything. I'm thinking maybe some blood has leaked through the floor from the butcher's above, or maybe rats or dogs or some shit come down here and I can go to town on them.

"Then I hear something banging around in the icebox. Remember, this is turn-of-the-century New York. We don't have big, metal, climate-controlled meat lockers, we have big, metal boxes kept cool with layer after layer of insulation and literal *ice* stacked in there to keep all the shit cool. I'm all out of my mind with hunger and it occurs to me that whatever's crashing around in there might well be alive, so I fucking dive in there like a man possessed.

"It's my fucking kids. It's fucking Ruth and Amanda.

"But what fucking choice did I have?" Blood-tears streamed down Chas's face. He glared at the road in the darkness ahead of him, as if he could just drive away from everything he had seen in the past.

"I'm sorry, Chas."

"Oh, that's not the end of it. See, they specifically *didn't* put my wife in there so that when I calmed down and they let me out, I'd have to go back to her. Well, I wouldn't *have* to, but they didn't want to make it easy or straightforward. If I killed my wife, too, I wouldn't have any choice but to move forward with my unlife. But they deliberately left her out there so I'd have to fucking tear myself up over what to do about it."

Silence hung over the car.

Minutes later, Isabel spoke. "And?"

Chas shook his head and sighed. "I had to kill her, too. I couldn't let her go on with something as fucked up as this completely changing her life. I mean, how the fuck do you *respond* to this sort of thing? Me, I've had to go on and come to grips with it, but that's because I fucking *did* it. When something like this just happens to you, what do you do? How the fuck can you even stand getting out of bed, knowing that something equally as fucked up or worse won't just arbitrarily happen to you the next day, you know? My fucking wife didn't do anything to deserve this—she married a Mafia guy. The worst thing that was going to happen to her was that I end up dead and she makes her own way or gets remarried. My goddamn kids—they didn't fucking choose to be born to Anna and I. They were just fucking born to the wrong guy at the wrong time and his fucking sick associates put them right in the path of totally wrong shit. Me, I fucking wake up with it every night for a hundred years—fucking get over it, you know?" More tears coursed down his cheeks.

"Yes, but you can't—"

"And that's basically why I'm following you around on this thing. Maybe it's not the most altruistic cause, you know, helping a bunch of fucking vampires figure out the thing that's coming after them, but it's a start, eh? It's making some kind of arguably positive difference. Frankie's dead. Fucking Victor's dead. It's not like I have anything to go back to except who knows how many more nights of hurting people and taking their shit when I feel like it, and this at least lets me feel like I'm contributing *something*.

"And that's what fucked me up the other night— seeing all those goddamn kids set up in neat little rows at Prudhomme's fucking school. *He* killed those kids. He fucking chose to do it. He went out of his way, selected *individual fucking children* and drank them dry. When I go to sleep at the end of the night, it's all I can do not to face the fucking sunrise for some shit that happened a hundred fucking years ago, that I had no power to control, and it's something that he can do and rationalize and get up fucking happy as though it's no concern in the world to him. My kids and my wife—I would have *destroyed* anyone who touched them. But it wasn't enough. In his case, he doesn't give it the least fucking bit of consideration.

"The son of a bitch."

Isabel knew she could say nothing that would change Chas's condition. This was his nightly demon. No doubt, when he saw the Beast, it wore his wife's face, twisted into a mask of betrayal. It spoke in the stereo voices of his children, asking *Why, Daddy, why; what did we do?*

Just then, Isabel's portable telephone rang. Chas jumped as the digital signal toned, jolted from his unpleasant reverie. Isabel answered quickly, "Hello?

"Where?

"Was he there the whole time?

"From Las Vegas?" She spared a pointed look at Chas.

"Right. Last night. No, this morning?

"All right. Thank you."

Isabel turned off the phone and looked again at Chas. "Well, I have another reason for you to stick with me."

"Oh, yeah? Great. What is it?" Sarcasm veritably dripped from Chas's voice.

"Our man Benito—he's dead."

Friday, 29 October 1999, 11:43 PM
Nussbaum Fuel
Outside Las Vegas, Nevada

Benito let himself into the bathroom, carrying his handful of newly purchased supplies. The entire trip from the storefront to the restroom on the side had been a protracted affair—the key was attached to an enormous old steering wheel and Benito's hands were otherwise occupied with the task of holding onto the toiletries he'd just purchased. After letting himself in, he checked the sole, dented stall to make sure he was alone.

Drawing the filthy sink full of tepid water, Benito looked at himself in the mirror. He was a mess. *First things first.* He took off his shirt and stuffed it into the trash receptacle. Lathered his hands with water and soap. Washed his face and the grime from his hands, arms and neck. Splashed a little water through his hair to loosen the blood and desert crud that had matted there.

Jesus, if I worked at a gas station in the middle of the desert, I wouldn't let me even come near the place.

Before beginning the shaving ritual, Benito put his hands on both sides of the basin and shook his head. What had led him here? He vaguely remembered talking to the stinking unknowns who had kidnapped him, but they had given him precious little about themselves. At this point, he wasn't even sure if they had been Nosferatu.

Bringing himself back into the present, Benito looked at the squalor around him. The door to the bathroom looked as if it had been bashed in and then bolted back into the frame. Someone had scrawled on the inside surface of the door

P.O.E.

O.P.E.

and a greasy tin of mostly used pomade sat on the sill where the sink joined the wall. A half-smoked cigarillo had been discarded on the floor, looking so dry that it must be at least ten, twelve years old.

Even the lights carried a sense of misery and despair—two of the six that lit the linoleum room had burnt out and the rest were so yellowed that they changed Benito's complexion from pale to jaundiced. Unwashed crusts of traveler's and gasoline filth accumulated in corners, crawled up the stall walls and filled the creases between the tiles. The Formica sink counter had been scored, burned by cigarettes, spotted with other mystery gunk and streaked with half-assed trails of tile cleaner.

Still, Benito had about half an hour before his car arrived, and he'd rather spend it making himself look civilized than hearing whatever hard-luck story or cinematic yarn "Dan" had waiting for him. He lathered his face with the soap and dipped his razor into the rippled water, preparing to cleave away the stubble that adorned his face this and every night since his Embrace.

"...Terrible place to die...."

Benito looked around. He hadn't heard the door open, nor had he observed anyone in here when he had first entered. *Must be someone outside*. Still, what a strange thing to overhear.

"...Elodie, Hazimel, Nickolai..."

This string of gibberish unnerved the half-dressed

Giovanni, though he recognized the last as a name with which he was uncomfortably familiar. He spun, hoping that he would be able to "see" where the voice had come from, whether via moving shadows under the door or, less possibly, someone who had hidden behind something in the restroom itself. But where?

"...Kiss like a spider..."

After this last strange pronouncement, Benito heard a *pop* and one of the four lit light bulbs in the restroom burst, showering him, the sink and the floor with a cascade of thin, jagged glass.

What the hell is going on here?

Pop. Another bulb shattered leaving the room illuminated only by a sickly half-light.

And then the door to the stall swung slowly open, creaking on its rusted hinge. Benito spun to watch it in disbelief—he had *checked* the stall to make sure no one had been inside.

From the tiny vestibule crept a form familiar but somehow different to Benito. What had once been smooth, swarthy skin had been crisscrossed by a lattice of livid keloid scars. The figure's eyes didn't match—one was the same as Benito had seen it before but the other looked as if it had been plucked out and returned rudely to its socket. The foreign eye veritably glowed red, brightening and dimming at seemingly random intervals. The clothes the figure wore were ragged, dirty, looking as if, since their owner had made the transition from his former self to this new...*thing*, he had forgotten all about personal upkeep. The hair was matted, the fingers longer and pronounced.

"*Leopold?*" Benito wondered, aghast.

"The same...same again and always. Leopold knows you. Leopold... So many nights wasted on you, Benito. So much time... your blood no longer cries out as it used to. Lost among the scum, Leopold—no! Benito! You traffic with those stinking rats?" Obviously, Leopold was rambling, probably maddened by whatever had wrought this hideous change upon him.

Benito took a step back, acutely aware of the strangeness of the situation. Here he was, in the middle of nowhere in a gas-station bathroom he had presumed—known!—to be empty, wearing no shirt, with his face partially shaven and some twisted Kindred staggering from a place it could not possibly have been only moments ago.

"Leopold, what are you talking about?" Benito asked slowly, hoping not to incite the ravaged Cainite to any rash act.

"I told you, this is a terrible place to *die*!" Leopold spat, his good eye, if such could be said, pinched shut in anguish. "Don't you listen? The names of the damned fall trippingly from the tongue!"

"This is nonsense, Leopold. What are you saying? Do you need me to understand you?"

"I don't need anything!"

"All right; all right. You don't need anything." *Then what do you want?*

"What do I want? I want you to die, but this is a terrible place."

Benito knew he hadn't spoken his last question aloud—or had he? Leopold was eating the thoughts that spun from his mind, approaching him with more and more malice. What had looked wretched and defeated seconds ago now seemed poised and malignant, a monster feeding on the fear and worry that poured from Benito's self.

"A terrible place? Why do I need to d—"

Quicker than Benito could see, Leopold lashed his arm forth, twisting it into a fleshy crescent crowned with a razored crust of bone. The tendril swiped across Benito's midsection, opening the flesh of his abdomen and spilling the withered remains of his once-vitals. Blood sluiced from the wound, covering the floor in a sticky sheen. Benito's eyes registered a horrid pain and shock, and he stumbled backward, willing what was left of the meager vitae in his system to close the wound. If Leopold intended to kill him, he had only little chance of overpowering the deranged Cainite.

The flight instinct took over. No matter Benito's relatively advanced age, his hunger prodded the Beast to flee. He spun, bringing the full bore of his undead strength to bear against the door, shearing it from its hinges and sending it flying into the parking lot. And then he bolted—

—but slipped in the pool of his own precious fluid staining the bathroom floor.

Leopold wasted no time in closing on his prey. His ribs erupted from his torso, lengthening and piercing Benito, splaying and spreading and rending their victim apart. A quarter of Benito's chest, the part attached to his neck, separated gruesomely from the trunk of his body. An arm tumbled to the ground, pried out of socket by Leopold's intruding bone and severed as the rib-worm curved over itself to reenter

Benito's body. Within seconds, what had been Benito Giovanni was nothing more than scattered piles of gore defiling a Nevada restroom. Presently, after the Final Death overtook him, Benito's remains crumbled to a greasy ash.

By the time the ash coated the floor, Leopold had vanished, but whether into the night or back to the realm of the unconscious from which he had surprised Benito, no one could say, for none saw.

Within the hour, Benito's cab arrived. The driver, a ghoul from the Scottish branch of the Giovanni family, knew exactly what he was looking at. With a careful mien, he scooped up enough ash to hopefully allow one of the accomplished necromancers to investigate the death of Benito Giovanni, and sped off into the night.

Dan Nussbaum scratched his head and cursed whoever had knocked his door from its hinges. Goddamn vampire hitmen.

Sunday, 31 October 1999, 12:21 AM
The Bourbon estate
Outside New Orleans, Louisiana

The remains of the Bourbon estate house—the home where Oliver Prudhomme had experienced his ordeal with Blind Tom and whatever it was that dwelt there—had fallen into disuse over a century ago. Terrorized by the monster that made its haven in the basement, the widow of the house and her servants had followed Oliver's example soon after he left, and abandoned the estate.

The swamp had since made every effort to reclaim the land that had once belonged to it solely. Creeping vines worked their way up the boggy hill toward the house, enveloping it in an organic cage of vegetative murk. Time and the elements had eroded the foundation and walls of the once-proud home, leaving breaches, rot and decrepitude in their wake. Although the air refused to move at ground level, some tremulous breeze passed through the shattered windows and splayed French doors of the house's upper level, moving the heavy burgundy drapes of the house so that they looked like lethargic black ghosts in the darkness of the night.

Isabel and Chas circumnavigated the enormous building, looking for whatever remained of the cellar Prudhomme had described in his letter or journal. Before long, they found it, a rude, rotten wooden affair laid over the gaping grotto that no doubt formed the cellar itself. No sooner had they found the entrance than the air came alive with a keening wail. Cold wisps of wind whipped across the grounds.

"The spirits of the restless dead," Isabel confided to Chas. "The thing inside has them bound to the house, serving as sentries or something. They're probably angry at its dependence upon them—I can feel that they don't serve it willingly."

"Can that help us?" Chas asked, with an uncharacteristic tone of hope. Since the latter half of the car trip he had been dour and withdrawn, affected by the ghosts that populated his own past and the death of the Kindred he had been initially responsible for finding, before everyone he knew who had been involved in the affair had turned up dead themselves.

"I doubt it," admitted Isabel. "The Kindred beneath the house is probably older than all of these spirits combined, and far more powerful. Even if they acted in unison, the monster could probably dissipate them with a wave of his hand or banish them into other realms. No, I'm afraid we're going to have to face this thing alone, and on its own terms."

"Well, fuck," Chas added. Isabel noted that at least this was in keeping with his personality.

Stepping carefully in the darkness, the two made their way to the wooden door that feebly shielded the world from the creature within. Chas pulled the door open on its rusted hinge, which gave a metallic shriek that sounded not unlike the voices of the unsettled ghosts wailing around them.

Beneath the house, the sedimentary rock of the Louisiana swamps formed a striated cavern. Here and there, great timbers or clusters of cypress wood spanned from the floor to the ceiling of the grotto, supports for the vast edifice above it. Wet vegetation crawled through various fissures in the ceiling, trailing slimy webs across the short protrusions that also roughened its surface. Pools of still water gathered in depressions that pocked the uneven floor and a still air suspended a subtle, cloying scent of decay. Chas's flashlight lit the darkness in a feeble cone, through which mist passed like the ephemeral bodies of the ghosts that had no doubt been barred from the ancient Kindred's haven proper.

Then the voice hit Isabel, resounding like a church bell through her head. It was neither male nor female, a heavy, uninflected boom through her mind. The Kindred taking its rest here knew that she and Chas had arrived, and it extended a telepathic tendril into her mind.

Why have you come? it asked.

Isabel replied aloud, so Chas would hopefully have some idea of what was transpiring. "We have come to ask your motives. We want to know why you have hunted down so many of our number."

Insolent childer, the both of you. Its affairs are its own. It needs explain nothing to you. You and your kind, who drove it so far under the caul of night—it does what it wishes.

"But, why? Is it revenge? Against the ones who hunted you in the past?"

Chas, regrettably, had failed to comprehend what was taking place. "The fuck are you talking about, Isabel?"

"It's the mon—the Kindred. It's talking to me through a mystic gift."

Who is with you? It feels anger from the other. It sees a limn of scarlet. Do not bring an angry guest into its home! You have transgressed already; you have violated the sanctity of its haven. Presumptuous and insolent!

"This is my companion, Chas. Chas protects me. We mean no threat to you, Old One; we know that you could destroy us at a whim. The both of us come only for knowledge. Without knowing the cause of your ire, we cannot end it."

"This is fucking creeping me out, Isabel."

"Please, Chas. I need to concentrate. You've dealt with this sort of thing before. Just let me talk to our host."

Your protector is impetuous! How safe can he make you? It expected only one....

"What do you mean, you expected one? You knew we were coming?"

It knows. It knows. It knows the end and the dark. But some things still surprise it. Even the voices from the cold failed to tell of the arrival of another. It cannot grant the same immunity the cloaked man asked for. William Burke! Go back and tell your master that I shall follow his request to the letter!

"William Burke? What do you mean, Venerable Elder?" Isabel was puzzled by the unseen presence's turn of words. "William Burke does not travel with me."

"Who the fuck is William Burke?" Chas demanded, a growl edging his voice. "Oh, now what the fuck is this?"

Isabel watched as the air around Chas grew hazy—dark and dense, a black whirlwind spun around him. A legion of otherworldly voices howled in chorus, sounding like the force of a gale wind outside. The air in the chamber was frightfully still, however, unsettling Isabel and Chas all the more; the storm overtaking him was unnatural, made up of a torrent of ghosts who did not disturb the world of the living in any temporal sense.

Still, it seemed that the ancient Kindred had sensed Chas's weakness, his proximity to the Beast. Isabel looked on as rage and anguish piqued Chas's face. His eyes sank in, growing dark, and his mouth gaped like a fish out of water, fangs exposed. His hands clenched into fists at his sides and then opened again, as if he was trying to grab hold of his wraithly tormentors, who eluded his grasp with ease.

The disembodied voice again resounded in Isabel's mind, a malicious tone with a tinge of mirth behind it. *The other has a short temper. We have sent it an offering to see how it reacts.*

As interminable seconds ticked by, Chas felt himself overcome by the emotional tide his attackers loosed upon him. The simple frustration of it ignited his ire, but the passion of the ghosts who whirled about him dragged him toward frenzy, an undertow of spectral turmoil and unleashed fury. *Get the fuck away from me*, he thought, and lashed out with his fist, striking nothing but a swath of cold air.

"Chas, keep calm. *Keep calm*," Isabel warned, but what the fuck did she know? The storm refused to break—Chas could see individual faces in the ghostly tempest, smiling, mocking and mouthing obscenities. Their shrieking echoed louder in his mind than his own thoughts. Again, he struck out, and then again, always failing to make contact. Chilling claws raked through his hair, lifted his jacket, tugged at his arms and battered him from beyond the veil of darkness between worlds. A torrent of individual words and curses rose from the cacophony—*cold, so cold, come, touch us join us be part of so warm, so much hate, so far from a man, can never truly, lost! too much black so away a little, hot black center.*

The swirl of bodies came together, converging to form...*something*. A face. Chas cast his hands out before him, hoping to disperse the forming face, but once again, his hands passed through the apparitions. The visage grew more distinct, a skeletal rictus stretched over prominent bones. It became more defined, and then the skull cracked, erupting into a laughing scowl, filling the dead air with its shrieking mirth—

—and then vanished. The cackling however, continued, becoming audible to Isabel, who covered her ears before it deafened her. The laughter faded into reality and dropped a bit, changing from the roar of the dispersed ghosts to the very real, very present laughter of something in the chamber itself. Chas's eyes narrowed to slits as he bristled. "What the fuck is so goddamn funny? What the fuck are you laughing at? You fucking...*coward*! Where the hell are you?" He lowered himself, looking as if he were about to pounce.

"Chas!" Isabel shouted. "Stay cal—"

Too late, too little.

Chas leaped forward into the heavy void of the grotto, followed closely by Isabel. A few yards deeper into the cavern, a vortex of darkness whirled, and the laughter took on a timbre that suggested it had dropped within. Chas seethed; Isabel leaped to restrain him, but he slapped her to the ground, lost in the throes of frenzy. From the floor, Isabel looked up at Chas, seeing the whipcord muscles of his thick neck bursting from his collar, his fangs jutting from his gaping maw, knowing that he was doomed. He sprang forward.

And stopped in midair, crashing to the floor.

From the vortex stepped a painfully thin figure, looking like nothing so much as an animated scarecrow, half again as tall as a man. It had no fingers, only long talons, and tatters of a shroud hung from it like the cowl of the Grim Reaper itself. The figure showed no face, wearing a cobwebbed black veil attached to a perfect circlet of small, humanoid skulls, each missing the lower mandible. As it stepped forth, the vortex closed, fading into the featureless darkness of the cavern itself.

The thing's head shook and the laughter continued. A bony finger pointed at Chas; the other hand waved capriciously. *It has walked with God. It has seen the sky rain blood. It has escaped a thousand-year hunt and then another. It has slept beneath the flesh of pharaohs and later beneath their lifeless bones. And one so young—this—thinks that he can destroy it. Not tonight.* More laughter. *Not tonight.*

Chas leaped from the ground, roaring, clutching hands outstretched—

—and transformed into a cloud of dusty ash. A few seconds later, the ash settled in a streak on the grotto floor before the figure.

It continued laughing. *Ashes to ashes, dust to dust.*

An anguished look crossed Isabel's face. Despairing, she sank to her knees, her hands leaving prints in the remains of Chas's body.

This is the might of it. This is what it can do, and will do. You cannot stop it; none can. It gives you leave, though. It wants you to know, and take back to your others, and tell them. The cloaked man would have you return to him, and it would have you do the same.

The dead figure stepped forward and stooped, grasping Isabel's slim neck in its infernally strong grip. It lifted her, bringing her up to where its face would be, cocking its head as if examining her. Then it dropped her to the floor.

It has been here for centuries and none have found it outside a cursed few. And see what has come of them? Maddened, prowling through a swamp. Dead, nothing but a streak of dust. Gone, abating its thirst for a few nights. It does what it will. As shall it always. It is outside of time. But its memory is long.

Take that back to your masters.

"But…" Isabel protested.

No. No questions. Don't coax it to prove the cloaked man's weakness and have its way with you. Return.

Isabel turned to look over her shoulder, back to the grotto's ingress. When she returned her gaze to where the figure had stood, all that remained was the still, black air and a feeble cascade of dust.

Thursday, 4 November 1999, 1:37 AM
British Airways Flight 2226
Somewhere over the Atlantic Ocean

Inside her rude pine box, Isabel opened her eyes and stared up at the veneer of wood that protected her from the attentions of the outside world.

Failure.

Utter failure.

Failure to resolve the fate of Benito Giovanni. Failure to take any hope back to the Giovanni concerning the ungodly potency of the cabal of ancient Kindred that would no doubt hunt them in the nights to come. Failure to prevent the sect war that would play out in the streets of Boston. Despite the fact that the Giovanni would maintain their supremacy in Boston, the conflict between the vampires of the Camarilla and the Sabbat would force the Giovanni underground for some time and necessitate that any action on their part be undertaken *very* carefully.

Still, Isabel comforted herself, wouldn't all of this have taken place with or without her? Could Benito not be replaced? Could Ambrogino really expect her to confound the actions of a Kindred who may well have walked in the shadow of the mythical Caine himself—assuming Caine had ever existed at all? Was survival in the Jyhad not itself the ultimate success? Didn't minor tragedies like these play out each night, winding through the unlives of the Kindred like the lines of incestuous ancestry in her own family tree?

After all, wasn't the entire, ages-old war a simple diversion from the unnatural act of rising, alone, from the day's rest to prey upon the mortals around the Kindred?

A single tear of blood trickled from Isabel's eye, staining the soft wood beneath her.

Thursday, 4 November 1999, 1:37 AM
The Mausoleum loggia
Venice, Italy

Ambrogino pushed the hood back from his head and lit a candle.

With a withered gray hand, he pulled two cards from the deck.

The Fool.

Death.

And then he looked to the mirror. No doubt someone—something—else saw the same reflection from the other side of the polished glass.

Tomorrow night, he would meet Isabel in London.

About the author

Justin Achilli lives at the bottom of a vodka bottle, where he listens to New Order and Morrissey. How he fit a computer and CD player in that bottle, he'll never tell. Justin may well be survived by his cat, Zöe.

The Vampire Clan Novel Series

Clan Novel: Toreador
These artists are the most sophisticated of the Kindred.

Clan Novel: Tzimisce
Fleshcrafters, experts of the arcane, and the most cruel of Sabbat vampires.

Clan Novel: Gangrel
Feral shapeshifters distanced from the society of the Kindred.

Clan Novel: Setite
The much-loathed serpentine masters of moral and spiritual corruption.

Clan Novel: Ventrue
The most political of vampires, they lead the Camarilla.

Clan Novel: Lasombra
The leaders of the Sabbat and the most Machiavellian of all Kindred.

Clan Novel: Assamite
The most feared clan, for they are assassins of both vampires and mortals.

Clan Novel: Ravnos
These devilish gypsies are not welcomed by the Camarilla, nor tolerated by the Sabbat.

Clan Novel: Malkavian
Thought insane by other Kindred, they know that within madness lies wisdom.

Clan Novel: Giovanni
Still a respected part of the mortal world, this mercantile clan is also home to necromancers.

Clan Novel: Brujah
Street-punks and rebels, they are aggressive and vengeful in defense of their beliefs.

Clan Novel: Tremere
The most magical of the clans and the most tightly organized.

Clan Novel: Nosferatu
Horrific to behold, these sneaks know more secrets than the other clans—secrets that will only be revealed in this, the last of the **Vampire Clan Novels**.

..........................**continues.**

The American Camarilla is reeling. Can they take advantage of the death of Cardinal Monçada to turn the tide back against the Sabbat, who have grabbed vast tracts of the Eastern United States? Despite the apparent efforts of Hazimel himself, the Eye of Hazimel is again in the hands of a once-pitiful Toreador named Leopold. Whose influence could be greater than that of the Methuselah from whom the Eye originated?

Some characters have yet to be introduced, while the stars of previous books will still return. Victoria, Hesha, Ramona, Jan, Vykos and others have ambitions and goals to realize.

The end date of each book continues to press the timeline forward, and the plot only thickens as you learn more. The series chronologically continues in **Clan Novel: Brujah** and **Clan Novel: Tremere**. Excerpts of these two exciting novels are on the following pages.

CLAN NOVEL: BRUJAH
ISBN 1-56504-825-3
WW#11110
$5.99 U.S.

CLAN NOVEL: TREMERE
ISBN 1-56504-827-X
WW#11111
$5.99 U.S.

Thursday, 21 October 1999, 11:14 PM
Broadway East
Baltimore, Maryland

The storefront blended in with the other buildings on the block: old brick, narrow, no exposed glass, just plywood painted black, a red neon sign that read just plain "bar." Lydia liked the sign. No cute play on words for the name, and the establishment followed the same no-nonsense suit. No bouncer, no line of beautiful people waiting to get in. Sometimes the random kine wandered in. That was okay. There was a bar stocked with liquor and beer for the minority of customers who could still drink that stuff. Everybody up front, either at the bar or at one of the few tables, knew to be on their best behavior if a "live one" was in the room. If nobody was too hungry, the kine might even wander back out after a few drinks. If somebody took a shine to him, however, he might be delayed in the back room for a few hours and wake up the next morning a few quarts low and with a hell of a hangover. Either way, none the wiser. So far, no mortals tonight.

Lydia had heard stories about Sabbat hangouts where kine, still barely alive, were kept hanging around—literally, on hooks—and the night crowd just dug in whenever they wanted. The idea repulsed Lydia. It seemed to her as bad as a gang bang, or taking a shit in front of somebody. Feeding was a private thing. She wouldn't go so far as to say spiritual, but she'd never had much appetite for feeding, or even hunting, in packs. Was it, she wondered, something about a Sabbat vampire's blood that led it to act like a fucking animal? That was tricky, because there were some Camarilla folks just as bad, or who would be just as bad if it weren't for the higher-ups threatening to kick their deviant asses. Was it just the social conventions, then, that set apart the Camarilla and the Sabbat? Most of the clans in the Camarilla, after all, had members that had bolted to the other side, *antitribu*, and vice versa for the Sabbat. Couldn't be the blood, at least not absolutely. Maybe bloodline set a general pattern, and some individuals strayed from that pattern.

Too bad Christoph wasn't around instead of doing whatever it was he did by himself. He'd probably have an interesting take on the question. But this was their first time off from patrol in four nights, since they'd gotten the car back from Slick's, just a few blocks away. Those four nights for her and her boys hadn't been boring either: five firefights, two confirmed Sabbat kills, three high-speed chases, one after Sabbat, one *from* Sabbat, one from cops. She'd taken a bullet through the face—damned painful, teeth splintered, took a chunk of her tongue. That had taken some blood to fix. Frankie had had his left hand cut off and still hadn't regrown all of his fingers yet.

Frankie was at the table with Lydia, as was Baldur. So instead of the chance to have a serious philosophical conversation with Christoph, she was sitting with the two members of her gang who were endlessly fascinated by questions like, Why do you drive on a parkway and park on a driveway?

"Hey, Frankie," said Baldur, "wanna go find a piano bar? You could play Chopsticks."

Frankie was less than amused. "Shut the fuck up, you ignorant fuckin' bastard."

"Was you givin' me the finger? I couldn't tell!" Baldur slapped the table at his own wit.

"Why don't you *both* shut the fuck up?" Lydia suggested. She wanted nothing more than to sip her drink—served in a dark glass, a small enough concession to the occasional mortal patron—and to ignore everyone else in the bar. "I can't even hear myself think."

"You must not be thinkin' loud enough," Baldur said, apparently finding something about his comment funny and laughing hysterically.

Lydia glared. Frankie glared. And Baldur, not as dumb as he seemed, shut the fuck up.

What was I thinkin'? Lydia wondered, deciding it was her own fault. If she'd wanted privacy, she should have gone someplace private. Any place with Frankie and Baldur was not private. And even with the two of them piped down, there were other people in the bar to aggravate her. People in general didn't aggravate Lydia; she wasn't one of the great loners, like Theo. But of the four Kindred in the bar other than herself, Frankie and Baldur, and the bartender, one of them was Jasmine. And that was a real pisser.

Jasmine herself was harmless enough. She was some hippie-throwback chick: long, straight hair parted in the middle; bell bottoms; cowboy boots; tight shirt and boobs perkier than they had a right to be. She was a powder puff as far as getting her own hands dirty, but she talked a mean game—mean, loud, and constant—and that's what she was doing now at the table in the corner.

"*We* shouldn't be doing *their* dirty work," Jasmine said to her small crowd of admirers. She jabbed her finger at the air at least two times every sentence to emphasize her points. Maybe she was trying to hypnotize her audience. It seemed to be working. The three Kindred listening to her were all guys. Lydia knew the type. They looked like jerks. In life, they would've been the kind to follow their dicks around, and now that those particular appendages didn't carry the same drive, the owners were pretty much without direction and susceptible to forceful speech. It didn't hurt that it was attached to a pretty face and erect nipples.

"If those *bigshots* over at the Lord Baltimore Inn are so worried about the Sabbat," Jasmine was saying, "*they* should be the ones riding up and down the highways keeping watch."

Lydia took another sip from the opaque highball glass half-filled with blood that she held in her hands. She'd heard Jasmine's rants before, directly and second-hand from Baldur and Frankie, but this time it bothered Lydia more. This time she had to restrain the urge to pull her .38 out of her jacket pocket and plug Jasmine one right in the forehead.

"*They* aren't taking any risks. *They* aren't putting their privileged asses on the line."

Let it go, Lydia told herself. *Everybody knows she's all talk.*

"*They* just sit up there and *talk*, talk, talk. *We* are the ones who do the *dirty work*."

Let it go. Nobody's listening. But they were listening. The three rebels without a clue were listening. Frankie and Baldur had listened, although they were oblivious to what was being said at the moment. Frankie was too busy brooding, and Baldur was occupied with making a tower out of salt and pepper shakers.

"What time is it, Frankie?" Lydia asked. Maybe there was a late movie they could go catch or something. Anything but staying and listening to Flower Child shoot her mouth off.

"About 11:30."

Baldur started laughing, tried to keep it in, unsuccessfully.

"*What?*" Lydia, against her better judgment, asked him.

Baldur forced a straight face. "You can ask him what time it is...but don't ask him to tie his shoe!" He couldn't control himself any longer and burst out laughing. He also ducked the angry swipe that Frankie sent his way.

Lydia's vision clouded over red. "Okay. That's it." She reached into her jacket pocket.

"It's not worth it to them," Jasmine said, "to risk *their* sorry hides. No, *we* are the ones they call—"

The wall right above Jasmine's head exploded in brick and mortar dust. The crack of the gunshot rocked the small room like a sudden clap of thunder. Jasmine flattened her face and arms across the table. Her admirers were on the floor. The bartender was out of sight. Frankie and Baldur just stared in dumbfounded disbelief as Lydia swaggered toward the other table, her smoking .38 held casually at her side.

"You talk *a lot*," she said.

Jasmine, her cheek still pressed against the table, slowly peeked over her own forearm. Lydia stood by the table, her gun in hand but not raised, so Jasmine cautiously sat upright in her chair. "There's a lot to be said," she responded, not, Lydia noticed, jabbing her finger at the air any more. One by one, each member of Jasmine's audience began raising his head above the table and glancing around furtively.

Lydia ignored them. "There's a lot of people busting their asses to make sure the Sabbat don't just run right over this place," she said.

"You're right," Jasmine agreed, some of her fire returning, "and those fat cats at the Lord Baltimore Inn ought to be *with* us."

"What do you think Theo Bell does every night?"

"He's a Ventrue lap dog," Jasmine said, jabbing toward Lydia.

Lydia pulled back the hammer on her .38. "Say that again." The three heads that had been rising above the table slowly sank out of view again.

Jasmine opened her mouth, paused, placed her palms flat against the table top. "He risks his ass," she agreed reluctantly, "but he's still just taking orders."

"You don't know what you're talkin' about."

"And you do?"

"More than you." Lydia eased the hammer back into place. As if on cue, the three heads slowly peered up over the table again. "What do you want us to do?" she asked. "Just give Baltimore to the Sabbat?"

Jasmine shook her head, said, "Of course not. All I'm saying is there's no equality. Pieterzoon and that crowd decide what's best for *them*. They don't give a rat's ass about us, but *we* are the ones who get cut to shreds every night when the Sabbat come creeping this way."

"How many of us have *you* seen get shredded?" Lydia asked. Jasmine didn't answer, didn't meet her eyes. "That's what I thought. Too damn busy bitchin' to get your hands dirty."

"That's not true!" Jasmine objected. "I go out. I patrol. I don't think it's as bad as they say."

Lydia crossed her arms, tucking the revolver under her armpit. "Why don't you make up your mind? Are we gettin' 'cut to shreds', or is it not as bad as they say? You can't have it both ways."

Encouraged by the lack of further gunfire, Jasmine's admirers eased back into their seats. The first and boldest of the three, a punk with a nosering, dusted off his shirt and smiled at Lydia. "I ain't seen that many Sabbat," he said.

"Then you been in the wrong damn place," Lydia said, gesticulating and inadvertently waving her gun about.

The punk shrank back. "Why don't you put that thing away, babe? You can't finish all of us with it."

Before anybody could move, Lydia had the .38 pressed up against the punk's nose. "No, but it sure would hurt a fuckin' lot, don't you think? Wanna give it a try?" She cocked the hammer again.

The punk's hands were in his lap. He didn't move a muscle. Lydia backed away slowly, let down the hammer, and then casually slipped the gun back into her pocket. She opened her mouth to call Frankie and Baldur over, then realized that they were right behind her already, both ready to back her up if there was trouble.

"Frankie," she said, "show this dumb-ass, peacenik bitch how safe it is out there."

Without a word, Frankie raised his left hand and started unwrapping the loose bandage that covered it. When he was done, they could all see the skinny, still growing hand, muscles and tissue not yet fully formed, fingers only about a third as long as they should have been.

"Don't you tell me it's not that bad out there," Lydia said quietly, threateningly. "Don't you tell him that. You just like to hear yourself talk and then blame other people for—"

A shrill chirping sound interrupted her. Lydia reached into her other jacket pocket—Jasmine and her admirers involuntarily tensed just the slightest—and pulled out a cell phone. She clicked it on. "Yeah."

"I need you to come over here," Theo's voice, still deep and strong if faint, said over the line into her ear. He gave her the address. "Don't bring your boys. Got that?"

"Yeah. No problem."

"Good." The line went dead.

Lydia almost took the phone away from her ear but then had a better idea. "Oh, yeah, Theo," she said to the phone, "You got a second? I got somebody here that has something to tell you." Lydia held out the phone to Jasmine. "Here you go. Your chance to tell it straight to the top…."

Jasmine stared coldly at the phone but did not reach out to take it.

"No?" Lydia shrugged. She put the phone back to her face. "Guess I was wrong. I'll be right there." Lydia clicked off the phone and stuffed it back into her pocket.

"I gotta go. You fellas mind keeping Jasmine and her boys company?" Lydia asked Frankie and Baldur.

"Sure."

"No problem."

"Good," Lydia said. "Tell her some war stories. Maybe tomorrow night we'll take her on patrol with us."

Thursday, 15 July 1999, 2:00 AM
Manhattan cityscape
New York, New York

Aisling Sturbridge sluiced through the rain-slick streets. The city towered above her on all sides in colossal glyphs of pitted steel and sizzling neon.

The jumble of arcane signs and sigils that assaulted her senses seemed haphazard. The city streets were piled high with half-forgotten ambitions rendered in concrete and raw altitude.

This was the Elephant's Graveyard—the place where the lumbering juggernauts of unbridled industry came to die. Sturbridge could feel the weight of old bones looming over her.

She ducked through a low archway and found herself in the midst of a vaulted colonnade of jutting ribs. Each of the gently curving monoliths was yellowed and pitted through long exposure to the elements. She absently ran a hand down the nearest ivory pillar. Its surface was encased in a nearly invisible envelope of cool water, tricking over the pocked surface in dozens of miniature fountains, cascades, waterfalls.

As if of their own volition, her fingers searched for and traced out the letters of the logo—the sacred name that the faithful had carved into the obelisk all those years ago.

The Plaza.

She smiled at a distant memory, recalling a lobby on the scale of a cathedral, filled with the luminaries of the American aristocracy gliding among peerless marbles. After only a brief contact, her hand fell absently to her side and she moved on.

In the rigors of the hunt, there was little room for nostalgia.

Through careful scrutiny, Sturbridge began to discern that hers was not the only sign of life among the ruins. She was amazed that the castoffs of two hundred years of avarice and ambition were not content to lie still and be dead. All around her, the city clamored heavenwards, clawing its way aloft, trampling upon its own shoulders in its upward rush.

The glass-walled towers seemed to shift like liquid under her gaze, flowing towards some unguessed sea amid the night sky. Experimentally, she put one hand out and broke the mirrored surface of the nearest building.

The tingling was not the expected rush of cool water, but something different—the scurrying of thousands of tiny legs across her skin.

The touch of Sabbat sorcery.

The vision shifted abruptly as the enemy attack erupted all about her. The alien mindscape pulsed like a migraine of flashing red lights. Fire engines emerged from the glaring light and screamed towards the Harlem River where a great funeral pyre tore free from the low-lying tenements. It cracked skywards like a whip.

There were figures among the flames. Long, lithe, gibbering figures. They danced the primacy of the flames—the legacy of Heraclitus.

In the beginning, there was the flame. And the flame was with God and the flame was God. The same was in the beginning with God.

Through it all things were made; without it nothing was made that has been made. In it was life and that life was the light of men. The light shineth in darkness, and the darkness comprehended it not.

Sturbridge could feel those flames reaching out to embrace her, to engulf her. She staggered, throwing one arm before her eyes to block out the light and heat. They bore into her skull. She stumbled against the nearest building, but its shifting surface would not bear her up.

Instead of the unbroken towers of still water she had envisioned earlier, the buildings now seethed in carapaces of teeming insect life. Sturbridge recoiled, stumbled.

She could feel the wave of scurrying life break over her. She felt herself going down beneath the weight of it—crawling, clinging, stinging. She sank to one knee.

Immediately, there were hands beneath her arms, steadying her. The ancient chant that formed the backbone of the ritual reasserted itself. The distant voices rose to a worried crescendo. Although the singers were all miles away, secluded within the walls of the Chantry of Five Boroughs, the voices imposed themselves upon the vision.

She could see the individual voices, distinct and radiant, like strands of colored light. They wrapped around her, supporting, caressing. Where they touched, the clinging insects burned away.

Sturbridge caught at the nearest snatch of song and latched on to it. Held firm.

She recognized something familiar in the bright

but tentative strand of amber light—it was Eva. Sturbridge smiled. She felt the novice stagger under the unexpected tug from no discernable source. Sturbridge could almost see Eva flailing wildly, trying to catch her balance and momentarily losing the rhythm of the chant.

The amber light flickered and vanished, but immediately there were a dozen others to take its place. Sturbridge could no longer see her surroundings for the glare of them.

She was exalted, bathed in their light. The adepts, Johanus and Helena, were twin pillars of smoke and fire, rallying and guiding the chosen. They shepherded the novices who could be seen to flicker uncertainly like fragile phosphorescent tubes. Sturbridge could not quite stifle a smile of amusement and pride in her young protégés.

But where was Foley? She took a quick headcount of her forces. He certainly could not have forgotten about the ritual. The *secundus* regularly regaled the novices at great length about his infallible mnemonic powers.

Her mind leapt to thoughts of treachery and then quickly discarded them. No, Foley was ambitious, but not so foolish as to attempt to dispose of his superior in such a clumsy, imprecise and public manner.

That probably meant trouble back at the chantry. It might be something as innocent as an unexpected guest, or an inadvertent trespasser. Or it could mean an intruder, a would-be thief, a Sabbat scouting party, or even an all-out assault.

She took another rapid count to be sure that no other forces were being withdrawn from the ritual to deal with the crisis at home.

No, everyone seemed accounted for, with the curious exception of Jacqueline. And here, at last, was Foley. His affected royal-purple glow was flushed and pulsating as from great exertion.

Sturbridge grabbed Foley and held him back from taking his rightful place at the head of the adepts. It was a gentle reminder that his absence had been noted and would be addressed as soon as the ritual was concluded.

Foley was unflinching in her grasp. His light grew more stable. Good, he was not wounded, at least. Nor did he try to draw her back to the chantry. Situation under control.

Sturbridge gathered the varied and multicolored strands of light to her. She stroked each one reassuringly, drawing from its strength, returning its strength twofold. She was the conduit. Her entire body thrummed like a taut string. Twisting. Tuning.

There. She was again perfectly in pitch with the pulsing lifelines and she rode the rising chant towards the very crux of the city.

The tops of neighboring skyscrapers rushed angrily towards her, intent on pinning her, wriggling, against the night sky.

But even as they closed upon her, she was already conjuring up her defenses. Her armor was forged of the materials abundantly at hand, the cast-offs of the city streets. She girded herself in the overturned trash cans, the abandoned cars, the gutted apartment buildings, the rusted iron gratings, the bodies (some stirring, some not) in the alleyways—the detritus of the city, jettisoned in its heedless skywards rush.

A vast pyramid of rubble and refuse was taking form around her. The vengeful thrust of the skyscrapers crashed against the sides of the pyramid but to no avail. They fell away harmlessly to feed the tangle of ruins below.

Sturbridge broke from the press of voracious buildings like a predatory bird rising above a forest canopy. Suddenly, she could see for miles in every direction. Any minute now... There.

She could pick out the main gathering of the Sabbat forces, down near the Battery. With elation, she soared higher still. At the very crux of the arc, she vaulted clear and watched as the mass of detritus tumbled in the air.

The twice-jettisoned debris reoriented itself under the pull of its several individual weights and plummeted smoothly, silently, towards the unsuspecting Sabbat forces below.

Sturbridge settled gently back down to earth. Her splashing feet broke the ghost images gathered in the puddles, scattering reflections on all sides.

Even having turned aside the worst of the Sabbat's mystical assault—and having arranged a nasty surprise for their more mundane forces—Sturbridge could not quite shake the feeling that something was still amiss.

She scanned her immediate surroundings for the slight telltale visual clues that might herald a new threat. Everything seemed normal enough for the moment.

Well, almost everything. Glancing down, she noted with some puzzlement that she seemed to cast two distinct shadows. A trick of the light? To be sure, she made straight for the nearest functioning streetlight.

No doubt about it now. Even under the glare of a bright single light source, she definitely had two separate shadows.

Her first thought was that she was being watched; or worse, followed. She was reluctant to turn back towards the chantry with an unwanted guest literally or figuratively in tow.

She assumed the worst. If this new presence were friendly, then why had it not identified itself?

Of course it was possible that the shadow did not represent any conscious entity at all. Perhaps it was simply a harmless side effect of the clash of arcane energies. Even old familiar rituals seemed to produce unanticipated results these nights. And the Sabbat sorceries she had faced this evening were an even more volatile element. When dealing with the alien conjurings of the Koldun, it could be difficult to discern between the enchantments themselves and their deadly afterimages.

She regarded the shadow with mingled curiosity and distrust. She half expected it to lunge suddenly ninety degrees to the vertical and go for her throat. After a few minutes of observation, however, she managed to shake free of this apprehension.

The shadow seemed to behave normally, if one disregarded the rather obvious fact that it did not appear to react to the presence, direction or intensity of light in the expected manner.

And the shape was not quite the same as her normal shadow. It was smaller and its contours were not quite right. The tiny limbs were more gangly, more girlish.

Recognition dawned on Sturbridge, accompanied by a cry of pure animal fury. She stomped angrily in the puddle as if to crush the shifting shadow underfoot.

The shadow wavered as the ripples rolled away from the point of impact, but the small fragile figure clung to her tenaciously.

Damn them.

She wheeled angrily as if trying to put not only the now-familiar shadow, but even the very thought of it, behind her.

It was a useless gesture. The little girl's shadow stretched before her on the pavement, taunting her, mocking her loss.

Sturbridge's shoulders knotted beneath the weight of the gathering forces. Her arms snapped forward and down as if hurling a great stone to the pavement. Rage erupted from her hands.

The asphalt cracked, smoked, boiled away. Still she did not relent.

She was blinded by the acrid black smoke. Where it touched her skin, it condensed and clung, burning like a liquid fire.

She broke off, stumbling backwards, one arm thrown protectively in front of her face.

But when she had fought her way back, clear of the deadly cloud, the shadow was there before her. Patient, tenacious, reproachful.

Her eyes stung with salt and smoke and her ears burned with the echo of distant laughter.